High Roller Airways
Ryan Surprise

High Roller Airways is a work of fiction. Names, characters, places, and incidents are the product of the author's imagination or are used factiously. Any resemblance to actual events, locales, or persons, living or dead, are entirely coincidental.

All rights reserved. No part of this book may be reproduced or transmitted in any form or my mechanical or electronic means, including photocopying, recording, or any information storage and retrieval system, without the written permission of the author, except where the law permits.

Please do not permit or encourage piracy of copyrighted materials in violation of the author's rights. Purchase only authorized editions.

Sale of this book without a front cover may be unauthorized. If this book is coverless, it may have been reported to the publisher as "unsold or destroyed," and neither the author nor the publisher may have received payment for it.

Copyright © 2025 by Ryan Surprise
Cover Design by Ryan Surprise

ISBN 979-8-9935818-0-4

PRINTED IN THE UNITED STATES OF AMERICA

Dedication
Jerry and Janice,
my loving grandparents

High Roller Airways

Chapter 1: Daydreams

Have you ever been to Buffalo? It's alright, but it feels like everybody's hometown they never wanted to come back to. Since Thanksgiving I've been taking overtime flights, holiday pay, double or triple pay because of the pilot shortage, and I still wonder if it's even worth it. Flying through duck soup on Christmas just to fall asleep in some hotel bed for a paycheck sucks, especially in a place that was cold, wet, and far away from home.

Ever since I was a kid I wanted to fly. I grew up near the grounds of the biggest air event in the US. Oshkosh, Wisconsin may not seem like much, but for a few days each summer the whole city would shut down. The rich folks would go to their cabins to escape the "noise" while my dad and I would walk around all day looking at old biplanes,

World War II bombers, and watch the acrobatic stunts of the Blue Angels that still make my mouth drop. Flying a 737 with a crew of five and a hundred passengers doesn't give you the flexibility to execute a tight barrel roll. When we couldn't get tickets to the show, my friends and I would bike around, and when we'd hear a plane flying overhead, we'd pedal as fast as we could, trying to keep up with the soaring jets.

    I remember my first time flying, my dad took me up to the cockpit and bugged the pilots to let me see what it was like. As soon as we walked in, the unfiltered sunlight brought my head down. I threw my arm over my eyes and looked up at the two shadowy pilots. One of them picked me up, letting me know the controls were just the way they liked them, and showed me the view above the clouds. It felt like being an angel, flying in the sunlight over the soft white clouds. They could be touched, flown through, and admired. Since then my favorite way to see the clouds is from above.

    After graduating from high school my dad woke me from bed and said it's time to get a job. He knew I wanted to go to flight school and that I would start in a few weeks, but he handed me a rake and a garbage can to pick up leaves and excess branches he just cut down from the tree out front.

High Roller Airways

That summer, and for the next two years, I worked while I went to flight school. The local warehouse needed help in receiving, so I'd go to work at six and come back at two, take lessons at three and be in bed by eight. Taking the flight exams always made me nervous, not because I was afraid of making mistakes, but because if I did make mistakes, it would be back to the warehouse. At the age of 20 I became a fully licensed pilot and gave my warehouse job two weeks' notice. For those last two weeks, every time I lugged a box over to be labeled and sorted, I knew I was closer to never doing it again.

Twenty years later, I'm still a pilot, picking up holiday shifts that pilots have crossed off their calendars every year. I'm not doing it just because I'm a nice guy. With the airline funneling me more money than I have ever made in a year, I'm saving up. Flying all the time has kept my life flexible. I sleep in hotel beds more than my own apartment.

I've had an idea of starting my own airline. It's not because I want to be the next Rockefeller. It starts off small. One private jet to take folks to Las Vegas, a private limo in the sky for a once-in-a-lifetime experience. They get the movie star treatment while I get to fly on my own schedule.

Plus, I get to hit the tables while I'm there, relax by the pool, and never have to fly on a holiday again. First, I had to quit.

High Roller Airways

Chapter 2: Crunching Numbers

After landing in Buffalo, I couldn't sleep. The idea I had was too enticing to let go. I used up half a pad of hotel stationery to come up with the plans. After a few winks of sleep, I made myself some coffee and looked out the window at the gray landscape in front of me.

I felt relief. In that moment of clarity I decided to call Personnel and hand in my resignation. My flight schedule had been completed for the month and thinking of flying to Cleveland or San Antonio on New Year's made my stomach turn. They fought against it.

"Think about your future. I know you. You're a pilot for life. You still have another twenty-five years left in ya."

"I know. I'm just trying something new."

"You gotta give us your two weeks' notice."

"I've been flying non-stop since Halloween, Bob. I've done more than enough for you."

There was silence on the other line. I held my tongue, hoping he'd have something to say. I'd been loyal to the company and worked lots of shifts I didn't want, but I liked Bob all the same.

"Alright, Dave, we'll send you the paperwork. Take some time off. If you ever feel up to it, we'll be happy to have you back."

I thanked him and hung up. I gathered my belongings and stepped into my uniform for the last leg of the journey. One stop in Chicago and then back to sleepy little Oshkosh.

In order to get this idea off the ground, I needed some help. I parked outside Oshkosh International Airport, the little eight-gate building on the edge of town, waiting for my friend Stan. Stan knew more about planes than I did, and I knew that he'd had a few private jets waiting in the hangars at the airport over his long career.

Stan came into view in a blaze orange golf cart that swung around the gate to the parking lot. He braked and waited for me in five layers of winter clothes, looking like an unhappy Santa Claus.

"How are you, Stan?" I asked.

"Freezing. I wish you'd waited until spring."

I chuckled at him and hopped into the seat next to him. He punched the cart into reverse, and we slipped past the attendant, who let us through before running back to his station. Stan gave me the grand tour of the airfield. The tarmac looked freshly plowed and full of tire marks. The snow made the massive gray hangars stand out above the rest of the flat empty landscape.

"So here's where we keep the big ones," Stan said, pointing to the hangar the size of several football fields. "The private jets are further down, I'll show ya."

"How much does one of those jets cost?" I asked. He looked at me incredulously.

"You can't make that much as a pilot, come on."

"I'm serious, I want to buy one."

"For what? It's cheaper to fly to Florida first class."

"I'm going to start an airline with my own jet."

"There are CEOs and old money around here that could use a pilot, why not reach out to them?"

"Because I don't want to work for somebody else. I want to be my own boss and make my own hours."

"Do you have any idea what these things cost? It's millions of dollars."

"How much for a down payment?"

"Down payment?" Stan scoffed. "Why don't you buy yourself a house instead?"

"I just need a small jet, something that can fit five, maybe six passengers."

"Look, Dave, even if it's used, it's going to cost you two million dollars, easy." That knocked me back in my seat. The cold whipping wind sobered me up. Maybe this was a pipe dream after all.

"I want to try," I said. "How much would it cost me, the plane, the maintenance, everything?" Stan looked over at me with his big shades. I could see the shape of his eyes, resting on me.

"Alright, the plane is going to cost you the most, but let's say you have the money for that. Then you'd also have to pay for the hangar fees, maintenance expenses, and, of course, the fuel."

As we drew closer to the private jet hangar, I started to calculate everything in my head. $2,000 for the annual hangar fees, scheduled maintenance of another $2,000 hoping that nothing goes wrong, insurance payments that cost $24,000 per year. That's already 30 grand without leaving the ground.

We pulled into the relative warmth of the hangar and saw three beautiful jets. Sleek, elegant, everything you could want out of one of these terrestrial rocket ships. There were two towering planes, capable of carrying more passengers and clearly more expensive, but there was a slimmer jet at the end of the hangar that caught my eye.

"What's that one?" I asked.

"That is an Embraer Phenom 100 EV," Stan explained. "It's got a single pilot cockpit with enough room for six passengers. It's the corporate jet for some gas station company. Apparently, the president is going through a sticky divorce. He's looking to sell it and stow away the cash in another bank account. I don't know the price or if it's still up for sale, but I could get you in touch with the broker."

"I'd appreciate that," I said, shocked by such a find.

"I don't know if he's willing to sell it to a civilian though," Stan warned. "It's a corporate jet and heaven knows there are plenty of CEOs who'd want to live it up on the company dime. It's not a slam dunk, but it's the best chance you have at something used and local."

I thanked him and told him to get me in touch with the owner. As soon as I got home, I looked up specifications for the plane, fuel tank and efficiency, cost per passenger to turn a profit, and what would it take to get this idea out of my head and onto the tarmac.

640 gallons per round trip x the price of gas ($4.15 per gallon) = $2,656. With those costs and the cost of the plane itself, it would be a miracle just to keep this business alive. A one-man operation with no income and a nest egg to cover the down payment? It'd be dead on arrival. I could go to the bank for a loan, but they'd laugh in my face. Taking a bunch of schmucks to Las Vegas while turning a profit? There's no way they'd give me the money, and if they did, I'd be in so much debt I'd never be able to pay it back. No retirement, no future, might as well beg for my job back at the airline.

After calculating and rocking my head back and forth, I came to the conclusion that there was only one man I could ask, but I didn't want a loan. If I wanted to work for somebody else, I'd start interviewing for another pilot gig. I needed a partner, somebody with the cash and somebody I could trust, or at least convince this would work in his interest, too.

I transcribed my chicken scratch notes into a legible document and dropped it into a three-ring binder to make it look presentable. I made a call to Jack Flambeau.

Outside the Chief Oshkosh Casino, I pulled up as close as I could to the front doors. I had an 11 a.m. meeting, and the parking lot was half full already. I looked down at my dress shoes that needed a shine months ago, and while I had gained a few pounds since I last wore the suit, I looked good. I looked like I meant business.

On the casino floor, the familiar tapestry of flowing greens and reds caught my eye before the eight-foot slot machines blazed their dazzling designs at me. The machines glowed like MACK truck headlights and threw cartoon characters at you to keep you sucked in. The old folks sat around, throwing in dollars a minute for the big jackpot. Through the maze of table games and ATMs, I reached the hotel's reception desk and asked for the Casino Manager.

Outside Jack's office, his assistant announced my presence. A voice mumbled on the other side of the large double doors. She led me inside.

The pale sunlight shone on the rich, hardwood walls. The rustic feel made me think I had been transported to a log cabin or some sweat lodge back in time, that was until I saw another wall covered with animal heads and trophies, photographs of Flambeau with rock 'n rollers and sports heroes. Jack was living large.

He stood by his desk, looking up from his documents when his assistant and I stepped into the center of his office. When he turned, his long, braided hair flew behind him. He gave me a devilish grin and stuck his hand out.

"Dave Jennings, it's good to see you," he said, his meaty hand covering mine. "Thanks, Alice," he told his assistant without taking his eyes off me. "How've you been?"

"I'm good. Thanks for talking with me," I said.

He motioned to one of the high-backed leather chairs in front of his desk. I sat down with my binder clasped in my hands. I felt like a kid handing in his book report, but Flambeau didn't seem to mind.

"You have something to pitch me," he asked.

High Roller Airways

"I do," I gulped. I set the binder in the next chair and stood up. Jack's eyes widened at the move.

"I've been a pilot for years, and I've loved playing at casinos across this country. You know that, and I thought — how could I bring those things together in a clever way that would be a good business? It's not a big casino in the sky, but the kind of experience people could only dream of, until today. Private jets don't have to belong to the rich, Jack. We can offer the jet set lifestyle to people for their next trip to Vegas. We fly them in a spacious cabin, with champagne and cognac, and they get to catch up before their bachelor party, their big convention on the Strip, or the gambler's vacation of a lifetime. We can give them that while still being profitable and inexpensive enough to bring in middle-class gamblers to keep the flight logs full."

I reached for the binder and handed it to him. His eyelids closed with a shade of doubt. I started to break down the numbers, but he cut me off.

"Do you have the jet?" he asked.

"No, which is why I'm coming to you for a partnership in this project."

"You want me to buy you a jet?"

"Fifty-fifty ownership of the plane and the business." His lips tucked in looking at the report. "You would own it for half, while still receiving profits, no upfront costs other than the overall sale of the plane."

"There's always costs," he insisted. He read the details, humoring me before closing it and slapping it on the table. "Listen, I've heard some hare-brained schemes, but this sounds like it just might take the cake."

My heart raced. Time to double down. "There's a jet in a hangar in Oshkosh with your name on it for a reduced price, and it can be profitable. I'm the pilot, the crew, the flight attendant, it's a one-man job, and all you have to do is collect the checks."

"How much are you willing to put in for this?"

"Half the down payment on the plane: $250,000."

He sat back in his seat, looking me over. "Maybe you're not just a dreamer. I know you. You're an honest guy and you don't flash your money around. I know I can trust you, but… people aren't going to spend, what?" He shrugged. "$5,000 for a plane ticket to Vegas when they can get an economy flight for $400? Nobody's going to do that."

"It's $1,600 per passenger, round trip, and with four flights in a month, I think we could turn a profit of half a million per year."

"You aren't going to convince fifty people to sign up for this in a year."

"Charging ten grand for a round trip with your best friends turns out to be only $1,667 per passenger, and thousands in profits per flight. That's totally reasonable for a bachelor party or a weekend of high-stakes gambling for executives in a mid-life crisis. We're creating an experience, not just a flight."

He scoffed at the idea.

"You know tons of celebrities and athletes that would love to fly in a jet without the costs," I insisted.

"Celebrities in Wisconsin?"

"Jack, you know who the heavy hitters are. They'd love to fly in a jet without the costs."

"I've shaken hands with lots of people, some rich, some lucky, but you want my money, and my resources, to fund this idea, Dave. And what's the price if you only have two or three passengers for a flight, huh?"

I cleared my throat. "The total ticket sales have to reach $10,000 per flight, otherwise the margins get thin."

"Agh!" he cried.

"By my estimates, each flight will cost the company sixty-five hundred dollars. That's four passengers at a minimum to make a profit."

"Agh!" he cried again. "No, I can't help you. You're a good guy, Dave. I've known you and your father for years. You've done right by us, but this is business. I need assurances, collateral, and I need more than a nice guy's pipedream."

That heavyweight gut punch sank in. He motioned me to go, so I stood. I had to stay alive and keep moving. I told myself I wasn't leaving without a yes. *I'm not giving up.* I sighed to myself and buttoned my suit. I stared down at him, trying to exude my best Don Draper look.

"Listen, it's a four-hour plane ride to Vegas from here. Do you really want to sit in a flying bus for that long? You're a tall guy. Those seats are torture. Or do you want to sit in luxury, sipping drinks you don't need to swipe your card on with some unconscionable upcharge. You get to fly like a boss. You set the rules. The world is your oyster."

"That sounds very nice for the average Joe-"

"No, for you. You don't have to sit in a crowded plane, waiting for anything, it's yours."

For the first time during the conversation, he didn't have a smart remark or a doubtful look in his eye.

"You can fly it whenever you want," I said.

"When there isn't a flight booked," he prodded.

"You could boot them and lose a customer, which would dip into your profits."

"It's not going to make money."

"It's going to make *you* money."

"Do you really want to be my chauffeur?" he asked.

"I want to be your partner in this business. You give me the fuel to get this airborne, and I'll handle the rest."

"My biggest concern is the clientele," he said. *I got him. Oh my gosh, I got him!* "We need high rollers, *real* high rollers. How are we going to get them?"

"I know a lot of pilots who love to fly to Vegas, sometimes they're scheduled for the weekend, sometimes not. We can fit them in during the week while most folks are going to want to go on the weekend. You know who your big spenders are here, around the state, and we can personally invite pro athletes from Green Bay, Milwaukee, Chicago, Twin Cities, you name it."

"Still," he pondered. "It's a lot of money just to pay for an experience. What about the hotel, casino, and all the other costs?"

"I'm sure there's a partner hotel you can reach out to, and we can make a deal."

Jack thought about it, paused, and thought longer about his next words.

"Alright," he said, leaning over his desk. "But this is going to be a process. It's going to take time, and a lot of things could go wrong. In that case, this whole project will be a thing of history, but if we can make it work, we'll make it work."

He extended his hand, and I shook the life out of it.

A few days later, I planned to see my dad. Whenever my dad or I wanted to talk to each other we simply called or knocked on the door. It was easier that way. We knew that we'd have something to tell each other every few months, and when either of us arrived on the other's doorstep, we knew it was as good a time as any.

On most of my visits I'd just wear whatever was fresh out of the wash, but I decided to dress for the occasion. I threw on my bomber jacket, my black boots, and a slim pair of Wranglers. I parked across the street from the old ranch house and ran through the rain, streams of rainwater rushing from the storm drain. There wasn't any cover by the door, so I waited with my hands in my pockets, enduring the cold rain dripping down my neck.

I listened closely between the raindrops smashing against the door. There wasn't any stirring in the house. *Maybe I should have called.* I waited before knocking again. It must have been hard to hear me at the door with the storm rolling through. More silence. The wind rose, cooling my neck with the help of the frigid rain.

"Forget it," I grunted. My feet pounded against the asphalt. I slipped around the car door and flung myself into the front seat. I begged for the heat to turn on and dry my shaking hands. I started the car before noticing a black hole appear across the white periphery. My old man stood in the doorway with a stern look for wasting his time. As soon as my hand could jut out of the window, I started to wave to him. The rolling window welcomed a sheet of rain across my arm and chin.

"Hey, Dad, it's me!" I shouted. His gruff appearance hadn't budged. I opened the door and rolled up the window.

It took a second, keeping my dad waiting. I slammed the door shut and ran back up the concrete path.

"It's been a while, Dad, do you have a minute?"

"I thought you were in Boston."

"No, no, I'm home."

"Well come in, don't stand out in the rain." He took half a step back. I threaded myself between him and the doorjamb.

The light in the house went out with my dad throwing the door shut. Not much had changed since I'd been there last. After I moved out, he had added his own little decorations, like a High Life beer sign, a framed Packers jersey, and a treadmill in the corner. The bittersweet, brown and gray familiarity disappeared when dad pushed past me.

We took a step down into the living room; I let him take his chair while I sat down on the old brown corduroy couch. I felt a relieved smile spread across my face. Dad rang with a loud groan as he descended into his favorite seat.

"How've you been, Dad?"

"Can't complain, not much happening around here." His eyes seemed fixed on some distant place.

"Are you seeing Boyd and Louie soon?"

"Yeah, yeah, we're going to Poto in a few weeks." His words hung in the air between us.

"Nice… that sounds like a fun time."

"Mmm…"

I held my breath, waiting for him to speak again. He sat, waiting. I felt my shoulders sink, but I had to tell him. He would enjoy hearing the news. He'd love it.

"I have something to tell you, Dad."

"You're not gay, are ya?" he asked, letting his eyes roll over to me.

I blinked. Was he kidding?

"I have something in the works. It's really big."

"Well spit it out, then."

"I'm going to start my own business."

"How're you going to do that? You have a job."

"Dad, I quit."

"What? Why would you do that?"

"I'll tell you-"

"Oh, boy…" He turned his body to the distant side of his chair. I perched up on the edge of the couch.

"I have a good reason, Dad."

"It sounds like you have one of those get-rich-quick schemes." He ended his statement with a low, dull sigh.

I fell back in my seat. "It's... it's not a scheme, Dad. I'm starting a business."

"It's not marijuana, is it? It's not legal here yet."

"Would you let me tell you about it?" I snapped. He sagged along the armrest, avoiding my stare.

"Look," I jutted my hands out, "I had this idea, I have a lot of money, right? I wanted to do something that nobody's done before but *could* be done if someone had the guts."

He waited for me to continue. His sagging gray eyes didn't make me eager to speak up.

"I'm starting a luxury airline, with Jack Flambeau."

"With that snake?

"Dad."

"Do you even know how to run a business?"

"We have a plane. He has clients. We're going to make this work."

"He's going to run you into the ground." His jaw swung left-right, left-right. My tongue dried up in a hurry. Nothing I could say would change his mind, but I had to tell him. I had to try to make him understand.

"If I fly out once a weekend every month, we'll be raking in the cash. It'll only cost us-"

"I don't need to hear the numbers," he muttered. He looked down at me, like I was a fool. "Plans never got anyone anywhere," he said. This time he sat up, pushed out his chin and held onto my gaze. "You're one man, with no customers, no money other than your savings, business goes south. What'll you do then? Those Wall Street guys play with other people's money, and Jack Flambeau isn't going to get stuck with the bill if you can't deliver."

I looked away first, straight to the floor. I could feel his eyes lingering on me.

"Well, Dad, I'll keep you in the know." I slapped my hands onto my thighs and rose above him.

He spread himself out against his chair, looking me up and down. "Don't go over your head, son," he warned.

"See you later," I muttered. There wasn't any point in defending myself to him.

The rain slapped harder against my shoulders, catching me in the eye. Just another slap in the face to pile on that afternoon.

I ground the key as far as I could into the ignition. I gripped the steering wheel until I heard the faint, dull tug of flesh against tight leather. What came next was a dreary drive through the rain where I'd be greeted with the bills my father warned me about.

After getting home and properly drying off, I parked myself at the kitchen table, combing through bank statements and invoices. I stewed over his words. My mutterings punched the air. The responses that came to me, far too late, occupied my mind; my pacing burned my bare feet with every about-face. I didn't recognize a peaceful moment in that evening until I rested my head for the night.

High Roller Airways

Chapter 3: Working Class Education

Why did I become a pilot? Why did I become a gambling man? Necessity. Working at that warehouse killed me. Every morning it killed me. I'd go in at 6 a.m. and come out worrying about how this would be my life. The only thing I had looked forward to was getting the chance to fly. Took me until I was 21 to get my pilot's license and pass the interviews to line up with Midwestern Airlines.

The job taught me a lot, like how to make a smooth landing with passengers and their baggage weighing down a multi-ton behemoth in the sky, and more personal skills like how to make announcements over the intercom without too many "umms" and "uhs". Truth be told, it took some time doing that.

That gig helped me travel the world, or at least see more of the world than I would have otherwise. As a rookie pilot they stuck me in one of the easiest flights out there, the commuter flight from Oshkosh to Chicago.

It takes about 30 minutes to get up in the air and touch down. It's a flight so quick the stewardess hardly has time to serve snacks and drinks. It was a great way to start out. I would work weekends, of course, but it gave me plenty of time to fly and practice that perfect landing, a landing so smooth that the people on the plane would hardly know we had landed until I told them over the intercom.

As a pilot you have a lot of downtime after flights. You can only fly so much before you need your regimented 8 hours of sleep, which gave us plenty of time to go to our hotels and let off some steam. Everybody had their poison — smoking, drinking, flight attendants, you name it. Sometimes my flight would lead me to an airport with a casino next door.

As a 21-year-old kid with no school debt and a few rough years in a warehouse under his belt, I was chomping at the bit for some real excitement. That's how Judd Thompson and I met. Judd was often the assigned captain of that little flight. He showed me the ropes and would make wise cracks about my inexperience.

"Next time try to sound like your balls've dropped," was a common theme, but I knew how to take it on the chin. It took a few flights together for him to really trust me, and I liked impressing an old veteran pilot like him.

He stood a full head taller than me, with a large block head, and was comprised of well over 250 pounds of toneless beef. Judd was a lot of things; he was a good pilot, a gambler, and a rolling stone in the worst possible way. He'd been divorced three times, and I never asked about kids. I assumed he had at least one, but he never talked about them.

After a month on the job, Judd looked over at me with a strange glint in his eye.

"When's your next flight?" he asked.

"Eleven tomorrow morning, why?" I asked.

"Perfect, we're hittin' the tables," he said. He pulled his jacket from the back of his chair.

"What?" I asked.

He gave me a squinty look as he threw his big arms through narrow sleeves. "What're you Mormon or something?"

"No, I mean, you're talking about the casino?"

"Yeah," he said, shocked by me missing the obvious. "It's right over there. Come on."

"Okay," I said, eager to go.

My dad was a gambling man. Some Sundays he'd leave the house to collect his winnings from his bookie or spend nights at the Chief Oshkosh Casino while I studied for school. I was surrounded by the concept of it but being out on my own and with more money than I ever had before, I couldn't believe I hadn't thought about it sooner.

After checking into the hotel, I stepped into the shower, spritzed some cologne on, and laid out the clothes from my suitcase. After traveling so much for work, I decided to pack everything I might need in a given situation. I pulled out the dress shirt and slacks I had packed with me. This was a special occasion.

Meeting Judd in the foyer, I straightened my back and gave a big smile, hoping he saw it as a sign of confidence. My grin faded slightly when I saw him wearing a Hawaiian shirt that could be turned into a tent. *Am I overdressed?* Judd's lip curled, and he took me under his wing.

"Lookie here, the kid cleans up good." His thick hand clapped the back of my neck, sending a sigh of relief out of my chest. Inside the taxi, Judd started interrogating me, seeing if I had potential.

"So, is this your first time?" he asked.

"Yeah, but I know how to play some games."

"Like what?"

"Blackjack, Poker-"

"What kind of poker?" he asked. His gray eyes stayed locked in on me.

"Uh… Texas Hold 'em."

"Three Card, Mississippi Stud, Omaha?"

"Umm, no," I muttered.

"It's alright. Just follow my lead. There are some rules in casinos that you have to follow. Unless you're playing poker, never touch the cards. Casinos are pretty paranoid about people marking up their cards, especially in Blackjack. If you have a fifteen or a sixteen, you should just stand so the next guy can get the ten he needs. Nobody likes getting their cards stolen. Don't forget to tip your waitress, and your dealer."

Stepping into the casino, the familiar asymmetrical carpet with musical notes and little red and black rectangles greeted our feet. Judd must have been there before because he walked in like he owned the place. One of the pit managers waved to him and he flashed her a smile.

"Good luck, Judd," she said as we shuffled down the game floor.

"That's my name," Judd said with a gloating grin.

Judd and I settled on an empty Blackjack table, and he dealt the dealer a wink. She had curly fire-red hair and blue eyeshadow. She could've been anywhere from thirty to fifty years old under all that gaudy makeup.

"Lady Luck is with us tonight," Judd said, nudging me with his elbow.

The dealer grinned and looked down at me. I looked at the cards. She let out a little laugh. "Where are you boys from?" she asked, shuffling the cards.

"New York," Judd said through his teeth. She gathered the cards into the shoe and handed me a yellow card. I stopped for a second before realizing she wanted me to cut the cards. I dug the card somewhere in the middle and let her hide it among the big deck.

"Good luck, gentlemen," she said. Her fingers held the cards lightly and landed them in front of us. They didn't budge once they hit the felt. My face couldn't hold back my excited shock when she laid down double aces in front of me.

"Hey, that's good, kid. Now put-"

I already had my pointer and little finger out and spread them apart, putting another bet on the split ace. She laid down a black queen and a red king, just like that.

"This boy's good luck!" Judd shouted. He shook me by the shoulders, and I laughed with him as I relished the sight of those red chips coming my way. The next deal started with a disappointing 6 but a 4 joined it a moment later.

"That's good," Judd started, but I beat him to the punch by doubling down on the bet. She produced a red 10 to settle me in at a comfortable twenty. Judd bounced his knuckles on the table and got his own red 10, sinking his chances. The dealer showed her hidden card, revealing a 4 to go with her ace. She drew a queen, still 15, but then slapped a king on top.

"For a rookie, you know what you're doing," Judd complimented me.

"A bit of luck never hurt anybody," I replied. As we were talking, the redhead delivered me a jack and an ace to seal the deal.

The night went on like that. Good cards and bad cards, but we loved to see the drama of the dealer's hand bust out of our unlucky 12s and 13s. The pit manager came over and gave her sales pitch to us to join their players club, offering us free drinks, and with that little commuter flight being on my schedule most of the time, I said why not.

After enough cards had been dealt for the night, we decided to take up those free drinks and chat at the bar. Judd was a connoisseur of bourbons, throwing back Wild Turkey neat while I stuck to beer brands I'd heard of.

"You're a good player, Jennings," he said between his second and third drink.

"Thanks," I said. "It's been fun playing with you. We made a decent chunk of change tonight."

"It's a good start," he dismissed. He reached for a pen in his shirt pocket, took a cocktail napkin down, and started writing.

"If you want to make some real money, here's what you gotta do." He wrote out the numbers 1, 3, 6, and 2. At first, I thought he was giving me lottery numbers, but he started to explain.

"Whatever your bet is, $5, $10, doesn't matter. When you win on your first bet, that's the one," he tapped with his pen. "Then you move onto the next step, betting 3 times your first bet. That way you're leveraging what you won from the casino against them, and if you hit 21 you're going to be making a lot more money. Then it's 6 times your first bet if you win, same rules apply, you have all that money stowed away at less risk to you, and then you just keep going until you lose a hand. Then you start back at one."

"Okay…" I said. I leaned in closer and listened.

"You start with $100 and bet $10. You win $10, so you have $110. Then you bet $30, so you have $80 in your pocket, and then you win that one, which brings you to $140. Then $60 which still leaves you with $80 that you had in your pocket before, but if you win that hand, that's $200. You've doubled your money by winning three hands of cards. A little risk has a big reward."

I smiled at the numbers on the page and how they felt real, like I could touch them. Judd looked at me with a satisfied grin.

"You keep up with that luck you had tonight, and you'll be peeling off Ben Franklins like a mobster."

The image of gangster movies like *Goodfellas* and *Scarface* came to mind. Those guys were living the life. They had no worries. They had everything they wanted, all the cash they needed on hand, so they could take care of their families. You need $50, you got it. It costs a hundred, you got it. Here's a few hundred, and their wallets would still be half full. I could make that happen, just from playing cards and piloting connecting flights to Chicago. I was going to have it made. Judd sighed after chewing on his last drink.

"You're a smart kid," he said blithely. He leaned closer to me and brought his voice down to a low gravelly tone. "Most guys, they pay for the thrill, but guys like us, we play to win. Look at them on the slots," he said. He jutted his chin over to the sea of retirees plugging away at the jackpot. I looked over. *Man, I hope that's not me at that age.*

"They're suckers. They come here thinking they can win, but the odds are only good at the tables. I'm telling ya," he said with his lip hanging over the glass. The clink of sliding ice filled the silence. "The casinos are only going to be slots in the future, because wiseguys like us know how to play the games and turn a profit. They're slaving away while we're playing it smart, remember that."

All said and done, I smiled at that. I'd never been to a casino before, and I earned $150 playing a game I only knew about in theory. Judd was right. I make some money here, pay for my rent back home by playing in the casinos.

I was on cloud nine.

"What time is it?" I asked him.

Judd looked at his watch. "It's… it's only 2."

High Roller Airways

My lips held my drink back. "I gotta go!" I turned to leave, but Judd caught me by the arm.

"Relax, finish your drink," he said. I lowered myself back into the stool. "Staying up a little later won't kill ya."

I stayed seated. Judd hung over his drink. I turned towards the bar and thought of questions to ask him.

"What's your family like?" I asked, unable to find a smoother way of saying it.

"They're alright. I've been married a few times. Tell me, Jennings, you have a girlfriend?"

"No," I said, trying to avoid sounding disappointed.

"Hmm," he muttered. I waited to let him speak, but it didn't seem like he was going to.

"It's just me and my dad," I mentioned. He looked over, waiting for more.

"Some fellas are family men, others travel the world," he mused. He held his glass up to mine. "Here's to traveling with you, kid."

I saluted his glass with mine and finished my drink. Not sure what else to say at Judd's sudden melancholy, I decided to say goodnight.

"Night, kid," I heard him say. I marched down the red and black floor but caught myself looking back for a quick glance. I saw him hunched over his drink, waving the bartender over. The way he called me kid made me think he hadn't any of his own. He was just an old man looking for a son to adopt after the last flight of the day. His head hung low over the bar. I told myself that next time I'd stay up with him and chat more over drinks. It's no fun being lonely, especially in a big city; you feel even more trapped.

The next morning I felt the spit stuck to the back of my teeth and rushed into the shower. I didn't bother to shave, and I didn't even remember to button the top button of my uniform when I reported for my next flight. There were a lot of mornings like that with Judd.

"Wild Turkey and some aspirin will put you right as rain," I recalled him saying.

The next time Judd took me down to the casino, I tried out his number method. Feeling more confident than I had before, made seeing the jazzy floors and the bright lights of the Chicago casino feel like home. We were welcomed as familiar faces, and we were lucky enough to find two spots at the Blackjack table.

High Roller Airways

One of the same dealers was the redhead from the other night. Her face erupted with a gleaming smile at the sight of us as she stepped up to our table.

"Hi, boys," she oozed.

"Hi, Donna," Judd said, lifting his drink. I put in $10 and waited for Donna to do her magic. Her red and white fingernails swung low over the cards. She launched them to us with a flourish.

The first hand was a pair of 10s, an easy way to settle into the game. She used her 7 to flip over the hidden card. 10. *Easy win, easy win.* She doled out my winnings and I stacked them before adding another $10 on top. A 9 and an ace, another 20. She showed her two 6s and slammed a 10 on top to nail the coffin shut.

"See, I told ya," Judd bellowed, shaking me like a palm tree. She slid over $30, and I kept it there. This was the big move. Half of me wanted to turn tail and run with what I had, but I was feeling good. Donna kept her warm eyes on me as she slid the next card out of the shoe. Double aces.

"Yeah!" I shouted. "Split 'em up!" I gave her the signal. A 9 and a queen landed in front of me. $90! $90 for being lucky while playing cards.

"Atta boy!" Judd pulled me in. I waved to her that I was standing on both pairs of cards. Her 6 flipped over an 8. *Don't be a 7. Don't be a 7.* She swung down the next card and her hand revealed a mighty king. She busted. I couldn't hear much after that. The whole table lost their minds.

$150, and we had just started. She placed a black chip and two greens in front of me. It felt like the whole place turned up ten degrees. My cheeks were red, and my chest was heavy. I hadn't expected to win that much in a night let alone five minutes.

"Remember to cool off, Dave," Judd reminded me. "Back down to twenty."

I raked in the black and green chips and stuffed them into my pocket with a canoe-shaped smile on my face.

A week later, at 1 a.m., I erupted from dreamless sleep and fell over myself, with my legs twisted in my bed sheets at the sound of my phone ringing. I untied the knots around my ankles and pinballed against the walls to answer it. I hoped I could reach it in time before the call ended. I snatched it up to my ear and answered.

"Dave, it's Judd. I'm calling from the Tiki Lounge."

"What?" I hissed.

"What's your schedule looking like for next month? Any big plans for the 28th?"

I rubbed my face, wiping crust away from my eyes, trying to remember what the white boxes of October said.

"Uh… the 28th? I can't make it the 28th."

"Oh come on, you can change your plans. Let's hit up the casino. You're my good luck charm."

"What? No, I can't. It's my dad's birthday, you know? It's just me and him."

"Alright, alright, but don't ask for any weekends off next month. We gotta hit up the tables sometime."

"Yeah, I'll leave it open, don't you worry," I said, a chuckle escaping my lips.

"Good, good, the hula girls are calling my name. I'll see you later."

"Alright, bye, Judd," I said. The dial tone hummed in my ear. I grunted and stretched my back before falling face first into my bed, drifting off to sleep.

Getting settled in as a rookie pilot came with a sense of security. I had my own place after flights, I had hotel rooms to stay in, I had a nice job, with good pay, and the casino winnings were just for fun, an extra drink here, a pair of new shoes there. But with all adjustments, things change. After we landed back home for a few days of R&R, Judd decided to change our plans.

"Dave, I got an idea for us," he said.

"What is it?"

"We're both in Oshkosh after the flight. You have off, and I fly out tomorrow afternoon. Let's go to Chief Oshkosh, try out the talent there."

"You want to go?"

"Yeah, I'm bringing Donna with us. A couple of good players like us, they won't know what hit 'em."

"Sure," I said. "Let's do it."

Why he was bringing Donna, I wasn't sure. I never thought of her as a player, only a dealer, and I know Judd had wined and dined her before, but it felt odd to add another player into our little gang. It was a two-man group, just a couple of pilots shooting the breeze. Either way, that was the plan. I joined them at the casino that night.

The Chief Oshkosh Casino itself wasn't much larger than your typical banquet hall. It had slot machines that nearly hit the ceiling, and the table games hung between the wooden support beams with green glass lamps, which gave it a cozy cabin feel. It was par for the rest of the places around town. Folks would go to their hunting lodges and little lake cottages and feel like they hadn't left.

I wore a polo shirt I had in my dresser from high school, hoping to fit in with the casual crowd. Judd and Donna decided to stand out from the others. Judd wore a matted black blazer alongside Donna's flamingo dress. I could taste her perfume on my tongue. I must have looked like their teenage son. Baby's first trip to the casino.

I tried to keep my head up and enjoy myself, but there was a different feeling in the air. Gambling in my hometown? People might recognize me, or see me as some kind of gambling addict.

I shook myself out of my head when Judd asked me what I wanted to drink. I muttered "Miller Lite" to the waitress and rested my arms on the table. We started with a few hands, winning some and losing some, but Donna excused herself and kissed Judd on the cheek. He shifted to the chair next to me.

A pair of 2s sat in front of me. Just not my day, I thought. I tapped the felt for another card. 10. *As expected.* I looked at the dealer's 9 and shook my head. Another tap on the felt gave me a face card. Busted out. I felt in good company looking over at Judd's cards, a 10 and a 6. He hovered his hand over the cards. The dealer moved onto the next player.

"Why didn't you go for it?" I asked. "He has a nine."

"I have a feeling it's not a ten under there," he told me. I shrugged and waited for the dealer to show his hand. He swept the hidden card up and over: 4. *Might be a bust*. He plucked a card from the shoe and slapped a jack on top.

"Sometimes you have to play small ball," he said. I placed another $10 on the mat and received another loathsome pair. 10 and 5, against another 9. I decided to play small ball and wave off the dealer. Judd had a similar hand of 14. He chopped into the table with his big knuckles. The dealer obliged and delivered a sweet, sweet 7.

"Twenty-one," the dealer declared.

"Man, you're on a roll," I said.

"I'm getting some extra luck tonight," Judd laughed.

The dealer motioned to the other players to make their move. They stood with what they had. The dealer turned over his card — a high ace: 20. He tapped a downward fist against the other players and gave Judd his money before taking mine. I was astonished by his luck and smiled down at my diminishing pile of chips. I wondered how I could turn my luck around.

High Roller Airways

I placed another $10 next to the card spot on the mat and looked around the casino. Donna in her neon outfit was at the table on the other side, playing some variant of poker. I gave her a nod and a grin, and her cheeks rose up politely.

I looked down at my cards. Two 8s, which wasn't so bad. I liked a nice split. The dealer had a 10.

"Let's try it," I told myself. The dealer split the pair and laid down a 3 and a 4, making 11 and 12. I stared down at them, thinking of my next move. I hit on the 11. 21. A win there, but hitting on a 12 always made me nervous, so I waved it off. The dealer placed his hand in front of Judd while I sighed through my nose and rubbed my eyes with my palms. Judd smiled at his 17. He pounded his knuckles down.

"What?" I gasped. "What're you do-"

The dealer extended a 4 to Judd's 17.

"Twenty-one, nice hit," the dealer commended. Judd gave himself over to a big belly laugh and a pleased groan as he watched the dealer slide him his winnings.

"Nice work, Judd," I said. My smile hung open as I waited for the next round, catching Donna taking a look at her cards just long enough to see them before folding. My brow furrowed. She didn't seem to like playing.

My eyes ebbed down to the dealer's hands. I traced the dealer's movements as he passed out the cards. An ace and a 10 landed in front of me but I didn't notice. When the dealer's hands rested over his own cards, he acknowledged the face-up card and took a look at the hidden card to know what to expect. My eyes snapped over to Donna. She had pulled her blood red nail from scratching the felt.

In that moment, she had given Judd a signal. I didn't want to look at him. I couldn't give myself away, so I glanced down at my cards. The dealer gave me a Blackjack.

"Hey!" I yelled. "Let's get the ball rolling," I said, rubbing my hands together. Judd didn't seem to notice. His cold gray eyes flicked up and down before settling on his cards. *Did he know what I saw?*

I tried to have fun the rest of the night, but the hair on the back of my neck stood up all night. My neck was red from me rubbing it for hours. I felt like a criminal, and even worse, he didn't even tell me. He didn't clue me in. I was losing money hand over fist, and he didn't try to save me.

I bowed out after losing a little too much for my liking and went to the bar. If those two were going to get caught I wasn't going to be thrown in the paddy wagon with them. I grumbled to myself over my suds and watched some college football team getting creamed.

"How'd you do, champ?" Judd asked half an hour later, saddling up to the bar with Donna in tow.

"I'm down a bit. Just not my night," I said. I let a beat of silence pass. "You were good out there."

"With my little luck charm, I can't be stopped," he chuckled, pulling her tight to his waist.

"Too bad you weren't with us last time, Donna. Judd, here, lost on three twenties in a row and nearly flipped his lid. I've never seen him so red."

"Just a bad night," Judd explained, a little louder than necessary. Donna patted his shoulder.

"The dealer thought he was rabid with the foam coming out of his mouth," I dared.

"That's enough!" Judd snapped. Donna's blue eye shadow retreated; her pair of hazels watched wide open. "Don't get bent out of shape because you lost your wallet, kid."

"Just a funny story, Judd, don't take it the wrong way." Donna's face chilled and she placed her hand on Judd's chest.

"It's alright, Judd," she cooed. "It's not a big deal." Judd's square jaw shut tight. He reached for his drink and Donna sat between us.

I sipped my beer with my lips curled. I liked getting under the old steer's hide. A little pride returned to my shoulders, and a refreshing "ah" escaped my lips. But I didn't hate the guy. He didn't seem any the wiser, but I still liked him. I offered a peace pipe for us to wash away the stale taste in our mouths.

"Wanna bet on the game?" I asked him. "Donna, how about you?" She shook her head. "Come on, who's going to score next?"

"You've been watching the game longer than me. You have better odds," Judd complained.

"Alright, how about position? Running back, receiver, or quarterback?"

"What about a lineman?" Judd pouted.

"That'll be Donna's bet. What do you say?" Their smiles came back. Judd looked up at the TV and saw the Tigers prowling the red zone.

"How much?" he asked.

I laughed. "Ten bucks."

"Receiver," he said.

"Running back," I replied. I turned my head to the TV and saw the quarterback ran through a big hole and march into the endzone. We both laughed. It was a good thing too — helped put the water under the bridge.

Two weeks later, Judd and I had the same flight schedule. Back to Oshkosh again. While the passengers filed out of the plane, I thought whether I should ask Judd about the game plan. I figured I should be prepared in case Donna came along to lay signals. Maybe it wouldn't be so bad, I thought. I didn't want to cheat, but knowing they'd do it was still enough to make me anxious.

"Just you and me tonight?" I asked.

"Donna'll be around. Don't worry, she doesn't bite."

"No, I know," I said. My nerves were getting to me. I felt like he could sense that I was jumpy.

"Ready to bust out in Blackjack," he joked. I chuckled along with him.

"Not if I can help it. You going to blow out the bank?"

"When you're my age, kid, you don't need luck," he sighed, putting on his jacket with a self-assured grin.

When we flew in that night, Judd and Donna wore more muted clothes, fitting in with the crowd. She wore a black off-the-shoulder sweater and that same pungent perfume, classy but still Donna. Judd wore a camouflage polo, which took me off guard. He didn't seem the type, but maybe that was the point, fit in with the regulars.

Before Judd and I took our seats at the end of the Blackjack table, he motioned to the dealer to come closer. "What's the maximum bet per hand?" he asked.

"Two hundred dollars," the old man replied.

I rested in my seat, my heart pounding in my throat as an old woman unburdened herself from the table across from us and graced Donna with her seat. *Like clockwork.*

"Let's make some real money tonight," Judd whispered in my ear. He handed the old-timer a fan of hundreds. I'd never seen that much money in my life. The dealer took Judd's money with great care, shouted to the pit manager the amount going in, and promptly shoved the money down into the slot in the table. Judd was locked in.

He started things hot off the bat with two green chips, while I was playing my normal ten-dollar hand. I sat back with steam coming out of my nose. My shoulders felt tight, but I tried to look casual.

High Roller Airways

Judd got 8 and 4 while I got a 9 and a 6. The dealer looked at his cards, revealing a card to Donna's wandering eye. She cracked her neck side to side and spread her fingers out. *Did that mean stand? Did it mean 5?*

I had no clue, but Judd went first. He held his hand over the cards. The old man gestured to me to make my move. *Crap! Don't cheat.* The dealer had an upturned 3, a bust card. *Oh forget it.* I tapped the table.

"What're you doing?" Judd asked.

"Just a rookie mistake," I said, wincing at the king the elder sent my way. He revealed his hidden card, a 2. 5 so far, then a 10, and then a queen, busted out. I kept my eyes on my cards, played a simple ten-at-a-time strategy to keep my cool. After a few hands, I looked at my watch. I hissed through my teeth and ran my hands through my hair.

"What? What is it?" Judd asked.

"I forgot to call her. I said I'd call her. I'll be back." I passed the dealer a chip. "Hold my spot for me, will ya?"

I didn't stay to hear what Judd or the dealer said after I left. I threw my chips in my pocket and streamed past the tables to a quiet part of the casino. Around the corner by the bathrooms was the pay phone. I sheltered myself inside, closing the door behind me. There was a plaque with numbers on the window for the hotel, restaurants nearby, the gambling addiction hotline, et cetera, et cetera. I called the hotel. I could feel the sweat starting to form in my hands as I squeezed the life out of the phone.

"Chief Oshkosh Casino and Hotel, how can I help you?" a voice answered.

"Hi, I'm calling from the casino. Who do I get in touch with about cheating?" Her pause told me she didn't know how to respond. "There're two people cheating at Blackjack. Who do I talk to about that?"

"One moment, please," she answered in a grave, measured tone. My swallowing ricocheted along the booth's walls. I kept an eye on the corner, expecting Judd to hunt me down and strangle me. I heard the phone leave its receiver on the other end of the line.

"Who is this?"

"Dave Jennings, I'm playing down at the casino, and I think two people are cheating."

"Who?"

"This guy in a camo shirt and a woman at the other table, black sweater, red hair, you can't miss her. The guy's, uh, white, two-fifty, maybe three hundred pounds, gray hair.

He's playing Blackjack and she's giving him signals from the table across from him."

I didn't hear anything on the other line. *Did I lose connection?*

"We'll take care of it." The dial tone droned in my ear. I took a breath and clapped the phone back in place. I smacked into the door and tried to open it the second time and found it successful. My shoulders were up, and my hands went cold. I had to chill out. I was a nervous wreck. Straightening my back and slowing my step, I returned to the table and folded my hands, waiting for the next game.

"Everything alright?" Judd asked.

"Yeah, yeah, I'm good."

"Is she happy you called?"

"Called?" I answered. My eyes grew like saucers. "Oh, yeah, yeah, she's happy. Dodged a bullet, I'd get an earful if I didn't call her."

The dealer doled out the winnings and pointed to the first player to make his wager. Judd adjusted his belt, shifting in his chair. His hot breath wafted toward me.

"Do you like this girl?" he asked.

"Yeah… she's nice," I added.

"Where'd you meet her?"

"At a bar, um, in Dayton."

"Dayton?"

"Yeah, it's in Ohio."

"I've flown to Dayton before," he growled. "I didn't know you had that route."

"Just one time, and she wanted to — she wanted me to call her."

"Well," he said, lifting his drink. "L'chaim." I knocked my drink against his.

As a welcome back present, the dealer passed me two queens. I started to feel a little more comfortable. I took a swig from my drink and let my muscles relax. The dealer awarded Judd for his bravery with green and red chips, and I let them sail past me like a ship on the horizon. *Nothing to worry about.* I threw in some chips, and the old man dealt me a 7 and a 3 in return. My eyes shot up to see what the dealer had: a 4.

"Let's give it a try," I said. I placed another bet next to my red chips and tapped the felt. The dealer swung low and showed me a dark black 3. I winced. *13, 13!*

The dealer swept a card out from the shoe. This was going to hurt. My elbows planted into the table and my hands cupped the back of my neck. *Please, bust out, please.* The dealer revealed a 5 to go with his 4.

"A nine? I'm toast," I groaned. The old set of hands threw down another low card, 6. "Okay, fifteen," I said. "We got this. Now big! Go big!" The line under the dealer's nose went crooked at my cries of hope. He tossed a 9 on top.

"Bust," he declared.

"Wow, that was close," I wheezed. Judd laughed.

"Big bet on Davey," he joked.

"I was sweating bullets," I laughed, miming the wiping of sweat from my forehead. We chuckled and looked to our drinks. *Nothing like a cold beer after a hard-fought victory*, I thought. After enjoying the spoils of war, in the midst of my laughter, my heart stopped. Two barrel-chested sheriffs stood behind Donna. She didn't know. She was looking at Judd. I almost forgot I called the casino. I didn't know they'd get the fuzz involved.

The dealer had a 3 face up, and he revealed a number to her. Whatever it was, she trotted her red fingernail into the felt on the other side. As soon as they saw that, they scooped her up by her arms.

"Judd," I muttered. A pair of hands clapped onto my shoulders. I looked up and another sheriff towered over me. "Whoa, what's going on?" I shouted.

Judd stood out of his chair with his arms behind his back. The wrenching sound of the handcuffs cut through the noise. Then I felt the cold metal trapping my hands. *Oh crap, I'm going to jail.*

"I didn't do anything wrong," I protested.

Judd kept his mouth shut. They shoved us forward. I couldn't help but watch the faces, the turning heads. My head slunk down. *We'll be out soon. Just ignore them. It doesn't matter.* But I felt like a criminal.

Outside there were three separate police cruisers waiting in the dark beside the curb. I wanted to yell at Judd, blame him for roping me into this, but that would've incriminated him.

As much as I hated cheating and wanted out, I still didn't want him to do time for it. The cop holding me opened the door and pushed my head down. I fell face first into the back seat and curled my legs up as soon as I could because the cop took hold of the door and slammed it shut.

High Roller Airways

Inside the tight space, I struggled to get comfortable. My shoulders were hunched and held tight, my legs, hardly fit between the seat and the wall between me and the cop.

I struggled to find good footing in that tight spot. I crawled further down the seat and used my shoulder to bounce myself up.

"One more," I groaned. I bounced and threw my weight with the momentum to sit myself up. I couldn't even relax against the back of the seat with my arms bent back. They had me folded up like a lawn chair and I was going to jail. They'd fire me. *I'm never going to fly again*.

My mind flashed back to the gray, lifeless warehouse. I struggled against the cuffs, but it was no use. They had me and were going to charge me.

With all three of us captured, the cars ahead of me peeled off. The cop in my car turned on the engine without saying a word. The car pulled forward, letting the other cars leave the parking lot, then we leaned to the right, down a path around the casino. *Where is he going?* There wasn't another exit that I knew of. My eyes squinted and my eyebrows came together. *What is going on*, I thought. He stopped on the other side of the casino and turned off the engine.

"What're you doing?"

He stepped out of the car.

"What're you doing?"

He slammed the door shut.

"What're you doing, man?" I fell out when he opened my door. He took me by the shirt and lifted me to my feet. The stitches of my shirt started to rip. His clenched fist told me I couldn't outfight him. The side of the casino seemed to have a strange addition to its wall. The thin line of a doorway became visible, then a silver keyhole. The sheriff flicked his ring of keys and found the right one in a flash. The door opened to a low-lit stairwell.

"Where are you taking me?" I asked. "What're you doing to me?" I cried. He forced me inside and frog-marched me up the stairs. I couldn't breathe. My throat closed up, and the spit choked me. Up a flight, he pushed me to a room full of cubicles. The corner office rushed up to meet us. The cop opened the door and threw me in. A wall of screens caught my eye. A native man sat with his back to me, carefully watching the casino floor.

"Sit down," the man said. The sheriff uncuffed me and pushed me down into the chair. I sat frozen, waiting for the man to speak. The pit of my throat throbbed. The sweat in my palms cooled my chair's armrest. The man turned to face me, rising to his feet in the same movement.

"Thanks for your call," he said, stretching out his hand. I heaved a sigh of relief and raised my hand to his. "Do you know those two?"

"Yeah, he's a friend of mine."

"Why'd you call us? I'm curious." He crossed his arms and leaned against his desk.

"You know, I uh... I just don't feel comfortable around cheating. I didn't want to be um..." His eyes hooked into me.

"I didn't want to play with a guy who cheats."

"But you didn't cheat?"

"No, I just like to play. Rules are rules." He turned his head, trying to read me. I felt like I would piss my pants at any moment. His arms depressed against his chest. He emptied his lungs, keeping me under his watchful eye.

"Have we met?" he asked.

"What?"

"How long have you been coming here?"

"Just a few times."

"You look familiar. You have an uncle who plays?"

"My dad, Ben Jennings."

The man clapped his hands and yelled out. "That's it. I know him. Yeah, how's he been?" Suddenly his eyes lost their hawkish intensity. It really threw me off.

"Uh, good, yeah, he's good."

"Yeah, you're good people." He laughed and shook his head. "You've saved us some money. How much did you have at the table?"

"Maybe one-fifty," I guessed. The man swung around his desk and wrote a number on a sheet of paper. When he handed it to me it read $250 with a thick signature underneath.

"Let's take a walk to the cashier," he said with a smile. "My name's John, but friends call me Jack, Jack Flambeau. If you ever need anything, just let us know."

Jack rolled out the carpet for me. I just had to hand the bartender the card, and he wouldn't ask me to pay for the drink. The first one anyway. Over the years, Jack and I would run into each other now and again, keeping the business going and remaining in his good graces.

For the following few weeks, I was nervous to fly down to Chicago, but I never saw Judd again. He never called to ask how I handled getting pinched, never called to threaten me for ratting him out, and I never felt guilty. I was put on the new Oshkosh-Detroit flight schedule, traveling the eastern United States for a spell.

Chapter 4: Big Bet On Black

After months of paperwork and finally buying the jet, we were in business. Jack whittled down the price to a reasonable $2.1 million and after we announced the news, we made the newspaper. I met with the mayor and the chamber of commerce, took a photo with the airport director on the tarmac with our lovely new High Roller Airways logo painted on the back fin.

We opened shop in March, and we quickly booked flights into May and received early reservations for the 4th of July. We had ball players, local executives, and retirees filling up our seats. Of course, not every one of our clients wanted to take a flight to Oshkosh, Wisconsin to board their luxury flight, so we flew to the airport of their choosing and slapped an additional fuel fee onto the bills of the pro athletes. They wouldn't mind an additional grand or two tacked on, it was peanuts to them.

The first party I flew was a group of middle-aged guys, a bit older than me, heading to Vegas for a boys' trip. When they met me on the tarmac, I welcomed them with open arms and a bottle of champagne.

"Welcome, gentlemen, this jet is yours for the weekend. You can leave your bags here, and I'll show you the cabin. Follow me." I waved them over, and they were right on my tail. After climbing the steps to the main cabin, I heard whistles and howls of delight. The champagne carpet blended into the walls with the fresh white seats that surrounded a drink table for them to congregate around.

"Feel free to make yourselves at home. I'll stow your luggage in the cargo hold and then we'll take off. If you have any questions before we fly, please let me know." I pointed to the silver box to my left and added, "Drinks are here, serve yourselves as you like, but only after we level out in the air. I'll let you guys know over the intercom. Sound good?"

"Yeah!" They shouted.

I left them to it. Lugging their suitcases into the cargo hold wasn't my favorite part of the job, but it's a luxury service to them and a business to me. Sometimes you have to add a little elbow grease to go the extra mile.

Once I settled into the cockpit, I felt compelled to take a moment to let it all soak in. Our maiden voyage, I wished I had my own champagne bottle, but I settled for the sound of whirring engines.

Jack made arrangements with one of the hotels on the Strip. The Blue Stallion Hotel was the last remnant of a tobacco magnate. Blue Stallion Cigarettes peaked in the 70s and went by the wayside years ago, but one spot of prime real estate they had bought was on the Vegas Strip. Rumor had it that the grandson of the family fortune would drink cocktails on the rooftop pool. I liked to imagine finding him poolside; maybe he was the Fat Cat with the unbuttoned Hawaiian shirt sitting in the sun, or the looming suit in the corner, sipping his drink. Either way, he ran a first-rate hotel for chumps, suckers, and wannabe high rollers.

I escorted the gang through the foyer of the hotel. I had spoken with the staff over the phone, but I had never stepped foot in the place. I took it slow, hoping someone would anticipate our arrival and give the guys the tour. At the front desk, two women tapped away on their computers.

High Roller Airways

The senior of the two noticed us. She had auburn hair that came down in waves that rested on her suit's lapels. She kept still and smiled, patiently waiting for us as we got closer.

"Welcome, you must be the Randall party," she said. I stepped ahead of the guys and spoke on their behalf.

"Yes, I'm Dave Jennings, from-"

"I remember," she smiled. "We spoke over the phone. Here are the room keys," she said, placing cards on the desk while focused on the screen. "We also have club cards for you," she spoke to the group. I stepped out of the way as the men sorted out which card was for whom. I looked up her lapel for her nametag. Susan. A familiar name from all those emails and conference calls.

"Rooms 211 through 213 are located to your left from the elevator," she said.

As I looked back to my clients a young guy in a blue polo and phosphorescent white pants had dropped in with a luggage cart. "What's your name?" I asked him.

"Mario," he said, caught off guard at someone asking him his name for once.

"Well, Mario, my name's Dave." I handed him one of my business cards. "These guys are my clients, so make sure they're taken care of. Ask them if they need anything, wish them luck, you know what to do."

"I will," he said eagerly.

"Thanks, are we all set?" I asked the group. They grunted and shifted their feet.

"Mario will take care of your bags." He started to pull suitcases onto the luggage cart. I slid over to the front desk and pressed my hands against the table.

"Is there any chance I could get one of those?" I asked with a chuckle. She placed another card on the desk. Near the blue horse head read the name "David Jennings".

"Jack told me," she explained with a smirk. "Enjoy your stay," she said with a bow of the head.

"Thank you, uh…" Her left hand clasped her nametag. Her lips curled in a mischievous grin.

"Susan," she said.

I remembered. "Thanks."

"Thank you, David."

Once the bags were set down near the door, the gang decided to hit the casino. They dreamed aloud of big wins and hitting the Strip. After entering the sprawling casino floor I turned to face them.

High Roller Airways

"Welcome to the Blue Stallion Casino, fellas. It's been fun being your pilot this evening. I'll leave you guys to it, otherwise I'll be around if you need anything else."

We went our separate ways. Taking in the enormity of the place, I wasn't sure where to start. With so many tables to choose from, I found a spot between some shoulders at the craps table.

"You're up, shooter," the dealer said, guiding the red dice with his crook. On the other end of the table, a young man lined up the dice just how he wanted them. His orange hair came out from under his pro fishing hat. He threw the dice my way, bouncing off the mat. The hollow cubes clunked against the back wall and turned over snake eyes.

"Two, craps, two," the dealer announced. I placed another $20 on the passline. *Seven or eleven would be nice.* The kid got another roll of the dice. He placed the dice into a neat row and pushed them into the felt twice. With a rush, the dice slammed against the wall.

"Three, craps, three," the dealer shouted. Grunts and sighs escaped from around the table. Even the kid started to sweat. I kept my eye on my chips. He didn't need another set of eyes judging him around the table.

The dealer's crook passed a new set of dice to the next player. He chose two and jingled them in his hand. I placed another bet on the passline. New roller means new luck. He was an older man with a combover. He seemed comfortable with the dice, placing additional bets with ease. I settled in and hoped to see a friendlier number.

"Go ahead, shooter," the dealer called. His tough yellow fingernails squeezed the dice. He wound up his throw and tossed them at me, almost jumping out of the pit. The dice bounced back and forth before sticking the landing.

"Two, craps, two!"

Feeling drained from the hole in my wallet, I looked around to see if I could find my clients. Even among the hum of the casino floor chatter, I heard an eruption of joy and groans near the roulette wheel. There they were. Now was as good a time as any to check in with them.

As I approached the wheel, I thought about the complex odds and wagers involved. Roulette's a funny game. It's all luck, of course, but every player has a strategy to edge the odds in their favor.

I remember blowing money on the roulette wheel while an old codger would always play the same bet: $10 on odd numbers and another $10 on red. The red squares have three more odd numbers than the black, and if the ball lands on black or any odd, it evens out. I don't know how often he hit an odd red number, but he seemed to be a part of the table, whenever I glanced his way.

Chris, the head organizer of this getaway, stood next to me rubbing his forehead. I leaned closer to him.

"Having a rough night?" I asked him.

"I'm down five hundred," he sighed.

"Just on roulette?" I asked.

"Poker," he said. "I thought this would be easier." Most folks play dollar chips and hope to get lucky. It's a slower game, less strategy. Pick a number, any number, but the roulette wheel always had poor Chris guessing.

"Hey, pal!" he shouted to the dealer. A fan of green rose to my eye level. Five big ones in hand, Chris looked to his friends. His tongue wet his bottom lip.

"It's time for a comeback." He threw the cash at the dealer, who pawed it with little effort.

"Twenty-fives, hundreds," the dealer asked.

"Hundreds, let's get some of those black chips."

My eyes watched the whole exchange. He was really doing it. Five hundred at once; I'd never known a player who wanted to flash his money around and play small ball. Chris rubbed his five chips in his hand. He turned to look at the screen near the wheel. The last six numbers that had been drawn shined into our retinas. The last three had been all reds.

"Let's put her on black. Big bet on black," he shouted. His hands came together with a big crack. He wiggled his fingers and muttered words under his breath. The tension weighed on all of us. With such big stakes, I didn't want to wish him good luck. This was a whole 'nother ball game now.

"No more bets," the dealer informed the players. The dealer looked at the black chips on the board and started the wheel. The ball whirred around the wheel. The droning noise sounded calm until the ball dropped onto the numbers. The clinking got everyone's hearts up. Which would it choose? I watched the black slots whizz by. The pebble stopped jumping and rested. My neck stretched to see the number.

"Seventeen!" The dealer exclaimed. All eyes went to the black seventeen.

"Yes!" Chris shouted with his fists above his head. He looked like he could lift a bus with the adrenaline pumping through his veins. His mischievous laugh knocked me out of my state of shock.

"Nice bet," I said. He placed the chips on the rail but kept his chips on black.

"Let's do it again!" Chris shouted. *Oh no.* "Ride my coattails, fellas!" He cackled and clapped his hands. I kept my composure at the sight of a probable trainwreck. Big risks mean big disappointments.

"No more bets," the dealer warned.

We're locked in now. I could feel my lips press together, holding my breath. The pill went down the chute and started whipping around the wheel.

"Come on, big black!" Chris shouted.

"Black!" His friends shouted. "Thirty-five!" Another shouted, pounding his hands together.

The words, "Black! Black! Black!" came out of my chest. "Come on, Black!" The little white ball chose her partner as it settled into place.

"Two!" The dealer cried. The whole gang jumped out of their shoes. The dealers started shoveling chips.

"This is the best action I've seen all night," I shouted to Chris over the whoops and hollers. Sweat started to bead through the wrinkles in his red face.

"I think that's the last of it for me, hooo," he exhaled into a laugh.

"If you want to cool off, there's a pool on the roof."

"I could use it," he replied.

They all huddled together at their collection of black chips and ran off to cash in their winnings.

After watching Chris narrowly escape a very difficult conversation with his wife, I decided to take my own advice and hit the pool. Twenty stories above the Las Vegas Strip was the glorious Blue Stallion hotel pool.

The string of lights wrapped around the glass wall surrounding the roof dwarfed in size compared to the city lights and neon signs of the other hotels around the block. The noise on the street didn't seem to bother the swimsuit-clad guests. Couples tread water in the corner of the pool while friends reminisced in the low light of the bar. I found an empty chair and stretched out. As soon as I got a good yawn in, a familiar voice piped up.

"Would you like something to drink?" Mario asked.

"Sure, I'll have a Manhattan."

"I'll be right back," he said. I looked out at the desert between the high-rises, wondering why of all the sand pits in Nevada, they chose this one. Before I could answer my own question with hypotheticals, Mario popped up again.

"What's your room number?" Mario asked.

"It's uh…" I patted my pockets and pulled my phone out of my pocket. *Did I even reserve a room?* "Wasn't there a room where you put my bag?" I asked.

"You didn't check in yet, so I put your luggage downstairs, behind the front desk." I squinted, retracing my steps. I could always sleep in the jet, I thought.

"I'll figure it out with Susan," I said. "But here…" I handed him a $20 bill. "For the drink, keep the rest."

"Thanks," he said with a bright smile.

I downed my cocktail and thought of my gameplan as I headed downstairs. Once the front desk appeared, Susan looked up to me. She juggled documents and gave me a look like I was slowing her down. I picked up my step to meet her there sooner.

"Hi Susan," I said, meekly placing my hands on the desk. "I thought I had reserved a room here-"

"I'm afraid not. Would you like to book a room?"

I surprised myself with a long pause. I tapped my finger on the desk and shook my head.

"Nah, I'll just sleep on the plane."

She flicked her eyebrow up and turned around. "I'll be back." She returned with my suitcase and met me at the edge of the desk. I pulled my gear from the ground with a toothy grin.

"Have a good night," I told her.

"Sleep tight."

After going through airport security in the wee hours of the morning, I settled inside the dark cabin of the jet — my jet. I threw a blanket on the couch and padded my clothes to form a pillow. My legs hung off the couch, but I couldn't care less. The distant sound of planes flying overhead soothed me. The lights on the tarmac and over the hangars kept a subtle glow under the cabin windows. I took a deep breath in with my arms behind my head. Flying sixteen hours a week, making money, and I own this flying can. I was living the dream.

High Roller Airways

Chapter 5: Bet Your Bottom Dollar

May is the biggest month on Kentucky's social calendar. Celebrities, horse breeders, and gamblers come together to witness the most-watched horse race in the world, the Kentucky Derby. This also makes May a busy time for the city of Las Vegas. Every sportsbook in town was prepared for every dreamer with an "inside tip" on the horses.

Logically, I was bringing in a new group of clients to celebrate. With the busy traffic to Las Vegas, taxiing into the hangar was a drag.

As soon as we got to the hotel, the feeling was electric. The biggest days in Vegas centered around sports betting: the Super Bowl, March Madness, and the Kentucky Derby just to name a few.

Mario was scrambling around the hotel with luggage carts and bags in his arms, keeping the blinders on until he reached the front desk to take care of my clients' bags. Susan, never wanting to keep a guest waiting, gave us our room keys and player cards while taking a pause before saying with a smile, "Good luck and enjoy your stay."

I refrained from making a little joke in passing, seeing how busy she was. After Mario caught his breath, we set our belongings down and followed the sounds of nervous bettors gathering in the sportsbook. Suddenly, we were engulfed by a flood of hotel guests. Even though it was hours before the race, the sportsbook was already teeming with hopeful bettors. We posted up at the bar, letting the younger crowd stand around.

I looked down at what I thought was a bar menu, but it was actually the list of horses and their betting odds.

Steam Engine – 4:1	Bucket of Mud – 5:1
Canadian Samurai – 5:1	Blue Mountain Mist – 6:1
Lucky Charm – 7:1	Horse Called Wanda – 8:1
Tom Boy – 9:1	White Wedding – 9:1
Scratch-Off – 10:1	The River Kwai – 11:1
Timbuktu – 12:1	Best Picture – 13:1

High Roller Airways

Casablanca – 14:1	The Grand Bazaar – 15:1
Old Frankenstein – 16:1	Gomez Adams – 18:1
Carpenter's Tools – 20:1	Baker's Dozen – 25:1
Bottom Dollar – 30:1	Logan's Run – 30:1

Who comes up with these names? History told me to always take the favorite. The names mean nothing. If you, like most folks, didn't have access to the horses' workout reports, you didn't have much to differentiate these bulking creatures. Pick a color, the symbol next to their name, or your lucky number, there's always a chance you'll pick the right horse, but the favorites are favorites for a reason.

The guys discussed their options. I heard nearly every name on the board thrown out at least once. There didn't seem to be any rhyme or reason behind them, but the thrill in the air couldn't be denied.

"Bucket of Mud, I'm calling it!" one shouted.

"Baker's Dozen!" another sounded off.

"Scratch-Off, that's a winner right there!"

I kept my eye on the big screen. The owners promenaded their horses on the muddy path to their stables. I laughed at the people in the stands with their big blue hats and mint juleps, knowing all the glamor would be wiped away as soon as the race was over. The pomp and circumstance of this prestigious event felt odd as I looked at sweaty, red-faced men yelling over the noise to the patient, unblinking kiosk attendants.

I leaned over to one of my clients, Greg, and asked, "Who're you betting on?"

"I'm not sure yet. Any tips?"

"Steam Engine has won a few races. Logan's Run only won a race in Arkansas. It's enough to qualify, but I wouldn't rest my hat on it."

He nodded, thinking. We looked down at the list of names we hadn't heard of before this weekend.

"I'd choose one of the top five to win," I suggested. "Otherwise it's up to you if you want to bet on who's going to place or show."

"Do you want to go in together?" he asked.

"I like the sound of that. Who do you pick to win?"

"It's between Steam Engine and Lucky Charm," he said, looking at the list.

"Steam Engine to win, Lucky Charm to place?"

"I like that."

"Want to bet on any longshots?"

"Bottom Dollar," he said without hesitation. "Just a feeling." I laughed and shrugged.

"Yeah, why not? Let's do it."

After having a few drinks and waiting for the line to the kiosk to get low, I made my way over to place my bet. The doubts swam in as I approached the desk. The attendant looked a little weary now, with tired, depthless eyes.

"Fifty on Steam Engine to win, twenty-five on Lucky Charm to place, and twenty-five on Bottom Dollar to show," I said.

"Alright," the attendant said, typing onto his computer. "That's 4 to 1 odds for Steam Engine to win, the payout would be $200. Lucky Charm to place is 6 to 1 odds, with a payout of $200, and Bottom Dollar has 8 to 1 odds to show, which makes it a payout of $150. Sound good?"

$550? Yeah, that sounds good.

"Yup," I muttered. He handed me the slips, and I returned to the bar to cool my nerves. I let the steam out of my lungs after the sip of a cold beer.

"How much did you put down?" Greg asked me.

"A hundred across the three bets," I answered. "How about you?"

"Five," he said, letting his head roll back on his neck. My eyebrows twitched.

"Five? Like five hundred," I asked. He just nodded and watched the TV screens.

"I have to save something for the craps table later," I said with a laugh.

"After we win, I'll join you," he said. The cool look in his eye didn't make me any more comfortable. I just raised my glass to him.

"To our horses."

"Cheers."

Before the race began, the lights of the casino dimmed. The chatter disappeared, the light from the TV screens shined brighter, and the commentary from Churchill Downs came in through the speakers.

"We're just about to begin the race, and you can cut through the tension with a knife," an announcer said. Every head in the room turned towards the massive TVs. I pulled the tickets from my pocket and looked them over.

"Alright, here we go," Greg said, blowing out a relieving sigh.

High Roller Airways

I took another nip from my glass and watched. The last of the horses were loaded into the starting gate. The door closed behind them.

"Logan's Run is the last horse in, and we're ready for the start," announced the commentator. There was a pause. The thunderous clap of open starting gates rang through the speakers. Hooves pounded into the dirt.

"And they're off!" The commentator's next words were mute. The whole casino jumped off their feet. Hands clapped together to nudge their horse along.

"Steam Engine!" "River Kwai!" "Timbuktu!" All were heard over the stampede. The jockeys edged their horses closer to the inside of the track, each finding their spot in contention.

"Canadian Samurai is off to a great start, Blue Mountain Mist cutting in front of Baker's Dozen," the voice announced. The bounding hooves kicked up circles of dirt, leaving a haze of gray behind the last of the herd.

"Canadian Samurai's in the lead, with Blue Mountain Mist, Steam Engine, and Tom Boy picking up the pace as we approach the first bend."

My heart dropped. The favorites were pulling ahead, but Steam Engine wasn't in the lead, and our dark horses were nowhere to be seen. In my mind, I screamed at the jockeys. I yelled at them to bend low over their horses, to crack their whips and get ahead. *There's no time to lose!*

Less than a minute into the race, the horses crossed the half mile mark. The positions hadn't moved much. The card on the screen showed:

1	Canadian Samurai	2	Blue Mountain Mist
3	Tom Boy	4	Steam Engine
5	White Wedding	6	Lucky Charm

Lucky Charm. Lucky Charm! There was a chance. He just got his chin over the bar into 6th. He and Steam Engine could make it if their jockeys had the guts.

"Come on, Lucky Charm!" I shouted. "Go, Steam Engine! Go! Go! Go!"

The pack was closing in on the ¾ mile mark. The lead horses slowed down, giving the others in the back hope. The jockeys buckled down and kept the pace. White Wedding and Lucky Charm fell off the board.

"Ahh!" I cried. Then two names replaced them: Timbuktu and Bottom Dollar.

"That's our horse!" Greg shouted. "Go Bottom Dollar!"

The bettors belted out desperate cries. Men swatted their tickets like riding crops; women clasped their hands and squeezed them tight. We all stood wide-eyed as the beautiful beasts reached the final, long stretch of the race.

"Lucky Charm pulls ahead of Timbuktu, while Bottom Dollar is neck and neck with Steam Engine! Now they're entering into the final stretch!"

The jockeys brandished their riding crops and delivered crashing blows to their beasts. Before that stretch, the horses seemed to be riding for their own enjoyment. Now with the herd collapsing again into a narrow point, it was all for keeps.

"Come on, Bottom Dollar, baby!"

"Give it some gas, Lucky Charm!"

"Go, Steam Engine, go!"

"Tom Boy is putting on his run. Here comes Bottom Dollar, pulling ahead of Steam Engine!" My back started to sweat. My scalp went cold.

"Go!" I shouted. "Do it! Go! Go! Go!"

"Timbuktu is making some distance with Lucky Charm, Steam Engine, Bottom Dollar, and Tom Boy are fighting to show! Bottom Dollar is in the lead for third!"

For the first time in a horse race, I didn't seem to care who won. It was all about who'd show. The three horses neck and neck for third pounded the dirt, not making any movement as they rushed down the line.

"Timbuktu is pulling ahead in the final sixteenth! Bottom Dollar pulls ahead from the pack. It's going to be Timbuktu! Timbuktu wins the Kentucky Derby!"

The cries from the crowd bellowed through the speakers, bouncing off the few disparate cries from the sportsbook. I turned to Greg, my newfound friend, and we screamed until the adrenaline ran out of our veins.

"Wooh!" I shouted.

My lungs couldn't scream any more than that. I held myself up with my hands on my knees. I patted down my pocket where the tickets were. I pulled them out and looked at the payouts. $350. *That's a lot of cash for watching horses.* Hats flew in the air, over the potent silence of saddened sighs. Losing bettors came marching back to the bar while the winners grappled each other and sang praises for Timbuktu.

"Drinks on me!" I shouted to the gang. I waved to the bartender and shouted, "Seven Mint Juleps!"

Chapter 6: Board of Directors

After a few busy months, I started to get the hang of it. Sometimes I'd be booked for a week solid, flying out Friday to Monday and then Tuesday to Thursday. As stressful as it was, I knew it meant more money was coming in.

After a busy 4th of July in Vegas, Jack called me to meet at his office. I had been flying almost non-stop since our announcement. This time I marched to his office with shoulders back. I knew who I was, and Jack was my partner. Nobody was going to question me. When I'd leave, the staff would ask each other with awe who I was. Jack's door was open, so I strolled right in.

"It's good to see you, Jack."

"Yeah, have a seat," he said, pulling himself away from the TV screens.

"I have good news. The Sebrings want to charter us again for New Year's."

"Good, good," Jack muttered. "Have you looked over our monthly revenue statements?"

"I have. We're doing very well so far."

He flipped through the pages of the latest report and placed one in front of me.

"34,300 dollars in profit," Jack said.

"Hey, that's great," I said. The look he gave me chilled my bones.

"That's 17,150 for both of us, in three months. How much were you making as an airline pilot?"

"But the amount I make per hour is better." The frown on his face straightened me out.

"You work two, maybe four days a week and then just lounge by the pool." The disdain in his voice hit me like a lead pipe. I resettled myself in the chair and took a moment to let the rage rush past.

"I'm the face of the company, Jack. You don't deal with clients, you're my partner."

He waved his hand.

I snapped. "And you sit here and collect the checks!"

"And without me, you'd still be an out-of-work pilot." The air hissed out my nose. I couldn't disagree.

"We both signed up for this. Once we pay off the plane, we'll be raking in the money."

"At this rate, we're looking at four years before we pay off the plane."

"Look, I know the margins are thin right now, but once we pay this off, we'll be making thirty grand more a month. We're starting off, but the future is bright."

"Flying by the seat of our pants for four years isn't very comforting, Dave."

"We're making money. We have customers lining up. We even have girls reserving the jet for photoshoots."

"How much are you charging for that?"

"$500 an hour, and they're paying it." He paused, considering the number. His sour tone didn't fade.

"How many super models live around here, huh?"

"I'm saying there are other ways to make money, and we're going to make more."

The disappointed silence filled the space between us. Suddenly, I felt like I had to convince him, but the other half of me wanted to storm out of there. I was the one working. He was an investor.

High Roller Airways

Jack said, "I'll reach out to the Packers. Their new draft class will be interested. Big, new money, Dave, that's what we need. Let's catch up in a few weeks."

"I'll keep you updated," I said, extending my hand. He gave it a respectful shake. I left the office less confident than I had found it. I still had someone else I could impress.

I stopped at the bank and the post office. On a tan envelope I wrote my father's address and shoved a roll of a thousand dollars inside and handed it back to the clerk. That'd be my warning that I was coming.

On the drive over, I pictured my dad waking up, late on a Saturday morning to find that envelope on his stoop with big black letters. As soon as he pulled it out, he'd know it was from me. I'd love to see the look of confusion on his face. *Eat your heart out, Old Man.*

Early on a Saturday morning, I slowed my car, letting it sink into a crawl before reaching my dad's front door. I popped out of the car and strolled to the stoop. I rang the bell and knocked on the door three times. I heard him shuffle towards the door at a quicker pace. That made me smile. He swung open the heavy interior door and watched me stare through the glass door. His hand stayed at his side.

"Morning, Dad," I said. My coy grin spread out into a wide smile. He pushed the door open a crack.

"Son," he said. "You know you shouldn't put money in an envelope. Postal workers might say it went missing."

"You should trust people more." My eyes flashed with new resolve, confidence. My dad's sagging eyes failed to register. He pushed the door forward and walked further into the house. I stepped quickly behind him before he turned around, making me roll back on my heels.

"So, what'd you come over for? To brag?"

"It's not a scam, Dad. I told you it wasn't, and I'm showing you now that it's a real business."

"You drop a wad of cash at my door and expect what? Some kind of medal?"

"I don't know," I answered defensively. I heard my hands slap against my legs. "Just say something." I saw him frown a little deeper. My anger started to turn. "Don't look at me like that!"

"You want me to tell you 'atta boy, Davie', because you made a few grand on this hare-brained scheme? That's not what a father does. You're in way over your head and you have no idea what's coming."

"Somehow, I think I'll eke out a living. I'm making money, hand over fist, and I'm working half as hard. I'm living on easy street because I took the risk."

"Oh yeah, you're a real entrepreneur." I raised my arm, ready to start up again, but he cut in.

"This is all just a dream. You're floating on profits now, but when things go bad, you'll have nothing left. You got a debt you can't pay back. You got yourself into a business that you can't sell. It's an anchor around your neck, David." The way he said it made a tear grow in the corner of my eye. I shoved my hand into my pocket.

"You just want to ruin what I've made for myself so bad, don't you?" He shook his head, eyes closed in disbelief. "Sorry I didn't want to work in a warehouse the rest of my life. Sorry I wasn't kicked out of the Air Force like you."

"You watch your mouth, boy." We both stopped in our tracks. His calloused finger hung between us. "Don't get too big for your britches. I'm still your father, and I've always looked out for you. I don't have to like the bed you've made for yourself. I'm not going to nod along like some clueless a—hole while my son throws away all that he's worked for."

My fists sank into my pockets. I looked around the treeless lawn. I had to think of something. It couldn't be another one of those "I told you so" moments.

"It doesn't matter what you think. I'm still going to put in the work; you just won't see it."

He sighed, knowing that I'd keep that promise. I kicked my foot, spiraling a rock off the stoop.

"I have your ticket for EAA, if you want it," he said.

"I might be busy. I'll let you know." I turned on my heels. When I reached the car, I slammed the door shut. My knuckles paled as I tightened my hands around the steering wheel. My eyes spanned the road as I took off down a country highway, flanked by tall trees and gray skies.

I'd have to turn this company into an undeniable success. I knew what I was doing. I drove my foot into the gas pedal, reaching 80 MPH and set the cruise control. The 55 MPH speed limit sign flashed by as I took the turns with both feet on the floor. I was in control.

High Roller Airways

Chapter 7: Lady Luck

Flying over the Rockies at night always stirred my nerves into a mix of fear and calm. Floating over the jagged mountaintops, only a few thousand feet below, should have filled me with dread, but in the cockpit with my hand on the controls, it felt cozy to coast over the mountain range.

Seeing the lights of Las Vegas below, I could anticipate the excitement on the ground. That weekend's cargo consisted of three couples touring the city. They weren't big gamblers but wanted to see what else Las Vegas had to offer besides casinos.

Angela, a straight-haired blonde somewhere between thirty and thirty-nine, seemed to be some kind of social media influencer. From her hair to her nails, to what she wore on the plane seemed to be from the cutting edge of today's fashion. She wore dark sunglasses on and off the flight. She kept her distance from everyone, made me feel like the help, even though I am the help.

Her husband, Madison, seemed to come from money at the start. He wore a watch with an exotic brand name, medically-assisted white teeth, and a pinstripe shirt with thick cuffs of the same glowing color. I always had doubts about rich couples, well, rich people in general, but I tried my best to see the people under their postured looks.

After sleeping in and taking a cat nap after breakfast, I decided to lounge poolside and get some sun. Most of the heavy drinkers and partiers hadn't rolled out of bed yet, so the guests lounging by the pool enjoyed their sun time in good health and easy relaxation. I looked around the chairs and the tiki bar.

There wasn't much seating despite being so early. That's the trouble with luxuries. You can never build a big enough pool, gym, highway, or airport. There's always traffic, no matter what you do.

An older couple in matching bathing suits decided to head back indoors. I smiled their way and threw a towel on the seat. Feeling the rubber straps on the lounge chair against my skin felt relaxing. Nobody was expecting me to chaperone, pilot, or guide them around today. It was lovely.

As soon as my eyes reopened to the crisp, cloudless blue, I found Mario standing over me at attention.

"Morning, Mario. What can I do for you?" He laughed at me answering first.

"Nothing, I'm good," he replied. "Can I get you a drink or something?"

"Mmm… Rum and Coke," I said aloud.

"I'll be right back," he said.

My head rolled back to the center of the lounge chair. My lips and tongue imagined the sweet nectar of that cheap tropical specialty. I exulted in the spices dazzling my tongue, and the bold taste of soda chasing it down.

I pressed my hat down over my face when I heard a sigh sit next to me. My little eye crept past the brim of my hat and saw Angela breaking open a magazine. *Just pretend you're asleep. No, you have to say something. Get up. She sat by you for a reason.* I rustled up in my seat and fixed my hat.

"Morning," I said.

"Oh, you scared me!" Her hand clutched her collarbone. "I didn't know that was you." *Dang it!*

"Sorry to startle you; enjoying the city so far?"

"It's better than home," she said as she leaned into her magazine.

"I love coming here. There's no place like it."

"I'm sure you do," she practically hissed. "You're here all the time, aren't you?"

"Always, I love sharing the city with new people. They're electing me to the tourism board in November."

"Mmm…" She returned to her magazine.

Mario, thankfully, came by to give me a suitable break from the conversation. "Here you go," he said, handing me my rum and Coke.

"Would you like one?" I asked Angela.

She looked over with her big, rimmed sunglasses. "No, that's alright," she muttered, returning to her pages.

I looked up at Mario with shrugging eyebrows.

"I'll have another one of these," I told him. He nodded and turned to leave.

Soon it was me and her again. My mouth felt like a desert that finally received some much-needed rain. I let the ice cubes rest against my teeth, the dark, crisp drink slipping past them. I sighed indulgently.

"I wish we had a pool at home," she said.

"Yeah, pools are nice to have," I said, running the ice cubes in circles.

"Madison said he'd buy a house with a pool. We've been married for two years, and I'm still waiting."

"If you're lucky tonight, he can get you two."

"It's such a waste. All he can think of is what he wants. He wants to go to Vegas, we go. He wants a BMW, he buys it. I don't even drive stick, but he buys one anyway. I want a pool, and I'm stuck here."

"By the pool," I muttered.

"What was that?"

I prattled on, "The shows here are world class. You should go to one."

"We have tickets for Celine Dion, balcony seats. Madison's so cheap."

I laid further back in my chair. Naturally, I couldn't leave the conversation without leaving the pool, and I liked the pool, but she was a client. I needed to serve her any way she wanted, even if it meant just sitting beside her, not making her feel unwanted.

"Big Celine Dion fan, huh?"

"Ever since I was a little girl," she said listlessly.

"There's always something for everybody," I said, looking for a life preserver.

"Madison chose the location; I chose the entertainment, it's the least he could do."

My eyes swung in a frenzy to find Mario, but I settled for the man of the hour, coming our way. "Speaking of…"

"Hey, sweetheart," Madison said, kneeling beside her. She offered him her cheek, and he kissed it, their little game. "How're you doing, Dave? Keeping Angela company?" he asked, flashing his ridiculous smile.

"We were just talking about some of the shows in town, singers, magicians, circus acts, you name it. Why don't you take a seat?"

"Aren't you staying?" Angela asked me from behind her shades. I could feel her eyes drilling into my frantic mind.

I gave a showman's smile and said, "You two have fun. I've had enough sun for today, take care." I power-walked to the elevators like an old lady the day after Thanksgiving.

The night before leaving Las Vegas, the couples wanted to try their luck at the casino. I met them down in the lobby, gave them the spiel, and probed their interest. They followed me inside. There's nothing like being the seventh wheel to make you feel lonelier and more burdensome, but once they made their decision, I was set free. I turned around and took a step away, but Madison clapped my shoulder.

"What's your game of choice?" he asked.

"You like to play craps?" I asked, jutting my thumb.

"I was thinking the same thing," he answered.

We gathered around a craps table and exchanged our cash for chips. I placed a bet on the passline and waited for the shooter on the other side to throw. The dice bounced across the green felt.

"Three, craps, three," the dealer announced.

"It's alright, just a bad roll," I assured Madison.

We placed our bets again. The red dice crashed against the backboard.

"Four!" The dealer said.

My head leaned back and forth. "We're still alive."

Madison was already claiming bets on the table.

"Bet on five," he said to the dealer. A hand took his bet and placed it under the 5 on the mat. "Bet on six and eight, too," he added.

The dealers communicated to each other about the bets being placed. He confidently stacked some chips on the Field. I joined him.

"Hedging your bets, huh?" I asked.

"I work in trading, I like to make sure I'm going to get some return on my investment," he said with a glowing grin. The thin crook escorted the dice back to the shooter. The fella shook the dice in his hands and lofted them over to our side of the table. The dice bounced and settled on opposite sides. The die nearest us showed 3. I looked up. *Not 4. Not 4. Not 4. Not 4.*

"Seven, craps, seven," the dealer announced.

Among the groans, I couldn't help but join them as I watched Madison's chips flee the table. I'm not sure if he could hear me sucking the air through my teeth, but his smile ran from his face in an instant. We got real quiet after that. I flagged down a waitress to take our drink orders, a reward for our bravery.

As a new shooter chose his dice, Madison and I shrugged off the last loss and hoped for future prosperity. The shooter gripped both dice, tapped them on the felt, then the backboard, and finally launched them across the green.

"Ten!"

"Wanna try it one more time?" I asked him.

He snorted with a grin. "I'm game," he said. We placed bets on 5, 6, and 8 and placed another bet on the Field. The crook swept the dice back to the shooter on the other end.

"Come on, shooter," a few guys howled.

"Give us something good," they wished. The shooter rustled the dice against each other between his fingertips. A pound on the felt, a smack on the back board, and whoosh. The dice came to earth and clinked against the other side.

"Three!" the dealer said. The other dealers placed identical stacks of chips to the winners in the Field box. Madison and I clutched our winnings and padded our stack on the railing.

"Do it again!" Madison bellowed.

"Make us some money, shooter!" I echoed. A crooked smile came across his face on the other side of the table. We were cheering him on. He ran his fingernails across the felt, back and forth, scooped up the dice, and tossed them down the lane.

"Niner!" The dealer shouted. The Field bettors got another neat stack next to their wager. Madison and I pocketed ours. I had a change of heart and took the rest out of the field.

"I think this one will be different," I said with a shrug. "Just a gut feeling."

"Scared money, don't make money."

"Shooter! Shooter! Shooter!" The fellas near the sparkling slot machines started to chant. The clink of the dice against chips caused every eye to look down.

"Eight!" The dealers swept the Field dry. Madison got his bet back from the 8, but it was a bittersweet victory.

The game went on like that. We won some and lost some, but ultimately Madison was down, and I was breaking even. As the dealers changed shifts, I took a moment to look around the casino, let my eyes gaze beyond a single table.

Angela was puttering away at a slot machine, not far from our table. I could see her eyes this time. They reflected the bright, dazzling lights of the fast-paced machine. She seemed either utterly enthralled or completely unamused. My bet was the latter.

The machine she was working must not have suited her, because she threw her hands up and ran her arm through the loop of her purse. Her mind was elsewhere until she saw that I was watching her. I was startled, too. My arm rose and beckoned her over. The listless stare she had didn't seem to change. She marched over promptly.

"Here comes Angela," I said to Madison, returning to the business at the table.

He looked around and caught her under his arm. "What's the matter, babe?"

"This place f—king sucks," she said. My face cringed. Thankfully, I was leaning over the table.

"Oh, it's not so bad," Madison assured her.

"How much money have you lost?" she asked. Another shocked expression ran over my face. I looked down at the chips and the crisp green mat.

"Only," he started, thinking. "Only a few hundred."

She gasped. "Now you're just throwing our money away. We should've gone to another show instead. It'd be more exciting than this."

You know, I thought she had a good point there, but, boy, was she a pill.

"Come on, don't be like that. Why don't you roll some dice for us," Madison suggested.

"No," she protested.

He swapped places with her. Suddenly she was looking at six red dice, waiting for her approval.

"Take two dice," Madison whispered in her ear. Her eyebrows rose with a displeased look on her face and picked the closest two.

"Now, aim it down there, but don't throw them too hard," Madison instructed.

Angela threw her arm and opened her hand mid-flight. "There," she said, crossing her arms. The dice jingled against the mat. Madison rubbed her arms and stretched his neck over her to see what the dice displayed.

"Seven, pay the line!" The dealer ordered. The dealers reached over with winnings to every player around the table.

"What happened? Was that good?" she asked.

"You just won us a hundred bucks," Madison explained.

"Really?"

"Roll it again, sister!" The howlers called.

She looked their way and the smallest curl formed on the side of her lips. The dice returned to our corner of the table.

"Do I have to roll the same number or a different number?" she asked.

"Yes, that number you just rolled and uh... five plus six, we'll win with those two numbers," I said.

"Five plus six? You mean-"

"Shh, shh," I stopped her. "We don't say the numbers here. It's bad luck."

She didn't like being scolded and shook the dice in her hand. She pawed them and let loose halfway over the table. The little cubes bounced across the mat and into the pit wall. The numbers tumbled, revealing five plus six.

"Yo-leven," the dealer sounded.

"That's good!" Angela cried.

"It's very good," Madison encouraged. "Look at the money we've won." The side dealers' hands stopped by our stacks and revealed another pile of winnings.

"Do it again!" The guys bellowed.

"Do it again, baby," Madison said. He placed two black chips on the passline. I hesitated but took the dive. I doubled my last bet and watched as Angela clutched the dice in her hands.

This time she threw them underhand. The dice skidded across the mat and slammed into the wall. The nearest die tumbled back to us. I saw a 4. *What's the other one say?*

"Seven!" The dealer called.

"Yes!" Madison shouted. He squeezed Angela tight.

"This is fun," she said.

I could see her bright smile and knew she meant it. "You're our good luck charm," I told her. "Let's see it again."

Angela pressed her hands together and rubbed them hot. The dealer shoved the dice back to her. She puffed out some air and plucked up the dice. Without hardly touching them, she launched them down the table. My throat closed. The lack of ceremony before the roll felt jinxed. The dice crammed into the corner of the table and ricocheted off. *Five plus two.*

"Seven!"

The whole table burst into cheers. The hoodlums at the other end shook each other and belted hardy laughs for the whole casino to hear.

"That's our girl!" one of the gang shouted.

The dealers scrambled to collect the winnings for everyone around the table. Players started asking the dealers to color them up. Greens and blacks started landing in front of the players. I pocketed my winnings like I was robbing a bank. Madison kept his cool and kept Angela close.

High Roller Airways

I never really saw it happen, but the hooligans at the table must have started jawing off to passersby. Players without a table began to close in. I turned around and two fellas crammed in behind me. My shoulders turned in like I was standing in the world's smallest phone booth. I leaned over the rail and waited for Angela to shoot her dice. Once the dealers had settled the bets, they pushed Angela her dice. Everyone's eyes were on her.

She held the dice vertically in her palm and thrust them forward. They crashed into one side and then rolled to the other. They came back together as a pair, with one die resting on the other. They stopped. Then the top die leaned, rubbing off the corner of its partner. It barrel rolled, ending up on the 3 side.

"Seven!" The dealer's voice sounded muffled under the riotous cheer around the table. She rolled again.

"Seven!" She rolled again.

"Seven!" She rolled again.

"Seven!"

The players could never have dreamed of this happening. The odds were always so stacked against you winning that getting away with this felt like winning the lottery. I even wondered when the dealers were going to change the dice, hand them off to someone else, but they didn't. They played it cool. I mean — they had to. Otherwise they'd have a mutiny on their hands.

"Let her ride, let her ride," the players bellowed. Another seven or eleven, I thought. Let's see ten in a row. Angela tucked her tongue into the corner of her mouth and lifted them above the table. The little red cubes came crashing down and almost flew out of the pit, but they plunked down again. Three plus… five.

"Eight!" The dealer called, almost too enthusiastically. My eyes caught a glance of the pit boss blowing a ring of fresh air. The howlers at the end took a moment to cope with the change of plans.

"Did we lose?" Angela asked.

"No, we just need you to roll that number again," Madison said, pointing to the 8. He placed some black chips behind his bet on the passline. "You got this."

She didn't seem unsure. "Easy," she said. She shook the dice and cast them down the table. The dice bobbled, every heart around the table throbbed harder, restless until the dice showed their numbers.

"Hard eight! Hard eight!"

High Roller Airways

"We won!" Madison shouted. He spun Angela around and planted a big kiss on her. Whistles and yowls shot out from the other side of the table. Angela and Madison took their chips.

"Let's celebrate," Angela told him.

"Anything for you, babe," he said with a sappy smile.

A laugh left my nose. I always loved seeing a happy couple, but enjoying the sight of a lovely pair was cut short. My attention was pulled back to the table as I saw the herd of red dice lined up in front of me.

"Your turn," the dealer said, reeling back her crook.

I put my hands up. "Oh no," I insisted. "That's a tough act to follow." The table shared a laugh, and I courteously gave my spot to one of the watchers behind me.

She had shot eight winning rolls in a row. I crunched the numbers to find out the odds on that: 1 in 500,000. Half a million chance, and we rode that wave like kings.

Later that night, she invited their whole group to the rooftop bar and ordered a trough of champagne on ice. Angela and Madison stood near the bar, entangled in each other. After a few sweet-nothings, I caught her eye, and she peeled away for him for a moment.

"David," she called. "I just wanted to say, this vacation has been so much fun, thank you."

"Anytime," I nodded.

"I know I've been hard to deal with on this trip. Please, have a drink with us."

"I hope he gets you that pool," I chuckled.

She smiled warmly and softened the look on her face. She took a flute of champagne and held it out for me. We clinked glasses and shared a drink together.

"I'll have to get this brand for the plane ride back."

High Roller Airways

Chapter 8: Ripped Tickets & Sportsbooks

As more and more states legalized sports betting, every homer with *Sunday Ticket* thought he could craft the perfect parlay. Seeing headline sports bets hitting gave every gambler the courage to place their ill-advised longshots, but I never really got into it. There were too many variables to consider, especially when I knew for certain that a deck always has 52 cards.

Some player gets injured in the game and changes the momentum. The late-seed underdog finally wins against the dominant favorite. Not to mention the spread or the over/under. How can anyone guess what's going to happen on the field? That's why they do it, because it's anybody's game, and the house always knows better than you.

One weekend, I had a round-trip flight with a trio of sports bettors. I stood in the hangar beside the jet, giving it the once over. When I was satisfied, I snapped out of my trance at the sight of three older men in bowling shirts standing waiting for me.

"Oh, sorry to keep you waiting," I explained. They didn't budge, watching me behind their aviators. "Just taking care of maintenance. We should be ready to go in a few minutes. Here." I reached for the door, bringing it down for them. The first man gave me a curt "thank you" while the other two filed in behind him up the stairs. After making sure the bolts were screwed on tight, I climbed the steps after them and gave my stump speech.

"Welcome, gentlemen, to High Roller Airways." I clapped my hands. The same stony stares stuck to me. I gulped. "We should arrive in Las Vegas about four hours after take-off. We'll have a shuttle take us to the Blue Stallion and get you checked in. We have champagne available as well as a full bar for you to enjoy. You can listen to whatever you like on the speakers. I will ask you to not drink until I click off the seat belt signal when we're stable in the air."

Their expressions hadn't changed.

High Roller Airways

"Any questions?" They looked at each other and shrugged. "Okay, I'll get us into the air. Enjoy the flight."

I turned on my heels and locked the cockpit door behind me, sighing. I put my mind on the flight and tried to motivate myself to enjoy the ride.

An evening of luxurious living at 40,000 feet had to be lived to the max, which means lots of empty bottles. During the flight, I would occasionally check the camera looking back at my passengers. The little box showed my three guests, sitting back, relaxed, pouring another round of drinks for themselves; then another and another... Still, I had to put on a smile, even though I worried about them staining the floor. I just hoped they could walk down the stairs of the plane without tumbling onto the concrete.

Once we landed and made our way to the hangar, I placed my hand on the cockpit latch. After opening it, a thrust of music swam past me. The Doors were trying to break on through to the other side while I caught them all in mid-stare. They must have been watching the door since we stopped.

"Hey, good to see ya!" one shouted. He sported big black glasses and thin hair. I'd learn that his name was Glenn.

"Have a drink with us!" Jim, already red in the cheeks, dared. "Do you have any more champagne?"

"There are two bottles in the fridge, did you check?"

"Oh s—t, we drank 'em both," Jim realized.

Before flying to and from Vegas, I always restocked the fridge with two bottles of champagne, a bottle each tequila, whiskey, vodka, and any fixings the previous group suggested I add. The shelf where I left the champagne was empty. I looked back at the spent bottles on the table.

"Looks like you boys can put 'em away, huh?" I joked. I remember hearing stories of kids getting their stomachs pumped for less than this. I strapped myself in for whatever roller coaster I was heading for.

After letting the drunks off the plane, I led them safely to a large SUV that took us to the hotel. I stood waiting for them to check in so we could go our separate ways.

My foot kept the tight beat of a snare drum watching the three old fogies ask questions about the accommodations and club rewards and champagne.

Susan wasn't behind the desk and Mario was gone, so nothing could soothe my anxious fluttering. Once they seemed to have exhausted their questions, they turned to look at me like I should have already had the answer.

"Well? Where's the restaurant?" Henry asked.

"There's two inside, the sports bar or the-"

"That one," he interrupted. They all laughed hollow, wet coughs from their chests.

"I'll show you," I offered. I could feel their eyes on my back all the way there, making me rethink my line of work in customer service.

I pushed the saloon doors open and welcomed the gang to a cozy corner with high-definition, retina-overloading TV screens. They unthinkingly sat down in their seats with saucer-shaped eyes locked in on the blazing colors.

"The best spot in town," I said with a flick of my salesman's tongue.

"Where's the sportsbook?" Glenn asked.

"In the casino, to the right," I said.

"Don't be a stranger, have a seat," Henry said, gesturing to the empty spot next to Jim.

I allowed as much of a grin as I could bear. As soon as I sat down, I was enrolled in what would be the *finest* lecture on sports betting I've ever heard, also the first, but every student needs to take their first class.

Glenn rattled off some questions to start. "You're a sports bettor, right?" he asked. His watchful green eyes shined through his big rim glasses.

"I've bet on horse races and Super Bowls, but not much else," I replied.

"We'll show you the ropes."

"But don't listen to Jim though," Henry warned. "He bet a grand on the Cowboys winning the Super Bowl."

"Don't talk about that. My wallet's still sore from last year." Jim chuckled.

Glenn was the analyst. He liked doing his research. "I have a list."

"He always has a list," Jim and Henry chimed.

Glenn shook his head like he hadn't heard that joke before, letting the well-mannered hyenas heckle him as he displayed his expert system.

"Record, injuries, home field advantage, points scored when they win, points scored when they lose."

"Seems pretty straight-forward," I said.

"Trust me. It's not." He lowered his glasses down his nose to show me I better wise up.

Jim was all guts. "I'm feeling an upset," he would say several times that weekend. He claimed to have dreams about big games the night before.

"And every single time the winning team won," he insisted. "The points were off, but now I know it's just the team that wins. There's a method to the madness."

Big Henry was the homer. Any home team, he would bet on.

"The home team wins five hundred and five out of a thousand games. That's an edge."

He also bet on his favorite teams because he couldn't root against them.

"You never turn your back on your team. It took fifty years for the Bucks to win a championship, and I'll keep betting on 'em for another fifty."

"You don't have to bet on them every time either," Glenn reminded us.

"But when those odds are calling your name..." Jim mused.

"Dumb money is what Vegas wants," Glenn explained. "Take the time to do the research and think with your head, maybe you can make some money."

I listened and nodded, drinking more beers than I had intended given that I wasn't doing the talking. The most I added was, "You think so?" or "Why is that?" Still, the looks on their faces, giving me all their hard-earned wisdom, made me smile. Sometimes it's nice to talk and have somebody listen, like you're appreciated. Somehow, someway, they pulled me in.

"They're the underdogs," I asserted. "It's a steal!"

"Vegas always knows the odds," Henry replied.

"They have it down to a science," Glenn extolled. "For the over-under, they're always off by one or two points. Always. You just have to decide which side of the numbers they are."

"Don't think you can guess better than the house," Jim chimed in.

"They do it for a living," Henry explained. "We're but humble day traders."

"Be smart, do your research, and stay away from parlays," Glenn interjected.

"You can do a small parlay," Jim hinted.

"No," Glenn said, pointing his finger at Jim.

"Oh come on, Pa, just a little." Glenn's face soured, muttering something under his breath. We couldn't hear exactly what it was with the hearty laughter bouncing out of our corner.

After dinner, some cocktails, and a touch of freewheeling at the craps table, I had a serious hangover. I slept for most of the day and by the time the Saturday games had started, I wiped the room service grease from my mouth and rolled out of bed. I stumbled to their door and knocked a few times. Nobody answered. I knocked again.

"It's open," one of them shouted.

I stepped through the door and saw a three-man gambling ring in progress. Glenn had several packets of paper printed out on the high-stool table, Jim had his bets already placed across the couch, and Henry, big Henry, stepped out of the shower with his towel hanging over his shoulder like he was walking a runway.

"Oh look, he's alive," Henry joked. They all bellowed. I averted my eyes and realized that their open window overlooked the casino.

"Let me get into something more comfortable," Henry said. He almost winked at me as he turned. *Is this what happens when you get old?*

"You ready for tonight?" Glenn asked. "I hope you did your research."

"A little, between migraines," I joked back. He grinned and waved me over. I gently stepped around Jim's laid out bet tickets and took a seat across from Glenn.

"Not a tree hugger, huh?" I jested. Glenn paid no mind and handed me a packet. It was a list of scores for the Chicago Blackhawks and Columbus Blue Jackets. All of their goals, wins, and other information Glenn was itching to tell me about.

"Clue me in, Glenn. I'm stumped."

"The Chicago-Columbus game is on tonight," Glenn explained. "The over/under is 6.5, and the Blackhawks have an average of 3.5 goals a game, and a goal average of 4.8 per game when they win on the road, so I have to figure out who is going to win and by how much."

"So who is going to win?" I asked.

"I don't know yet," Glenn admitted. "I have to crunch some more numbers." His pen carved black ink into the margins of his sheets.

"How many games are you betting on here?"

"Three tonight, six tomorrow," he said, pulling more packets out of his duffel bag. "Serious bets mean serious decisions," Glenn declared.

"You must have an industrial printer at home, huh?"

"No, I did this at the library," he stated, then ducked his head down to his papers.

Taken aback, I turned my attention to Jim as he read the ink-printed rolls of paper at his side.

"Who are you betting on tonight, Jim?" Jim's round head peeked up at me. He noticed a change in the atmosphere.

"Blackhawks, Bucks, the Canadian Jets, the Wild, Houston Rockets, and Cleveland. I have a parlay on all of them, so if it hits, it hits big."

His greedy grin made me laugh. Glenn swayed his head at the decision.

"That is if you hit all of them."

"You'll have an old-fashioned on me to go with eating those words, Glenn."

Glenn couldn't hide his laugh behind a swatting, dismissive hand. Henry strolled out of the shower with pants and an unbuttoned Hawaiian shirt, looking expectantly at us.

"You fellas ready to make some money?" he asked.

"Let's do it," I replied.

"Atta boy," Henry said with a thunderous clap on my shoulder. Jim gathered his tickets in his hands and methodically folded them into his breast pocket.

"What about you, professor?" Henry asked Glenn.

"Give me a minute," he said, flipping through his pages of statistics.

"Have you ever heard of paralysis by analysis?" Henry asked with a contagious laugh.

"Wise choices take time," Glenn replied.

"Wise choices? This is gambling! It's all heart. Isn't that right, Jim?"

"If they're on the field, they have a chance."

"There's your one-bit wisdom, eh, Davey," he clapped my back again.

After a few more jokes and betting tips, I escorted the guys down to the sportsbook where every inch of the walls was covered in TVs and projector screens. No matter where we looked, we could see each shot, pass, and goal as if we were on the field.

I decided to join in on the fun and put some money on the Bucks to win, being the slight favorite. I'd almost double a $50 bet if I won, nothing too crazy. As these old timers' eyes locked in on the screens, I leaned over to Jim.

"How much do you have on the Bucks tonight?"

"One," he said. My eyes squinted.

"One?" I asked.

"One thousand. I have five on Winnipeg beating San Jose, and another thousand on a parlay."

"How much is that total for tonight?"

"Uh…" he looked at the tickets in his breast pocket. "Twelve," he said.

I almost swallowed my tongue. "Good luck," I said as confidently as I could. His eyes stayed on the screen, while his fingers stuck the tickets back in his pocket.

Watching with those guys, knowing the money they were throwing around, made every play seem like a fighter landing or dodging a punch. The Bucks ran up their lead by 20 and the guys hollered. When the Jazz cut the distance, even by a 3-pointer, I shifted away from the table after feeling their iron fists crashing down on it. I looked over at Jim refreshing one of the scores on his phone every few seconds.

It started to make me sick. It wasn't feast or famine, it was staying on course or spiraling towards disaster. No joy, no hurrahs, just white-knuckling stress.

As the games came down to the final period of play, I could feel all of us on the edge of our seats.

Keeping his eye on the Bucks-Jazz game, Henry started shaking his head. "I don't think I'm making the over on this one," he muttered.

"There's still five minutes, a lot can happen in five minutes," Glenn explained. Even a methodical thinker like him had to get his hopes up. There was too much on the line to be a cynic.

Jim checked his phone again and jumped out of his seat. "Yeehaw!" he cried.

"What happened?" I asked.

"Winnipeg's up by two goals. I told you it's a lock."

"How much are you going to win?" I asked.

"Twenty-five hundred clams," he answered, slapping his ticket on the table. "Now we just need the Blackhawks to win and I'm up five grand!"

Our attention turned to the Blackhawks. The game was in the final two minutes of play. The score was tied 3-3. The Blackhawks' winger chased the puck out of the zone. The Columbus defensemen skated back, closing the space between the winger and the wall. The puck tapped off the winger's stick before the defenseman flawlessly took it in stride, spinning and launching it across the ice. Time ticked down. The puck got caught against the wall, two, three men stabbing at it with their sticks and skates.

The Blackhawks' left winger pivoted his hips and threw the puck down ice behind the goal. The keeper guided it safely to an uncovered defenseman. One of the Columbus players took the bait and sailed past the defenseman who then passed it to the next free man. The Columbus player skated back as fast as he could to recover his team's defensive numbers. The two teams squared off. The wingers passed the puck to the center, trying to gain another inch on the ice, pinning back the defenders.

The Columbus center charged. The puck flew through his legs, ahead of the winger and the man marking him. The puck slapped the backboards. The goalie kept his head on a swivel, not letting up that side of the net. The Columbus defenseman flung the puck down ice, less than a minute to go. Columbus pressed up as Chicago brought the puck back to center ice.

The Blackhawks maneuvered in a triangular formation, keeping distance between the Columbus players. They passed the puck, back and forth, skating ahead. Columbus pushed closer together, making a large half oval ahead of the goal. They watched the puck with their eyes, not overstepping this time. A Blackhawk tried to separate himself from his defender, make some distance. He looked back for a through pass and got it. The center slid the puck past his opponent and had it lined up with the winger. He placed his stick down, but the puck ran off his skate into the goalie's stick. Without thought, the keeper flicked the puck over to a defenseman. He was ready.

With his hips at full torque, he zinged the puck upward, aiming for the sprinting winger further down the ice. The Columbus player caught it, laid it down, and the Blackhawks' defenseman missed! He threw his body into the wall, leaving Columbus one on one with Chicago's goalie. He puffed out his chest, taking up as much of the goal as he could. The winger wound up and slapped it. We could hear the crack on the ice from our seats. Top left corner. Red buzzer. The Columbus Blue Jackets chevron swept in from the side. 2.5 seconds left.

"Ugh!" we cried, our hands in our faces. Jim swore into his shoes. We sat in heavy silence. My weak, defeated eyes looked up to the Bucks game and saw the Jazz had taken the lead by 4, with 28 seconds to go.

"That's about it," I said. Jim looked up at the game and watched a Jazz player sink one of his free throws. 125-120. Henry leaned back in his seat with a breathy sigh.

There were two more games we watched together, but the energy had dimmed. There were some wins and losses, but everyone seemed quietly content by the end. Maybe it was the drinks or riding the highs and lows of professional sports.

The fellas brought me back to the hotel room, and I didn't object. I could live vicariously through them. Almost immediately, the old geezers drew themselves a hot tub and stripped off their clothes. Glenn and I sat aside at the table to give them their space.

"There's more than enough room, boys," Henry guffawed from the small triangle of steaming hot water. I peeked over out of morbid curiosity and saw rolling blocks of ham, slow cooking in the corner of the room. I don't know much about those European bathhouses, but this seemed to fit the description.

"How'd you do, Glenn?" I asked.

"Lost some tough bets, close games, but I think I can turn it around."

"How's the damage?" I asked, prodding.

"Eh," he bobbed his head, not wanting to answer. "About three grand, but we'll see how tomorrow goes."

I nodded, dreaming the same dream. Somewhere behind me was this strange, high-pitched noise. I looked back at the bathing hippos and saw it was coming from two grown men, already finished with their first round of beers.

"Oh, Davey!" Henry's deep voice climbed an octave.

"Do you need help getting out?" I shouted.

Glenn snickered behind me.

"Could you be a pal and grab us some beers from the fridge?" Glenn asked.

Suddenly, I was the go-fer again, the help. That feeling didn't lift my spirits, especially as they kept shouting my name as I moved toward the fridge.

"Dave! Dave! David!"

"David, please hurry. We're thirsty!" I bucked up and turned their way with a pair of cold ones in tow. I took slower steps to get there, out of pride.

"Do you want me to open these for ya?" I joked.

"Yeah," Henry said, surprised at being relieved of the smallest inconvenience.

"My hands are all wet," Jim alleged. I tucked the bottles into my shirt and twisted free two bottle caps.

"All yours, gentlemen."

"Thank you, David," Henry said.

I stepped toward the fridge and reached for two more. "Do you mind if I join you?" I asked.

They raised their bottles, exposing their wet, wrinkled arms.

"Cheers!" Henry shouted. "There's more money to be made this weekend." I let the booze do its work and excused myself when they stepped out of the hot tub. I had plans most of the next day, but I'd join the old fellas the day we'd fly out.

The few hours between checking out of the hotel and getting to the airport on time are the riskiest hours to gamble. You have nowhere to go besides the massive TSA line or the tables to gamble away the rest of your stake. Some guys get the idea that it's their last chance to cut and run with some big winnings. Others have to fight the itch to put their mortgage on the roulette table.

I was struggling with the same feeling. I was down that weekend, pretty bad, and told myself firmly that I wasn't going back to the tables. I had some moneyline bets on a few football games before we had to head out, but the worst part was, I had to wait for them with no escape in this house of temptations.

I met the guys down in the sportsbook, looking over the odds before pulling the trigger on their favorite underdogs.

"Any hot tips I should look into?" I asked the group. Nobody responded. I looked down at my phone again, looking at the odds. There were some early basketball games alongside the football window, with some pretty one-sided matchups.

"Are the Spurs really that bad?" I asked.

"What're the odds?" Jim asked, politely looking over at my screen.

"+385, that's like four times your money," I explained.

"Who are they playing?"

"The Pelicans," I said. "They're only .500, so they're not *that* dominant on the court."

"Why are the odds so lopsided?" Henry asked.

"They only have 5 wins on the season, they're bottom of the barrel," Glenn warned. He flicked through his papers, then reached for his phone, possibly looking into it, just in case.

"Those are nice odds," I muttered. "And they're not getting blown out in every game, they just can't finish."

"How about injuries?" Glenn asked.

"Their rookie center is back, I don't know how to say his name," Henry said, adjusting his eyes to see his screen.

"Those odds are too good to pass up," Jim said. "What do you think, Dave?"

"I'll put some money on that," I smiled.

"I'll stick to football," Glenn muttered.

"You and me, Jim?" I asked.

"Let's do it," he grinned, extending his balled fist. We made our bet on a fist bump.

Four quarters and a possible overtime is a long time to play, lots of baskets to score. I looked down at the kiosk screen and selected the game, the moneyline, and then at the over/under. 231.5, so 116-117 would be over, 115-116, would be under.

How both teams can score over 100 points in a game never made sense to me, seems too inflated, but if a cellar-dweller like San Antonio was going to pull off one of their few wins this year, it was going to have to be a big shootout.

"What do you think about the over/under?" I said from the side of my mouth. Jim stood over the next kiosk and prodded through the options.

"231.5? That's a lot of points," Jim said, a little wary.

"But if the Spurs win, it might go to overtime, which almost always means an over." His eyes shifted back and forth. The idea crawled in his mind.

"You betting the over?"

"I'm betting the over," I echoed. "Let's do it!"

I pressed the button, bringing my $10 bet to a possible $85 payout. *$75 for maybe 15 minutes of strategizing?* It's a good day's work.

I placed my picks for the first window of games. When I assessed my choices with the rest of the gang, they all seemed to have different answers. With competitive matchups and a chance at the playoffs on the line, it could go anyone's way.

I learned quickly that watching football games with sports bettors was not relaxing. Curses, armchair coaching advice, and deep stat sheet analysis jumped up around me. No matter what happened, someone was groaning. Every play mattered, every point was for or against their hopes and dreams, their late-night strategies. Every broken pass, every field goal, every cheerleader dancing in frame mattered to these guys. I thought I was above the fray, safe among the clouds, until a star quarterback crashed down, out of bounds... and didn't get up.

"That's a late hit!" "Where's the flag!" "Oh, the refs are in on it!" "What did I tell ya!"

We all looked at our bets and tallied the damage. Tennessee was part of my bet, and their seasoned veteran was limping to the bench.

"There goes my parlay," I griped.

"Don't rip it up yet," Henry advised. "It's not over until it's over."

It was actually refreshing to hear some optimism from all the protests and grievances.

As the games went on, I checked a handful of scores on my phone. The Spurs and Pelicans were duking it out on the court, but the score had evened out at 60 apiece. Maybe this was it. Maybe they could pull ahead.

"The Spurs and Pelicans are tied," I said to the gang.

Glenn rolled his head towards me, eyeing me up, while Jim rubbed his hands together. "This could work, what's the score?" he asked.

I hesitated, not remembering, and refreshed the score. "Pelicans 54, Spurs 50, at the half."

"What was the over again?" Glenn asked.

"231.5," I muttered.

Henry couldn't hold back a grimace. "That over bet is not looking good," he said.

"Anything can happen in the second half," Glenn replied with confidence.

Jim stood and waddled to the kiosk and placed another bet. As he was tapping the screen, I hoped he wouldn't put any more money down. From what I could tell, his bets already weren't looking as secure as he let on. A new ticket draped out of the chute, and he waved it around to knock the bad luck off the thick printer paper.

"Who'd you bet on?" I asked.

"I don't think the Spurs are going to hit the over, so I just bet on them winning. One hundred to make five hundred," he said with a chuckling sigh. He could sense me worrying when he added, "More money on 'em gives 'em better luck."

Suddenly I started to lose hope in our little scheme. We were out of our depth. Chasing your losses is one of the many workplace hazards of gambling. For a guy who talked a big game, and I didn't judge him for doing so, he was having a bad day. With a quarterback down, another underdog being put in the pen, it was looking like Las Vegas was bleeding him for all he was worth.

I could see the dejected look on his face. His eyes looked gray and hopeless. His jowls sagged against the palm of his hand, keeping his head up. I was rooting for him, cheering when his team forced a turnover or sank both free throws, but still, we saw his odds plunge deeper and deeper on his bets.

As the afternoon rolled on, the Spurs-Pelicans game was coming to an end. The Pelicans were up by 10. The Spurs point guard took the ball to mid-court and assessed how the New Orleans' defense was moving, covering his teammates. He whipped a pass to another player just outside the three-point line. He leaned back and fired a desperate shot under heavy pressure, still able to finish his follow through. The ball dove into the net, putting three more points on the board. 111-118.

We kept silent, watching for the anticipated comeback bucket from New Orleans. Their shooting forward put his hands up for the pass. His mouth called out something but got caught slack-jawed as the San Antonio forward snatched the ball mid-pass and charged into a fast break.

He lunged down the court so fast that the other players slowed down to wait out the inevitable. The dunk slammed through the speakers. Jim and I roared and roared. *It's destiny. This is it!*

113-118. New Orleans took a timeout as soon as they crossed into the Spurs' side of the court. The giants huddled together to change up their game plan. Once a decision was made, they jogged into their positions and swung the ball around the arch. Hesitant and unsure, the offense couldn't penetrate the redoubtable defense. The shot clock started to constrict their passes. The point guard pivoted for an opening and threw a weak fadeaway shot as the buzzer rang. The ball tapped the rim and fell into the greedy palms of a defender.

There was only a minute left, and the game was within striking distance. San Antonio took the time to move down court and communicate their strategy. Time was fleeting, every moment another opportunity wasted as they side-stepped and bounced the ball around. The shooting forward decided to get brave, juke his defender, and lob a ball toward the net. The net jumped as the ball ran through it.

High Roller Airways

"Yes!" I heard myself scream. Jim and I clutched each other and saw the 116-118 scoreboard. We weren't out of Dodge yet. We sobered ourselves with the ticking clock, only 45 seconds left. If the Pelicans scored, that might be the dagger.

The Spurs kept a man down court to pressure the two players. He slowed them down, waving his hands, staying between them. A harsh throw got the ball onto the other side of the court. The New Orleans shooting guard kept his dribble low and tight, looking for an opening. Thirty seconds to go. I rubbed my numb cheeks, groaning in miserable fear.

The shooting guard didn't find anyone. His shoulder rammed into the defender to make space and fired a shot. The ball reached its peak before sinking fast, finally ricocheting off the rim and bouncing out of play. *20 seconds to make a miracle*, I thought.

New Orleans pulled all their men back. The Spurs moved down court but faced a tight wall of goliaths along the three-point line. The point guard hurled the ball out to the right side, but the defenders swarmed the center. He threw his elbows back and forth, trying to see a friendly jersey beyond the fray. He delivered a bounce pass that nearly flew over his teammate. Bringing it down, he got swarmed too.

He gave it back to the center, who had to dribble along the sideline, all the way to center court before flinging it over to the point guard again. 8 seconds left and it looked all but over.

The guard looked to pass the ball to the other side, but his defender stepped into his path. Coming to the rescue, the center landed a sturdy pick. The defense threw their arms up as they leaped forward. The point guard was already in motion. He jumped and flicked his wrist, sending the ball into a back spin. My mouth was catching flies, gripping onto Jim's shirt. The ball sailed to the net. It crashed into the rim like a springboard, towering hands reached for it, escaping their fingertips.

Baaah! 116-118, final score. 234 total points. They hit the over.

"Ahh!" I sagged, sinking into myself.

"Tough luck, boys," Henry said.

"Vegas is always so close, either way," Glenn said.

Jim gave me a knowing look. Our tired eyes looked at the rest of the football games on screen. We checked our bet slips and started tearing them up.

"How'd you guys do?" I asked.

High Roller Airways

"Tennessee lost, so there goes that bet," Henry read from his slip, splitting it in half. "Jacksonville and Houston lost, so there goes another."

"I also had Houston winning," Glenn said. He crumpled up his bet receipt.

"Did anyone win?" I asked. My question was met with immediate silence. Somehow, we all went bust. One leg went wrong here, two over there; not even Glenn's bean-counting could save us from a miserable last day in Vegas. We walked back to the lobby with nothing, just a hole in our wallets, full of regret.

Chapter 9: Kabaddi Nights

Whenever I thought of high rollers, I thought of old guys with young girls on their arm, or upper management snobs looking for the nearest putting green, but everyday people squirrel money away and nobody's the wiser.

"Good morning," I called to my clients as they approached the plane. My contact for the group waved his hand and jogged ahead of the rest. "Are you Vihaan?"

"Yes, I am," he said with a hardy handshake.

"Good to meet you. Why don't we do some introductions before we board?"

"Ah, yes," Vihaan said with a little bow before sweeping his hand out to include his fellow travelers.

"This is Deepak," he introduced. Deepak was a round man with a square mustache, older than Vihaan.

"Rahul," Vihaan said. Rahul greeted me with a charming smile and a double-handed shake. He was closer to Vihaan's age, a little younger than me. He had an eager look in his eye.

"And Manish," he said, sounding like "Maneesh". I jutted out my hand. Manish slowly uncrossed his arms enough to let one free to give my hand a shake, before recoiling it back into its previous position.

Their shirts and slacks made them look like typical office workers, maybe coming off of work directly. In my experience, four fellas from India never really seemed like the heavy hitters Vegas was accustomed to, but looking down at their Coco Chanel shoes and the slim gold chains they wore made me think these were guys I wanted to impress.

"My name's Dave Jennings, I'll be your pilot this weekend. There's plenty of drinks inside for you, including four bottles of champagne, so sit back, relax, and we'll get there around 8 local time."

Deepak and Manish kept their straight, stern faces, while Rahul looked like he'd jump into the cockpit with me.

"Follow me," I said with a chuckle and led the fellas up the stairs.

Once I gave them the whole spiel about flight safety, I disappeared into the cockpit. The runway had a refreshing look with some midday rain. I could smell the grass through the open window. I took one last noseful before slamming it closed and taxiing my craft out the hangar. The slick gray concrete shined ahead of me. Up above were white clouds and bright blue skies. Not a bad day to fly.

Once the wheels lifted from the ground, I did my best to get us to the top of the jet's altitude range. Fuel wasn't any cheaper this week, so we climbed up and up to about 37,000 feet. The thin air barely laid a finger on the wings; no turbulence, no problem.

Then I heard a knock on the cockpit door. I manhandled the radio.

"Feel free to open the mini fridge, fellas. It's all complimentary," I said to the radio with a satin tone.

"Hey, David, can we see the cockpit?" Vihaan's voice eked through the slits around the doorframe.

"What?" I shouted, hoping he'd change his mind.

He repeated himself. "Can we see the cockpit?"

I turned back in my chair, trying to bring my confusion to a heel.

High Roller Airways

Oh crap, is this a hijacking? No, come on, they're harmless. They just want to see the cockpit. But why do they want to see the cockpit? Because they want to see the clouds like anybody else. What if it's not? Why would they pay so much just to take down this plane? Is it racist to not let them in the cockpit? Do you want to be a dead bleeding heart or a living racist?

"David?"

"Just a second," my voice cracked as I tried to stall.

Now that I thought that I'll have to live with it.

I pulled the cockpit door just open enough to sense if there was any resistance. I felt nothing. I yanked back the door and saw all four passengers looking past me, bobbing their heads for a glimpse of the afternoon sky.

"Here," I motioned. "One at a time." Vihaan was the first to step forward. The cockpit started to feel crowded with the two of us standing. I sat down and manned the controls. Vihaan pressed his hand on my seat and leaned forward, seeing the streaking clouds and square farmlands below.

He kept his hand on my headrest. My head turned at a tentative speed. I'm sure my eyes looked worried or bothered with him looking for so long, but when I saw his eyes hang open, I knew I had a fellow traveler by my side. The memories of boyhood swam through my mind.

The first time I flew, my parents took me to Florida. I remember them asking the stewardess if I could see what it was like from the cockpit. It was the '80s, so it was fine. Dodging the cigarette smoke the best I could, my dad took me to the front of the plane. The two grinning pilots had called me "champ" and suggested to my old man that he pick me up for a better view.

He had hoisted me and saw the control panel rush down to make way for the wide-open skies. I knew I wanted to be a pilot, and now seeing Vihaan, a grown man like me, experience the best view in the atmosphere, made me realize I had made the right decision.

Once Vihaan took in an eyeful, he let Rahul take a turn. He was impressed, but once he saw the flat plains to the farthest horizon, he decided to duck out of the vestibule and make room for Deepak. I could feel his gorilla-like strength as he gripped my seat.

He had an undeniable, boyish glisten in his eye. He saw me looking up at him, grinning, like I caught him in the act. He looked away like he didn't notice, leaving the strong, silent Manish to take a look. After looking out at the clouds, he grunted and turned back. Once they sat back in their seats, I took hold of the radio.

"Make sure to look out your windows and see the sights from thirty-seven thousand feet. Enjoy the champagne, fellas." Settling back into my seat, thinking of them back there warmed my heart, highlighting this routine flight.

After touching down in Las Vegas, my passengers wanted to get to the casino as soon as possible. In the lobby, Manish and Deepak threw their bags on the luggage cart, nearly pushing it out of Mario's reach. I gave Susan an embarrassed and shocked look. She placed the player cards and room keys on the table without a word.

"Guys, here are your keys and player cards," I said, fanning them out. They plucked their cards out of my hand and distributed them to their rightful owners.

"Follow Mario, rooms 431 to 435." My clients formed a tight scrum behind Mario as he heaved over the heavy loaded cart. I looked back at Susan with a reluctant expression.

"I'll keep an eye on them," I said.

"I'm sure you will," she replied. I remained undecided on whether she meant it or not.

As soon as the bags were delivered, and Mario was properly tipped, by me, the group aimed straight for the elevators. I squeezed through the doors, narrowly avoiding a metal pinch as I entered.

"So… what's on the menu for tonight?" I asked. Manish's arms held their typical tight curl. Deepak looked at Vihaan and Rahul to answer.

"David," Vihaan turned to me. "Can you show us to the sportsbook, please?"

"Of course. I'm not sure what sports are on this late, but there's always something." As I finished, I felt a shoulder in my back and stepped quickly out of the way. I guided them to the hall of glowing TV screens and let them choose a spot.

In the booth, I let them settle in as I waved down a waitress. She followed me with a pitcher of beer and glasses for us. They looked like they hadn't moved since I left them, staring at the screens with magnified scrutiny.

"What're you guys betting on?" I asked, letting the waitress pour our drinks.

"Australian horse racing," Rahul piped up.

"Gold Coast Raceway," Vihaan said.

"Do you guys follow racing much?" Their eyes held onto the plain, dry grass course. For a horse race, I thought it would be more of a show, but there were just a measly six horses trotting behind the starting gate. It looked like they made a track in someone's backyard, which gave me another business idea. But I had spectators of my own in the booth with me. I cleared my throat to cut through the silence.

"So what do you guys do for a living?" I asked. Manish turned his head to Vihaan to explain.

"I'm the head of IT at Alpha Insurance, Manish is Director of IT at United Supplies, Rahul is IT Coordinator at First State Bank, and Deepak is IT Manager at Great Lake Financial." I gave a surprised nod and looked back at the turf track. The names of the horses came up on the screen.

1. Sambuca Surprise
2. Tokyo Tea Party
3. Gus Bus
4. Boxer Shorts
5. Penn Station
6. Queensland Express

"Who do you think is going to win?" I asked them.

"Red looks pretty good," Deepak said, pointing at Sambuca Surprise.

"Blue is my lucky color," Rahul countered, chuckling at the name Gus Bus.

"As good a strategy as any," I heard myself say. The timer on the screen showed five minutes.

"Let's place our bets, eh?" I suggested. I stepped out of the booth and put $20 on Queensland Express to win. I stepped to the side and caught a glimpse of Manish unraveling a wad of hundred-dollar bills.

Once we settled into our booths, I waved the waitress over for another round. The trainers filed their horses into the gate. The camera changed to watch the animals from the front. *Here we go.*

The gates flung open. Penn Station flew out the gate and closed the inside track. Queensland Express stretched her neck out in front of Gus Bus, keeping out of last place. The riders whipped their horses down the first stretch before settling into their arched form, gliding over the grassy backdrop. With so few horses, any error would be catastrophic. Queensland Express ran behind Sambuca Surprise, the race favorite. I swallowed a crisp mouthful of domestic beer and watched the horses bob along the ring of the track. Tokyo Tea Party and Boxer Shorts ran neck and neck behind Penn Station.

"Come on, Queensland!" I shouted.

"Go Tokyo!" Rahul shouted. The blue horse's legs pounded into the turf. Harder and harder the riders whipped them. Their strides' inertia seemed to propel them around the final bend.

"Queensland! Come on, Queensland!" I shouted. She squeezed her flanks between Tokyo Tea Set and Boxer Shorts, leaving Sambuca Surprise behind.

Then a voice like a rifle crack erupted near my ear. "Boxer Shorts! Boxer Shorts! Boxer Shorts!" Manish shouted, pounding the table. I reached for nearby glasses and kept them off the quaking surface. The last hundred yards came into frame. *Give her more time*, I thought.

"Stretch that neck out, Queensland!" I cried. "Faster! Go! Go! Go!"

"Tokyo!" "Sambuca!" All the names jumped out around us and echoed in our booth. My eyebrows reached for the sky. I felt like I was ready to pop and then… Boxer Shorts stretched his neck across the line.

"Ugh!" we groaned, except Manish who hollered from the depths of his chest. He growled like a tiger and pushed me out of the way to the kiosk. I pardoned him, seeing the stone-faced giant turn into a kid at the candy store. The other winners joined him, reveling in their shared victory.

After the seventh race, I started to sag into the booth. The rest of the gang scanned the screens for the next set of races.

"Are you guys staying up?" I asked. "It's my bedtime."

"I'm going to bed, too," Rahul said, stretching out his arms with a big yawn.

I slid out of the booth and waited for Rahul to join me. I led the way back to the lobby elevators. Down the long hallway between the casino and the lobby, a hot blonde came down the other way. She walked with purpose and held her head upright, glancing at me before holding a stare. She raised her eyebrow slightly, daring me to come closer.

As I conjured a charming line in my head, Rahul whispered to me. "I forgot something. I'll be back."

"Oh," I said, taking my eyes off the woman. "I'll see you tomorrow." I looked back and she swept past me like a platinum flash of lightning.

"Good night, David," Rahul said under his breath.

I marched to the lobby, feeling my eyelids sag. Then I saw Susan at the front desk. *One last thing*. With one witty line in the chamber, I strolled to the front desk, but she saw me approach. Too far to speak, too close to change direction. I grinned and cocked my head at her.

"What're you doing here?" I asked, like a sarcastic dad. *Idiot*. She chuckled anyway.

"Just got done with welcoming some very important guests. Any luck at the tables?"

"Nah, just horse racing tonight. I'm good at picking fourth-place horses."

Her lip curled. Her mouth opened to say something, but Rahul laughed aloud with the blonde on his arm. Glancing over my shoulder, I squinted, wondering how a guy like that could pull a girl like that. *Ohhhh*. I looked back at Susan, a little embarrassed.

"I'll look after him," I said.

"Mhmm," she replied.

"Do you... have you seen her... here before?"

Susan looked at the happy couple disappear into the elevator. "Lots of people come here," she replied.

"Uhuh," I said. She playfully looked away.

"You don't think she's a prostitute, do you?" I asked.

"Prostitution's illegal in Las Vegas," she stated.

"Uhuh," I muttered. "Do you know about that one? You know, just so I can better protect my clients."

"I don't think you can save that one, David." Her smile smoothed into a flat line.

I stepped closer to the desk and lowered my voice to a whisper. "I think you should tell me if you know about her… work history."

She leaned closer to me. "In the hospitality industry, we don't ask women whether they're prostitutes." She had pretty emerald eyes.

"Maybe you could confirm for a friend." She leaned away and shuffled some documents.

"Good night, David." She turned and disappeared.

"Uhuh."

Lying in bed, my head, shoulders, and torso were sapped of all energy, ready to fall one inch deeper into rest and plunge into dreamland. My legs, on the other hand, kept fidgeting and twisting to find the right spot under the covers. I tried throwing the blankets over; no good, too cold. I tried my left, and then my right side.

My legs still had energy running down them while the rest of my body couldn't possibly stay awake. I grunted in defeat. I checked the clock next to my bed. 4:00 in bright red looked back at me. *When in Rome.*

High Roller Airways

I walked down to the casino in yesterday's clothes, with my morning stubble settled in. *I wonder if they serve beer this early*, I thought. *It's five o'clock in... Hong Kong?* My thoughts about time zones washed away when I saw Vihaan walking out of the sports book.

"What're you doing up so late?" I asked. I chuckled at the parental concern that sprang from my voice.

"Hey, you're up," Vihaan cheered, welcoming me with open arms. "We have a table set up just for us, come on. You'll love it."

Vihaan led me to the same booth; they hadn't moved the whole night. A waiter caught my eye.

"Can I get a cup of coffee?" I asked.

"Yes," he said without stopping on his way back to the bar. Looking around the booth, I saw two sleeping tigers: Manish and Deepak were taking a big cat nap, mouths hanging open, and their heads leaning back.

"Should we wake them?" I asked. Vihaan looked at the TVs. What he saw caused his eyebrows to jump. His hands slammed together.

"Jaago!" He shouted. Deepak's head stayed still but his eyes sprang open. I felt my footstep back. He blinked repeatedly and did a double take, seeing me stand there in yesterday's clothes.

"Good morning," Vihaan said with a bright smile. Deepak sat forward, rubbing his temples.

"Good morning," Deepak muttered politely. Manish cracked his neck and knuckles before finishing the beer he left for himself before his trip to dreamland.

Vihaan and I sat down at the edge of the booth. Vihaan rubbed his hands, looking like a kid on Christmas for what was happening. I looked at the big screen in front of us, playing some coverage from a gym with no players nearby. A confused frown grew on my face. I leaned closer to Vihaan's ear.

"What sport is this?"

"Kabaddi."

"I don't think I heard you. What was that?"

"Kabaddi, it's a sport from India. You'll see."

"I didn't know you could bet on… Kabaddi?"

"Only in Vegas, it's not very popular here; but in India, it's massive."

"So is it like football?"

"No, you'll see, watch." He pointed to the big screen as seven men in light blue uniforms ran out onto the court.

High Roller Airways

The screen introduced them as the Bengal Warriors, with an animated tiger head roaring in approval. There weren't any hoops or goals, and the court was maybe 20 yards across. My eyebrows creased as I scrutinized what I saw on screen.

A poorly animated 3-D tiger with blue stripes roared at a mustached man with a swirling, silver club. *What is this?* I wondered. The referee, with most of his weight sagging over his belt, waddled from center court to his position only inches off the field of play.

Seven men stood on each side of the court at once. The referee blew the whistle and gestured for a player from Haryana to cross to the other side of the court.

The seven opposing players formed a red rover line, but instead of a group of boys on the playground, it was grown men on their toes, fighting for advantage with the cheers of thousands echoing across the ceiling.

Pairs of men held hands, ebbing away from the opposing player encroaching on their side of the court. This opposing player, called the "raider" in bright red letters on the screen, approached the line of defenders. The defending team formed a crescent, a wall of eyes watching for the raider's next strike. Where the raider went, the opposite side of the crescent moved in, shrinking the field of play.

The raider shifted his feet, catching a pair of defenders off guard. They jumped backwards to the corner of the mat. Like an outnumbered tiger, the raider backed away shifting his eyes all around. The line slowly formed into a crescent again. Seeing no way to make inroads, the raider stopped his attack and returned to his side of the court, joining the chain gang.

"How do you score in this game?" I asked.

"The raider has to touch an opponent on the hand or foot to receive a point," Vihaan explained.

Now it was Bengal's time to strike. Their raider kicked his foot out, missing a backpedaling defender. He prowled the edge of the zone before giving up and returning to his side. *Is this a low-scoring game?* I asked myself. *Are these guys good? It shouldn't be that hard to tag a guy.*

When the crowd appeared on screen, old ladies in saris watched with dazzling smiles. Old men whispered to each other with brooding eyebrows and square mustaches. It was like discovering a new world.

High Roller Airways

This entire ecosystem existed without me knowing about it, never even hearing of it, with millions of fans around the globe talking about this game.

The opposing team, known as the Steelers (not from Pittsburgh), sent another raider to the other side. He shifted from one foot to the other, watching the line of defenders adapt their position. He threw his leg out and then back behind him, switching his hips. The crescent started to constrict. The raider swiped at the nearest player's arm. The player's arm jerked back but he lost his footing. The raider dove at the player's foot and stayed on all fours to return to his team.

The ref blew the whistle and raised one finger in the air, pointing to the Steelers. 1-0.

"Seems like a pretty simple game," I said.

"You like it?" Vihaan asked.

"I think so…?" Nobody could pull my eyes from the screen as I soaked in the game.

Then it was the Warriors' turn to pull a raid. The offensive player bobbed and weaved, hoping the defense would bite. He pushed on the right side, pressing them into the corner. The Bengal player leaped out along the sideline. Then the Steelers clamped down on his leg, twisting him out of play. The raider's face slammed down on the mat first, causing spectators to jump out of their seats. Half the faces shouted with shocked expressions and others looked around, hoping for some correction to the cruelty. The referee awarded the defending side with a point. 1-1.

By the end of the second half I was enthralled. I thought I had found all the sports that were meant to be played, but now, I had a new game that I could explore. I sat up watching while the others slumped back in their seats. The Steelers were up by 10 with one minute left. The fat lady was just about to appear on stage. Seeing my clients look defeated I decided to lean back and borrow Vihaan's ear for a minute.

"Bad luck tonight?" I asked.

"Bengal was the favorite, so there our money went. Manish and Deepak had some wins earlier, but I've been a little off each time."

"Where's Rahul?"

"He wanders off at some point during the night. He'll be back before the big game."

"What's the big game?"

"We're from the same city back in India. Patna is playing Jaipur today. We're on a winning streak, which reminds me…" He leaned forward, looking at Deepak.

"Let's place our bets," he said in an unusually firm manner. Deepak grunted and slid out of the booth, followed shortly by Manish.

"I'll come with," I said. Vihaan looked taken aback. "Really?"

"Yeah, I kind of got the point of it. Patna, you said?" Vihaan's shocked expression vanished before making room for a cheery smile.

"Yes, welcome to the team," he said. He patted my arm before quickly jerking it back. We weren't that familiar yet. His arm hung at his side, but I chuckled and warmly clamped down on his shoulder and flashed him a big grin to reassure him that I was having fun like the rest of them.

I found an open kiosk and scrolled through the options. *Kabaddi. Kabaddi.* I pulled up the game and looked at the odds. Patna and Jaipur, cities I had never heard of, but were probably metropolises on the other side of the world.

To me they were names associated with odds. Patna was an evenly matched underdog, with +120 odds versus Jaipur's -110. I wanted to go with the group, but there was something else in the air. Maybe it was my delirious mind at 5 AM, but I bet one hundred. *Eh, why not?* Two hundred on

Patna. I walked back to the booth with the ticket in my hand. Deepak and Manish opened their eyes.

"Let's go, Pirates!" I shouted, my fist pumping in the air. Manish and Deepak's big hands slammed together, welcoming me to my spot at the table.

As the cameras swept the arena, familiar sights came through the screen. The little kids jumped with excitement for the start of the game. The referees prepared for the teams to claim the court. The little spotlights started to flash squares and patterns around the court, signaling the show was about to begin.

Through the gate, the Jaipur team ran onto the court in neon pink jerseys. Air rushed out my nose at the stern faces the men wore in their bright flamingo colors. Then the animated mascots popped up on screen. The Patna Pirates' mascot looked like the green giant, if he were a pirate at all, while the Jaipur Pink Panther had rippling muscles and a sultry look in his eye. As the lusting creature disappeared from the screen, a familiar face appeared at our table.

Rahul wiped his nose and opened his eyes wide. "Hello, hello," he said, seating himself at the end of the booth.

"We were afraid you weren't going to make it," Vihaan chuckled. He pointed to the kiosks. "Did you bet?"

"No, I'll do that," Rahul said with an aimless look in his eye. He rubbed his hand under his nose and shuffled over to the row of screens.

"You guys must really love this game to stay up all night for it."

"We do," Vihaan confirmed. "It reminds us of home, and we have lots of fun memories playing this game."

"You played it during recess, growing up?" I asked.

"Deepak played professionally."

My eyes turned to headlights and swept over Deepak's sagging, tired face. "You used to play, Deepak?" I asked.

"I played for the junior Patna team before university," he replied, eyes tracing the players on screen.

"What happened?"

"Happened? I went to university. No time for sports," he grumbled. Rahul came back with his own bet slips in hand, chuckling to himself before letting his face drop as the game began to unfold.

Jaipur sent their boy over. He wasted no time shifting to the middle of the court, jumping back and forth, trying to catch the defenders slipping. He threw his hips open and stepped backward. With proper footwork he could cut down the distance and reach out. He lurched at one defender. The defender's hand flew up and pivoted himself away from the Jaipur player. His partner flew out and raised both his arms out to catch the raider behind his knees. The raider jumped back and lost his footing.

His arm held him parallel with the ground. Turning, wrenching out of his opponent's grasp wasn't enough. Another defender wrapped up his arms. Another took his waist, weighing him down. The Jaipur player struggled toward center court. With one slow move, he fell like a piece of lumber and crashed against the mat.

The ref pointed to the Patna Pirates and raised one finger in the air. 1-0. The thunderous claps from Manish sat me up right. I joined the round of applause from the table.

"Aggressive," Deepak said, nodding, impressed.

"They read his attack, no hesitation," Vihaan added. I smiled at the familiar sport talk I had heard in countless variations over my years in bars, basements, and living rooms.

Next was Patna's turn. The excitement welled up in my gut. This new team was the gang's favorite, and I had a hefty sum on them winning. My gut started to turn as the first raider hardly left the line as he crossed the court. I needed a sign that this was all going to be OK.

The Patna raider marched closer, keeping his steps short and spry. He reached out, sweeping his arms to catch a lazy defender. He jumped to the left and the defenders he moved from closed in. He shrugged his shoulders, looking to strike. The raider donkey kicked and caught a defender's hand, launching it to maximum height. The Jaipur defense stretched for the wayward leg, but it retracted as fast as it left and carried the raider to the other side of the court. 2-0.

Suddenly, Jaipur's seven men narrowed down to five. Patna was winning. We were winning. *We*. The weight of doubt on my shoulders felt like a silly memory.

Jaipur came back with a few successful raids, whittling down the Pirates to five men. The burliest Patna player crossed the center mark and crouched, elbows over knees, hands up like crab claws. His eyes darted around, checking where the hands and feet of his competitors swung in the rhythm of this cat-and-mouse game.

The strapping Patna player flexed his back against the sideline, watching for the right opportunity. His feet swept to the middle but ripped from the mat as two Jaipur defenders lunged at his legs.

The 220-lb muscle-head pushed off one defender's back and landed on all fours, shifting back to the centerline, totally unscathed. Out of honor, the leapfrogged player put out his hand for the raider to tag, giving Patna the point.

He rushed back to his chain of teammates as a Jaipur player lunged across the line. The pairs split up and chaos swarmed the Patna side. Deepak and Manish groaned at their defense, totally caught off guard. The Jaipur raider tested the waters, finding his advantage. With his head turned to the corner, the big Patna player laid into him, decking him like a MACK truck. The other players dog piled on top, ensnaring him in a bramble of arms and legs.

"Oh man!" I shouted. I didn't know they could hit that hard. The fans on the screen booed and threw up their hands in disgust. Jaipur was down and soon they were reduced to one player on their side. When the Pirates had to send a raider over, the last remaining Jaipur defender gave himself up. The raider reluctantly reached out, taking his time to tag his opponent. The ref's whistle screeched. The referee raised three fingers and pointed to the attacking side.

"Three points for that?" I asked. "I mean, I'll take it." I never got a response. I looked over at Deepak and Manish. They watched on high alert, tracing the players' feet bouncing up and down the court. The Jaipur defenders returned with all seven players to their court. 16-7, Patna.

Rahul snorted and cracked his neck. A waiter came over with a notepad. Rahul stood, using the waiter's shoulder to straighten himself out.

"Some beer for the table," he said, limply pointing at us. "Room 432." He excused himself without saying a word. The sleep in my eyes started to come back, heavier and more suggestive than ever.

"I gotta wash my face," I said to Vihaan, sliding out of the booth. "More coffee," I told the waiter.

I stumbled my way to the bathroom, trying to remember I had to keep my eyes open to weave through the slot machines.

In the bathroom, my eyes blinked like crazy at the sight of the white LED light bulbs shining off the starch white walls. I told myself I could sleep after the game and looked at myself in the mirror.

The gray-blue veins under my eyes looked deeper and harsher under those heavy bathroom lights. I rubbed my eyes, letting the crisp, cold water splash off my hands. The water refreshed my skin and made my hair stand on the back of my neck.

As I looked up, I saw the black stall door open behind me. Rahul looked up and stopped in his tracks. He wagged his nose with his hand, inhaling with a brusque sound. White powder frosted his nose.

I slid over to him, catching him mid-stride. I caught his shirt in my fist, holding him upright.

"I don't like drugs on my plane."

"I don't know what you're talking about," he protested. I shook him and stepped closer.

"You bring a whore back to the hotel." I took his hand, feeling the ring rub against his finger. "You snort coke. Did you bring drugs on my plane?"

"No, I got it from her. Relax."

"I have friends at this hotel. You're f—king up my business, and I'm not going to have a coke fiend cost me my license either. You understand?"

"Alright, alright," he said, squirming back, still caught in my grasp. I pushed him back.

"They're waiting for you in the booth," I said.

But… that didn't happen.

High Roller Airways

The truth is I clammed up, feeling like I should have apologized because I'd walked in on something I shouldn't have. We both looked away. His footsteps beat behind me. The door swung open. I didn't even watch him go. The water flicked off my hands; I avoided my own stare in the mirror.

By the end of the second half, the game had tightened up. Jaipur sent their top player across the line to secure a point to tie the game. He moved like he had in the first moments of the match. He shuffled side to side, throwing the defense back and forth, like rolling waves along the court. He kicked out his foot at the winger, catching his little finger. The tacklers came in and shoved to the sidelines, but he reached out and slapped his fingers on the other half of the court.

The referees awarded him with a point for his narrowly successful raid. All tied up, Patna sent over a lanky young fella. The camera changed to a closer look. His eyes checked the corners of the mat, but he seemed nervous. We crossed the minute mark, only a few more phases in the game left. The slim Patna player threw his limbs around the mat, avoiding an overextension. He switched his hips and ran to the opposite side of the mat.

A Jaipur defender stepped forward, planting his feet for a big tackle. The tall raider followed his instinct. He shot out both his feet at the defender. His feet leaped off the defender's foot like a springboard, and he catapulted to the center line.

"Yes!" Manish roared with baring teeth. The silly Patna Pirate animation did the "robot" on the screen. Deepak shot his fists up in triumph.

The Jaipur players protested with wagging fingers, but the ref had blown his whistle as the Patna player crossed the centerline. I watched the clock, ten seconds left. 29-28, Patna. I felt the weight drop from my head. We were going to win.

"Let's go!" I shouted, shaking Vihaan like a ragdoll.

Jaipur sent over their last man. He ran the lengths of the mat, jutting in and throwing blind kicks, just to make contact. There's no time. It's over. Double zeroes. The ref raised his hand.

The guttural screams of joy blew the roof off that sportsbook. I bet passersby thought we had just won a horse race, but no. It was some silly game I couldn't pronounce, and we had all won big. I stepped up and lifted my head above the booth, finding the nearest server.

"Let's get some beer over here!" I cried. Deepak and Manish gripped each other, their eyes wet with tears.

High Roller Airways

♠

We seemed to reach the peak of the weekend after that match. For the rest of our time there, we alternated between playing the tables, lounging by the pool, or napping throughout the day. When it was finally time to go, my stomach started to churn. Rahul looked too casual, too unsuspicious for my liking. The back of my tongue dried up at the thought that he'd sneak some of his white powder onto my plane.

As soon as security cleared me, I looked back at Rahul standing in line. Backup plans sped through my mind as he glumly set his belongings into the heavy gray trays. They waved him forward. He had a confused look on his face. He raised his limp hands, not sure what to do next. They started to pat him down. *Make it through, you son of a b—h.*

Vihaan and Deepak distracted me from my obsessions with the flight plan. I informed them that we could cut some time off our flight going with the Jetstream. I looked back at Rahul and saw security point to his pocket. *Don't do this to me.* Rahul laughed and retrieved his keys from his pocket. The security team was just as relieved as he was. The tension slipped off my shoulders, and Rahul joined us without issue.

"Everybody ready?" I asked.

I let my clients sit inside the plane as I did the necessary inspections of the aircraft. My inspections were always thorough, for my own sake, really. With wildcards like Rahul, I couldn't leave anything to chance. Every turn around the plane, I thought I might miss something, and this whole scheme might go up in smoke, literally. I held myself up by leaning on the plane. The thought of crashing just to keep from working a regular gig made my head swell. But then I thought, it's been worth it. It's been worth it every day.

I gripped the rail on the stairs, gave her one last look, and ascended into my prized jewel. The High Roller Airways logo was emblazoned on the side. It was the throne that I'd built for myself, David Jennings, no one's subordinate. After shutting the door, a smile leapt across my face, thinking about my happy passengers.

"It's been another crazy ride, gentlemen. I hope you had as much fun as I did."

"Thank you again, David," Vihaan piped up.

"Take off is in thirty minutes." I turned to my quarters but stopped to listen to a deep voice behind me.

High Roller Airways

"Can we see the cockpit again?" Manish asked. A warm chuckle erupted from my chest.

"Sure thing."

Chapter 10: Jonesin'

After the first few months, gaps in my flight schedule started to show. We were still turning a profit, but I felt nervous having such thin margins. I decided to try my hand at earning some money on the Strip. To save money, I decided to fly economy to Las Vegas. Some things are worth every penny.

The ceaseless waiting and crammed conditions sank me into a vicious gloom. The gaps in the calendar made me think this whole project would backfire. Then I'd have to fly everywhere like this for a vacation, if I could even leave the state with all the debt I'd be in.

As much as I love going to Vegas and trying to win some money, I was going for work, not pleasure. I had to make some serious money, which I never liked thinking of doing. Desperate players make big mistakes, but so do big bettors. I just didn't know what else to do.

I could chat up players from the Midwest who wanted their next trip to include a private jet, maybe find some models who would pay for a chance to do a photoshoot inside the jet, or anything that could turn a profit.

At the Blue Stallion Hotel, I approached the front desk and received my key from the receptionist. I just had the one bag, but I saw Mario pushing his luggage cart back toward me.

"Hey, Mario, how've you been?"

"Hey, are your clients checked in already?" he asked.

"No, it's just me this weekend. Here," I plopped my bag on the luggage cart. "I'm in 323." Mario picked up my bag and slid the cart against the wall by reception.

"It's not too heavy." Mario smiled.

He escorted me to the elevator and to the third floor. I let my shoulders relax. This was a vacation. It was for pleasure. *Loosen up.*

"So you apply to any schools yet?" I asked.

"Yeah, Western Nevada, Reno, you know, cheap colleges around here."

"Have you heard back?"

"Not yet, but I'm hoping soon. Here's your room."

"Good, let me know when you know and uh… I don't know, I'll give you a firm handshake and 'congratulations.'"

He let out a little laugh.

"Have a nice stay," he said.

"I'll see you around."

Later that night, after a hot but lonesome meal in the hotel restaurant, I decided to find fellow travelers at the tables. I came back to my usual haunt of Blackjack and set a few hundred on the table. The dealer punched the bills down into the table. I placed $25 on the table and waited for my cards. The guy next to me put his hand through his stringy gray hair and looked down at me with his long nose.

I kept my eyes on the cards. The dealer slipped me a Jack and a 6. He placed his 8 under his hidden card. I sighed and rubbed my forehead, tapping the felt. A 2 landed in front of me. I swiped my hand above the cards.

"Nice hit," the long-faced guy said to me.

I grunted my thanks and watched the dealer hand out more cards. The two other players at the end of the table stood up after some friends pulled them away. My neighbor winged out his elbows, cracked his neck, and placed down three separate bets. *Big shot*. I placed my usual wager.

The dealer slapped down two 6s in front of me. *Not great*. I glanced over at this high roller's cards: 18, 19 and 20. The dealer had a 5. I waved my hand. He flicked his hand three times, wiggling his fingers like they were a flock of birds. He kept his toothy grin the whole game. The dealer flipped his hidden card, 10. He slammed another 10 on top of it for 25.

"That's how we do it," he whispered to me. I chuckled and shook my head.

"That's some good luck," I told him.

"My name's Tre," he said. His hand flopped in front of mine. I gave it a good grip.

"David… you're an adrenaline junkie, huh?"

"No guts, no glory," he said with a shining grin.

"Where are you from?" I asked.

"Chicago," he answered.

My eyes lit up like a wolf in a chicken coop. My exact clientele. "Oshkosh," I told him.

"Uh oh," he chuckled.

"Out here that makes us neighbors," I said, extending the olive branch. He chuckled warmly and pointed to my side of the table. The dealer waited with his open hand for my wager. I placed my usual bet. My eye caught Tre placing another stack on top of his latest winnings.

"Let 'er ride. Let 'er ride." His hands sounded like sandpaper rubbing together. The back of my neck started to radiate heat. I wasn't betting much, but I was getting nervous for him. Two 10s slipped in front of me, and the tension in my shoulders fell down a notch. I took a big sip of my beer as I waved my hand and watched this goofball try his luck.

He had 16 on one hand, two 7s on the other, and an 18 on the last. He flicked his hand over the first one and split the 7s. My eyes jumped from his cards to his stacks. He had over $300 on this game, and he was battling uphill.

On the two 7s, a 10 and an 8 landed. 16, 17, 15, and 18 all in a row flanked by green and red chips. He hit the 15. The snap of the card pull from the shoe widened my eyes. A red jack, holding a dagger to the heart. *Paints a picture, doesn't it?* He waved off the rest of his hands and the dealer showed his hand, 14. He swiped another card from the shoe and smacked it against the felt. His hand's shadow left the card as he raised his hand. A big red 5. That 19 beat my tablemate's four hands.

High Roller Airways

The dealer swept his hand over Tre's chips, pulling them into the grooves of the table. Tre promptly replaced his bets, three hands again. The back of my teeth started to drip. *Another sure-fire client. If I play my cards right, I can get back to a busy schedule.*

The cards flew out to meet our chips. I had a safe pair of kings, so my eye wandered to Tre's hands. A cool 19, matched with a delicious 11, and flanked by a respectable 18. He stood on the 19 and doubled down, $75, on the 11. The dealer flopped a 10 on top of his 11.

"Woo!" Tre bellowed. His voice crashed like a cymbal. It spooked me, and as I glanced around, I could see the floorman looking our way.

The dealer showed his ugly 13. The next card shot out of the shoe. The dealer's hand slowly turned it over his fingers and planted it down with his thumb. 8.

"Twenty-one," the dealer muttered. He took my stack and pounded his fist in front of Tre's one hand, before clawing at the rest of his bets.

"Are you sure you shuffled?" Tre said to the felt. The dealer's salt and pepper mustache hid his lips, holding back his tongue. I felt my neck sink into my shoulders. Tre clicked his teeth with a disapproving smack. He took out what he had

175

in his wallet, a few hundred dollars at least and threw it to the dealer's side of the table.

Tre slapped his chips on top of each other for three individual bets. Tre glared at our dealer, who, with a steady hand, divvied out the appropriate number of chips. The green fan of cash got shoved down the chute, and the dealer's open palm laid itself out to me.

"Just bad luck," I said, betting $50. "Let's turn this around." Tre's scowl started to soften, and he rubbed his fingers, anticipating a lucky set of cards. A red six slid into my chips, *not great*. Its partner followed behind it a few moments later. *Also not great*.

I turned my head to see what Tre had on his hands. 16, 17, and 18, not a bad hand when compared to the dealer's uncovered 5. I could do a number of things, hit and hope I got a 9 or lower, which wouldn't be a bad idea, but if I got a lower number off the board, Tre would be up a creek without a paddle. If I split, I could wind up with two 16s and leave the small cards to the dealer. Figuring I wanted to schmooze Tre, I decided to let him take the driver's seat.

"I can beat a fifteen," I said, waving my hand over the cards. Tre looked long and hard at his cards. His gray, slick hair started to shine from all the heat that was coming

High Roller Airways

off him. He stabbed his middle finger into the table. The hand plucked a red-backed card from the shoe and placed it in front of him.

"Twenty-six," the dealer said and swiped the bet away. Tre threw himself back in his chair with a pained look on his face. He folded his arms and waved off the next two bets. The dealer paused before revealing his hidden card. He lightly flicked it over and spread them out for the table to see clearly. 15. Before we noticed, his left hand brought another card down on top of the 10.

"Nineteen," the dealer declared. He swiped our bets. I wasn't even concerned that I had lost $100 in a few short hands, but Tre had lost a good amount more.

I watched him cover his face, his fingers digging into his skin. He put down the rest of his chips in three different bets, another $100+ per hand. He started to pace behind the seats of the table. It made me feel nervous. I wanted to hitch my wagon to this money fountain, but he might have been a loose cannon, and I knew I didn't need that kind of attention.

I looked up at the dealer, whose eyes swung like a pendulum. His cold grays watched Tre sweat over his next bet. I turned to Tre and waved him over to the table.

"Sit down, man, let's turn this around."

Tre turned on his heels and gunned right for his chair. I placed my bet down and shook my hand for the dealer to speed up the process. He quickly doled out the cards and waited at the ready with an uncovered 8.

A 10 and a 9 greeted me when the dealer signaled it was my move. I waved my hand. *Come on, Tre, don't screw this up.* I was rooting for him. That's the messed-up thing about sore losers, you want them to win so they can ease up, like a drunk father who stops trashing the house to go to sleep and leaves your family in peace for a few hours. *Maybe I can be a calming influence on this gambling fiend*, I thought.

I blinked and noticed Tre was still making his move. He stayed with two 18s and pawed the table for another card on his 8 and 7. A black queen squashed his 15, pushing him over the top. The dealer made his pass over the chips. The dealer's wrinkled hand pinched the corner of the hidden card and laid it out for us to see. A black, venomous ace, enough to tear your heart out.

The cold fist of the dealer pounded in front of my cards and carried the rest of Tre's chips to join its compatriots. Tre pulled at his hair, fuming. Spit jumped off his lips and four-letter words cut through the air. He started pacing again.

"Color me up, will ya?" I asked. The dealer nodded and swapped out my reds for greens and blacks. I dropped the new chips in my front pocket and took Tre under my wing. "Let me buy you a drink, pal," I suggested. "Relax."

He shook his shoulders and wiped his nose. I hurried to the closest seats at the bar and signaled the bartender over.

"What'll you have, Tre?"

"Coors," he muttered, trying to reconcile with the burnt hole in his wallet.

"Two Coors," I told the bartender. She stepped over to the cooler and pulled out two ice cold bottles. As soon as I knew the drinks were coming, I settled myself with a great sigh. My head turned over to a low-looking Tre. As soon as I heard the bottles scrape against the bar top, I took them in my hands and pushed a beer in his face.

"It'll be alright," I assured him.

Tre rose up by taking air into his lungs. The wet shine in his eye dimmed as he poured beer down his throat. His melancholic appearance seemed even more dejected when I heard his dull gulp. "You're right. I can always bounce back," he muttered. I pointed my bottle his way. He tapped the neck of the glass against mine, and we shared a drink.

"So what do you do for a living, Tre?"

"Real estate," he answered.

"The market's red hot," I added. "You must be doing well for yourself."

"Lots of folks moving to the suburbs," he said, his tone distant from the conversation.

"Which airline did you fly with?" I asked.

"Chicago Skies," he answered, pressing the bottle against his lips.

"Not bad, but it's a long flight, eh?"

"Yeah," he muttered. "The seats are so small on those planes," he said as he adjusted in his chair. "Bunch of cheapskates."

"I don't know why they can't make seats for people taller than kindergartners." I laughed.

His lips lifted and showed he was still listening. "More seats, more money," Tre answered.

"Mm," I said, nodding. "I've flown for lots of airlines, and it's like they squeeze, squeeze, squeeze," I complained with my hands closing in.

Tre's head bobbled a little, the wheels turning around in there. "Did you say fly for?" he asked.

"Yup, I'm a pilot, over twenty years' experience."

"So you must've traveled a lot."

"Oh yeah, mostly regional stuff, all over the Midwest, but I always make an excuse to come out here."

"Did you ever ask for Vegas flights?"

"I did, but with seniority all the old-timers got them first." We shared a laugh and the soothing balm of an ice-cold beer.

"Do a lot of pilots gamble?" he asked.

"I can't think of one who doesn't." I laughed wildly. "If airplanes could fly themselves, casinos would be the first thing to go out of business."

That knocked the rust off us two losers, just chuckling over some suds.

"Next time you want to go to Vegas, give me a call." I handed him my black business card. Boy, it's the prettiest thing when I pull it out of my jacket. He took it by the corners and looked it over. He chuckled at it.

"Private jet, huh?" he asked.

"Free drinks on every flight," I added. His lip curled. Always happy to see that smile when I sweeten the deal.

"I'll give you a call next time out. My buddy's getting married next year, so we'll have to fly in style," he said, placing the card in his wallet.

"I'm your man," I said with a little salute. Tre pushed himself away from the bar and dusted himself off.

"Heading back out there?" I asked.

"Yeah, you comin'?" he asked.

"I'll finish my drink and find ya." He gave me a thumbs up and trotted down to the tables. *Another satisfied customer.*

After throwing back a few beers, I thought I had played enough for one night, up a few hundred already and made my way back to my room. I patted the button outside the elevators, taking a deep breath and cracking my neck. *Long night's work.*

As the door slid to the side, I opened my eyes to Tre sitting on the floor with his face in his hands. He didn't even notice the doors had opened. Instinctively, I reached around the door and pressed my floor number, covering him from any passersby. As soon as the doors closed, and I felt my stomach lift, I turned to Tre and touched his arm.

"Tre, what's the matter?"

"I lost so much, man. I don't know what I'm going to tell my wife. She's going to leave me, man." His eyes held a gloomy haze. His tears shined off his cheeks. I hesitated, searching for the right way to answer. It's never easy to tell your wife that you lost a large amount of cash on stupid games, especially at his age. I imagined the bitter fights they must have endured up to this point, arguably because of his foolish decision-making, but... I still felt sorry for the guy.

"How much did you lose?"

"I lost 10K, I screwed up so bad," his throat reverberated inconsolable sobs. We reached my floor quickly. I gave him my hands and leaned back to get him to his feet. I took him by the shoulder and kept him close.

"Let's go back to my room and try to calm down, huh?" I rubbed his shoulder. I kept a bright smile for the both of us. I felt the corners of my smile lift higher as we walked past an elderly woman who was watching us with slow shock and concern.

I marched with Tre until we reached my room. Inside, I sat Tre down on the couch. He pushed his hands across his face and hair. He sniffed hard, trying to hold onto any semblance of pride he had left. I pulled up a chair and sat across from him. I tried to console him, but no words came. How many times does this happen to anyone? All I could see was this desperate, helpless man sobbing in the dark.

"Listen, Tre, it's bad. It's really bad, but it's not the end of the world."

"It's so much money, man."

"Yeah, there's no way around that, but you just have to say you screwed up and face the music. It'll be okay."

"She's going to leave me," he cried. I put my hand up to protest, but he beat me to it. "She's going to leave me, Dave. She doesn't need me. She doesn't want to be chained up to some loser like me."

"You don't know that. We can't think of the worst possible outcome."

"You don't know what she's like. She complains about everything I do all the time. This is going to kill us."

"You can get through this, Tre. You have to admit that you messed up, but if you're willing to put in the work to repair the damage, who knows what can happen?"

Tre cried into his hands, sinking into depths of despair at the hopeless state of his marriage. His sobs ricocheted off the walls. His soft howls echoed like a lost wolf in the wilderness.

"I can't live without her. It's all over, man."

"Don't talk like that…" I couldn't think of anything else to say. Here was this guy, his life in shambles, and I couldn't think of a single word to tell him that his life was worth living.

I ran my hand across my jaw, trying to think of a plan. As I contemplated my next move, Tre's whimpers started to die down. I watched him slowly tip over, spreading onto the couch.

"Yeah, just get some sleep, buddy, you'll be okay." I raised my hand to pat him on the shoulder but thought better of it. I stepped outside and closed the door as soon as my body passed through. I checked the halls to make sure no one was around. Tre didn't need any more people to feel embarrassed around. I saw one man down the hall. I tried to put on a smile but realized I didn't need to put on an act. It was Mario. He was coming my way, so I jogged over to cut the distance.

"Hey, Mario, how've you been?"

"Not too-"

"Good, good," I said, leading him with my arm around his back. "Listen, I could use your help. This is the most important thing you will do at this place."

Mario's mouth hung open, trusting me, but I could see the fear and calculations running through his mind as we walked to my door.

"My friend Tre has lost a lot of money. I'm going back to the casino to win it back. I need you to stay with him and watch over him, because he might be a suicide risk."

Mario stepped out of my reach and put his hands up.

"I can't-"

"Look, Mario, I need you. He needs you. This is more important than folding towels. This is a man's life. Please…"

Mario nervously licked his lips and let out a sigh.

"Alright," he said. I rushed him into the room. We found Tre pressing his face into the couch. His eyes rolled up to see his new friend.

"Hey, Tre, this is Mario. He's a good friend of mine. He's going to sit with you for a bit while I take care of some things downstairs."

I don't know how Mario looked being left in a hotel room with a suicidal man twice his age, because I closed the door behind me and ran to the blackjack tables.

I squeezed through the elevator doors and had a mind to march straight to the casino, but Susan was standing behind the front desk. There were no other guests around. I noticed I'd slowed down. *I have to do this first.*

High Roller Airways

"Susan," I said a little too far away from the desk. She tilted her head in my direction. An alert and cautious expression covered her face. She waited to answer back before I slapped my hands on the desk.

"David," she said smoothly. "What can I do for you?"

"I need a player banned from the casino." Her hands dropped to her sides, waiting for me to explain. "Listen, it's not for a stupid reason. The guy has a gambling problem. He just lost a ton of money. I think he's a compulsive gambler."

"Did he ask you to do this?" she pondered.

A chill sat on my shoulders. "Does he need to do that on his own?"

"If he wants to be barred from the casino, he has to ask, otherwise we're happy to let him play."

"Come on, he's not going to do that. He screwed up and he needs some help. Can you please put him on your list or something?"

She crossed her arms, deep in thought. Her index finger tapping her arm, hopefully conjuring up some loophole to help out a desperate man. "What's his name?" she asked, stooping down towards the computer.

"It's Tre uh…" *He told me his name, right? Oh come on, Dave, get it together.*

"He's from Chicago, he probably comes here all the time. You know him."

Her back craned upward, standing firm, with a solemn look on her face. "If you can't even give me his name, there isn't much I can do."

"He was playing with me at the blackjack tables and at the bar, just look at the security tapes and you'll find us."

"David, I know you're concerned, but some guys-"

"He's in my room right now, wondering what he's going to tell his wife because he lost-" I looked around to see no one was near enough to hear. "Ten thousand dollars," I whispered. Her face softened.

"Please, just help this guy out." I let out all the air in my lungs, waiting for her answer.

Her tongue twisted against her cheek. She stepped away from her desk. "I'll check our files and find your man."

"Good, I appreciate it, Susan."

Her sullen face kept its shape. "Go upstairs and get some rest," she added.

"No can do, I have to win him back his money." The chilling shock on her face gave me nothing but confidence that I was doing the right thing.

I've never needed the money, not like this. Most trips I spend all night playing, winning and losing, but it's for fun. Sure, I come out on top all right, but having to put in the work and grind out thousands of bucks on the casino floor? That's another story.

Tons of players teemed through the game floor. If I wanted to do this, I needed a table to myself. I liked getting cards fresh out the shoe, so no rookies would screw up my game by taking any tens heading my way.

As I prowled around the tables, I checked to see the highest table limits available. I had to bet $100 a hand. I found one table that had a minimum of $50, which would keep out most players. I needed to win big and win fast. I threw $2,500 down on the table.

"Let's get this going," I sighed. The dealer took my money without a blink and handed me the necessary chips. I thumbed a black chip into the felt. I stared down the dealer and waited for him to do his worst.

The first three hands came out to 17, 18, and 19, all to be beaten by two 10s, a king and a queen, and a lethal jack and ace combo. Down $300 in three hands made me swelter under the lights. I cracked my neck and breathed through the grilling heat to place another black chip down.

The ebb and flow of the game kept me a few hundred under for an hour. Down $200, down $100, down $200, down $300, down $400, push, push, and down $300. No winning streaks to pull me ahead. Maybe I could play it big, put down big bets, but something wasn't right. Rarely does needing a win bring one, so I tried my luck at another table.

I sat in an empty chair with a thud, the fake leather seat stretching under my weight. I held my face up with my hand. My eyelids felt heavy and irritated. The dealer seemed inappropriately alert for this. I looked her dead in the eye and placed a black chip down. *$400 down*. I felt like my body was collapsing into ooze in my chair.

"What time is it?" I asked. I received no answer other than a king and an ace sliding my way. That perked me up.

"That's a good start." Another black and two green chips joined my wager. Then I had the devilish idea that made my rational side white-knuckle my brain stem. *Do it. Let it ride.* I placed another black chip on the pile in front of me. *$500 down. $350 bet.*

I sat up and fidgeted as the dealer divvied out the cards. She'd awarded herself with a 9 and a mystery card that I had to assume was a face card, even with my impressive 18. Do I lay down like a dog and take an easy beating, or do I risk it since I'm a lost cause anyway? I needed to turn this three-fifty around. My talon dug into the felt two times. Between the first and second time my finger hit the table, the next card from the shoe slipped on top of my hand. *2, which makes 20.* I threw my hand out and sucked air into my lungs.

"Nice hit," the dealer muttered. *I think she's trying to beat me. Look at that look on her face, those eyebrows. She wants me to lose.* At this point in the game, I had lost myself to petty paranoia.

She showed her hidden card, 9+3=12.

"Easy," I murmured. Then she laid down a three on top of the nine. *15, okay, don't panic, Jennings.* Then she laid down the bust card bringing it to 25.

"Yes!" I let out with my hands raised over my head. My little noises must have made me look like a madman, but I kept playing it fast and loose for Tre. The dealer knocked a few black chips into her palm and placed them next to my stack. $700 right at my fingertips. I pocketed the greens and replaced them with a black chip. I stacked another four black chips on top.

"Come on, baby!" I smacked my hands together. It was the biggest bet I had ever made. Looking at the chips, I thought they would jump at the earth-shaking beat of my heart. $1,100 on the table, $900 down, which was about a third of the chips I had set aside for this whole trip, all on one hand. I kept my eyes wide open, staring at the shoe. I didn't want any surprises. I wanted to know the odds. It was like looking into a magic eight ball.

My eyes fluttered as the cards jumped at me. My heavy eyelids darkened my vision of the clear-cut numbers in front of me. A 10 and an ace. I threw my head back in shock. The numbers on the cards stayed the same. My throat gave out a soft, hyena chuckle. My forehead fell into my arms on the table. I couldn't stop laughing. I was almost hyperventilating; my heaving chest carried my desperate, panting laughter out just for me to hear.

Before I could verify what had just happened, my dealer placed a stack of six black chips before putting the cherry on top. A purple chip, $1,000, all mine fair and square.

"Wheh," I exhaled. "Just give me a second," I asked.

She smiled as if to say, "Of course."

That one pair of cards was worth $1,650 in winnings, making me $1,850 in the black. The trouble was, as I was doing my calculating, I still had a mountain to climb. Winning a down payment on a car in one hand, based purely on luck? That wasn't going to cut it.

Tre owed much more than that, and I only had about two grand for him. This whole trip would be one big goose egg for me. I noticed my dealer was patiently waiting for me. She also gave nervous glances towards her pit boss, probably wondering how she was going to explain losing two month's rent on her watch.

I looked at the treasure beneath my fingertips, and it felt like I had nothing, like I was starting over. I placed down one black chip, like a punk. Suddenly, I had this expectation for myself to bet the farm, but I had to keep something for myself, something to show for it. I pulled out my phone and read the time. Like a knockout punch, the numbers read 3:18 a.m. I cursed under my breath and looked at my cards. Two sevens versus an eight. I split the pair.

Another 8 and 7 came my way, 15 and 14 to make an unsavory set of hands. I tapped the table. The sharp thwack of the card sounded doubly harsh as it pushed me over the edge. My hunchback sank into the table. She took my chips.

"Second time's the charm," I muttered to myself. *Tap tap*. An ace, 15 still. I sighed even deeper. *Tap tap*. Another $200 down the drain.

After a few more bouts with my stalwart dealer, I asked her to color me up. I headed to the bar and asked for their phone. The bartender handed me the phone installed to the wall with an ungracious look. I dialed my room number.

"Hello," Mario whispered.

"Mario, it's Dave, you're still there?"

"Yeah, he fell asleep a little while ago. I have to get back to work."

"You're doing good work helping me out like this Mario. I owe you."

"No problem, did you make any money?"

"I made some, but I'm gonna need a lot more. I'll check in on him in a little bit. You do what you gotta do."

"Thanks, Dave, good luck."

By the time I had played my last hand, I could hardly keep my head up. My skull felt like a hot air balloon. If I looked at another pair of cards, I felt like I'd puke a whole deck. As my legs carried me out of the casino, I saw the hotel's front doors. I could see that the sun had started to rise. The hard black night turned into dull gray morning.

The elevator carried me to my room. As I crossed through the threshold, the room was unexpectedly silent. Tre had nuzzled into the couch where I had left him. He'd wake up in a few hours, which gave me some time to lay down and sink into the black.

I twisted my head at the sound of Tre gathering his belongings. He stood, hunched over, looking back at me in the chair. *I fell asleep in a chair?* I rubbed the sleep from my eyes. He avoided my eyeline.

"Morning," I coughed. As I took in my surroundings, he slunk back into the bathroom with his old clothes in hand. He came out dressed as he was the day before. His head bobbed low when he came back to the living area of the room.

"Listen, Tre…" he looked up at me like I was about to give him the death sentence. I paused for a moment.

"Here," I said, handing him a thick white envelope. "There's fifty-five hundred in there. I know it's not all of-"

"No, no, I can't take your money."

"It's not from the bank. I won it in the casino." His eyes widened. How could that be? I chuckled at the incredible run I had to get there, and I was giving it away.

"I wanted to soften the blow."

He hugged me so hard it shook me. It was like he was using me to stand straight. He shook me again and whispered, "This is the kindest thing anyone has ever done for me."

I patted him on the back. Gave him a squinty look that said, "Don't sweat it."

"Just wanted to help you get out of a tight spot."

"Thanks," he sighed. He crumpled the envelope as his hands came together. His eyes shined bright past the tears.

"I don't know what to say," he barely uttered.

"It's still going to be a tough conversation, but… don't come back to this town ever again." His lower lip tightened.

They were hard words to hear. He patted my shoulder playfully with the envelope. He made his way to the elevators. I was down $2,500 and didn't have the energy to try to make it back up. I lounged out on the roof, sipping refreshing cocktails as I waited for my four-hour trip to limbo before landing back home.

Chapter 11: Bachelorette Party

"Security!" A bartender screamed. Stools flew back, rocking on the floor. The hotel staff behind the bar braced for impact. I put my arms out, ready to pry them apart. I felt a splash from someone's drink on my face.

"Hey, that's enough!" I shouted. Two glasses smashed against the floor. Spinning around I could see all eyes had snapped onto us. A hand gripped my sleeve, twisting it like a vice. My eyes shot open, and I held my breath, waiting for the worst.

This was going to be a rough night.

At some point in every service industry, you run into bad customers. Most folks are responsible, in-control adults, but it's something about the allure of Las Vegas that makes people lose sense of themselves.

I've heard all kinds of wild stories come out of Sin City, fellas running off with cocktail waitresses, parking lot beatdowns, and drinkers jumping from great heights into crowded swimming pools, but nothing prepares you for when those wild nights are your problems to solve.

When someone reserves a flight, they don't tell you why. They just give you their money and a way to stay in touch. On one particular Friday night, I stood on the hard concrete floor of the hangar, waiting for a new group of passengers. They were scheduled for a 6 p.m. flight, but it was 5:57. A mix of worry and relief churned in my stomach. I didn't offer refunds, but no word from them made it seem like they were going to be late. I don't like late people.

I like living on Island Time as much as the next guy when I'm on vacation, but when we agree on a time, it's a contract. If we can't rely on what we agreed, then there's no trust. I grumbled to myself as the clock struck six. I looked at the number on the invoice and gave it a call.

A woman's voice answered, "Hello?"

"Jennifer?"

"Yes, who's this?" *Who's this?*

High Roller Airways

"It's your pilot, Dave Jennings, where are you?"

"Our pilot…" She tasted the words on her tongue. "We're coming soon. We're just getting here now." I closed my eyes and stifled a deep, dreaded sigh.

"Alright, I'll be in the hangar."

After a very long fifteen minutes they rolled their suitcases up to the side of the jet. They looked like they were hitting the Strip right off the plane. I cleared my throat.

"Welcome aboard, ladies!"

"Wooh!" It sounded like they had the first round on the way over.

"Just a few rules before we get started. Do not leave your seats until the light goes on. That is when you can get up and get your drinks-"

"Yeah!" One of them shouted. I couldn't help but laugh. One of the girls kept staring at me. Even when I looked around, her eyes were still there. *Oh boy*.

"There's a restroom onboard too, and uh…" She still kept looking at me. "I'll take your bags, and we can get you to Vegas," I said, wrapping up. I started packing their bags away, but the one who kept staring was wearing a hot pink dress that stopped beneath her fingers. She handed me her bag, looking me up and down.

I raised my eyebrows and pointed her to the cabin stairs. A grin creeped up her face as she climbed the steps. She was going to make things interesting.

As soon as I felt the wheels leave the ground, I heard a muffled noise behind me. I checked the security camera looking into the cabin and saw them cheering and chatting amongst themselves. I squinted to look at their faces. None of them seemed to be nervous to fly. I felt a smile spread across my face. I focused on bringing us up to the right altitude as smoothly as possible. I pictured me and a few high school buddies drinking champagne in the back. It warmed my heart to make their little shindig a bit more exciting.

Just as I began our descent, nature started calling. There was no way I was making it to the hotel, and I wasn't going to pee in a bag. I checked the camera looking into the main cabin. All six partygoers were chatting away. I bit my lip and got us into the hangar safe and sound.

When I opened the cockpit, I heard a little gasp. Their wide eyes locked on me. I raised my hands.

"Welcome to Las Vegas."

"Woohoo!" They cheered.

"Have a drink with us," I heard in an enticing tone.

High Roller Airways

"I'll be back in a sec," I said, excusing myself.

"Where are you going?" A coy tenor slipped into my ear. Some of the girls formed the slightest channel for me to pass through. I felt my cheeks burn from forming an embarrassed smile.

"Just a minute," I reassured them as I pulled the door shut. I slid the lock into position and looked at myself in the mirror. My shirt was white and bare. *Wasn't I wearing a tie?*

I exited the facilities, and the girls hadn't moved. They were waiting to form another gauntlet of embarrassing, inappropriate behavior. I shuffled through sideways; a few sets of eyes looked me up and down.

"Did you wash your hands?" The loudest one, Jennifer, joked from her chair.

"A good boy always does," I said, tipping my hat. *Ugh.*

"I was hoping you'd be bad," the same suggestive voice I'd recognize as Kelly's curled behind my ear. I tried to play it off, but my eyebrows were touching the ceiling. I looked back and could see her spread against the couch with my tie around her shoulders. She flashed her smoky eyes at me, knowingly. I ignored their little comments and opened the cabin door.

Most guys would be flattered, but knowing these kinds of hen parties, their insincere advances are spurred on by little dares. Being close to the brink of a life-changing decision, like marriage, makes people stir-crazy. Not me. I just go with a full head of steam. Want has nothing to do with what needs to get done. I ushered the girls out of the jet. As I gathered their suitcases, I took a moment to wonder: how did she got so close that she could swipe my tie?

Our two SUVs rolled up under the marquee of the Blue Stallion Hotel. My passengers looked up at the blazing neon horse and the shining lobby inside. After helping them with their luggage, I escorted them to the front desk. I felt a jolt of excitement as I led another group of travelers on their next adventure. Mario stood by, as if on cue; I waved to him.

"Hey, girls, this is Mario. He'll take your bags." They greeted him with warm smiles and lugged their big suitcases onto his little trolley. Susan stood behind her desk, clacking away with her keyboard. She wouldn't typically allow guests to reach the front desk without her notice.

"Susan, hi!" I said to get her attention. She looked at my bright smile. "I've brought some new customers for ya."

"Yes, we have their room keys and player cards here," she muttered, casting her hand over the little envelopes. I didn't want to prod her into being in a better mood, but there was something off about her today. I glanced over at the party waiting for their luggage to be thrown onto an overcrowded luggage cart.

"May I?" I asked Susan. She helped me collect the room keys and player cards.

"I have your room keys here," I said in my best public speaking voice. Jennifer stepped closer and took them.

"I can take it from here, David," she said with a put-on smile that seemed to come naturally to her.

Seeing the luggage stack up, I turned to Susan. "Do you have another luggage cart back there?" She looked back and uttered an unconfirming sound. She disappeared before flashing back into view, empty handed.

"That's alright. I can take care of the bags." Before she responded a freshly empty cart rolled out of the elevator. "There he is."

I bounced off the desk to hoist the remaining luggage onto the newly discovered cart. I slapped the side of it when it was all full.

"Mario, take my clients to their rooms," I declared, enjoying the authority ringing in my voice.

The caravan of suitcases rolled to the elevators. The girls chatted a bit, so excited to finally arrive. Kelly threw her blonder hair over her shoulder, glancing back at me as I watched them go. *She's trouble*. Still, feeling a spring in my step, I turned back to Susan. We had the lobby to ourselves.

"First bachelorette party on my plane," I said.

Her attention stayed on the computer screen as she replied, "I see you have female clients for once. Congratulations, you finally integrated."

"Come on, you don't have to be so snippy."

Her unconcerned eyes jumped up to meet my nervous set. "Just keep them under control."

"I will," I said, taken aback. "Are you alright? You seem a bit edgy… edgier than normal, I guess."

"Please excuse me, Mr. Jennings, I have other matters to attend to." She whirled away from the desk and moved to disappear behind the wall.

"Since when did you stop calling me David?" She stopped in her tracks. She gave me a chilling glance and carried on. Not even a witty remark. Something was wrong. The walls seemed colder without her behind the desk, so I preoccupied myself with recalling which floor my clients were staying on.

I guessed a few floors in the elevator where they might be. I jumped out of the elevator, throwing my head up and down the corridor. After the fourth attempt on the 9th floor, I found two empty luggage carts standing halfway in the hall.

"Hey, Mario!" I called. I squeezed past the cart and felt my eyes widen at the sight of the suite. The length of the exterior wall was one pane of glass, looking at the sprawling main drag. Headlights, neon signs, and hotel rooms lit up the black desert city. Seeing the rushing nightlife stirred excitement under my feet, far from the peaceful feelings of the sleepy Midwest.

Some members of the bachelorette party stood around, chatting with Mario, taking in the view.

"Can you believe this place?" Jennifer asked me. I had never been in one of the suites before, so I swiped the amazed look from my face.

"It's one of the best in town," I said with a cheesy grin. "I have to say… you have impeccable taste."

"Thank you," Jennifer said, holding her hand to her heart. "As Matron of Honor, I only want the best for this trip. Speaking of, do you have any recommendations?"

"I already have a few places in mind." I smiled. As I said it, I saw Kelly leading Mario and some of her friends back into the main space of the suite.

"Back for more?" she asked. Her sly look curled the corner of my mouth.

"Do you still have my tie?" I asked Kelly. She let it unravel from her perched hand. I took it delicately, matching her mischievous look. Mario came to my side as I rolled the tie around my fingers.

"I'll text you a few restaurants around town," I told Jennifer. Her cheeks flexed with her growing smile.

"Come on, Mario, my room next."

"You got it. Enjoy your stay," he finally mentioned to the girls. They waved us goodbye as I shut the door behind us. The fun stayed in the room. Now it was just me and a friendly bellboy. I stretched out my loose tie between my fingers. I caught Mario looking down at it. His eyes shifted away to the empty length of the hall.

"Make sure you walk out with as many clothes as you walked in with around these girls," I joked. He felt no inhibition as he let his teeth shine in the light. I swiped the room key and led us inside. I heard a long sigh erupt from my lungs as soon as the relaxing abode opened up to me.

"Man, what a day." I stretched my arms out.

Mario flipped on the lights and unloaded my gear onto the floor. "How long were you flying?" Mario asked.

"Four hours on the nose."

"I bet you're tired," Mario chuckled. "Are you still going out with those girls?"

"Oh yeah, part of the job, not that I can complain."

"No, you can't," Mario said winsomely.

"How's the college search going?"

"It's going. Here and there," he muttered.

"Here and there?" My voice curt; a radio squawked behind him. I forgot he wore one. He slipped it off his belt and answered in code.

"I'll have to catch you later," he stated.

"Don't work too hard," I sighed. I fell back on the couch and rested my eyes.

Once we settled in, I led the girls to the casino. They were interested in the slots, so I quickly dropped them off at grandma daycare before heading to the tables. I was interested in something with a little more strategy.

After an hour of losing, I felt a presence fly to my side.

"Mr. High Roller, himself," I heard Jennifer whisper in my ear.

"Oh, hey," I said, shoving my chips in my pockets. "How are you, having fun?"

"I know a few girls who would love your company," Jennifer's sweet talk made me look around the gaming floor.

"I'm sure there are. Where is everyone?"

"We're over by the slots. Come on, I'll take ya."

"One last round here, it's my turn to roll."

"New dice!" the dealer shouted. She pushed eight identical green dice my way. I picked one on either corner of the stack and let the dealer take the rest back with her crook.

"New shooter!" the dealer sounded.

"Here, give us some luck," I leaned back to Jennifer.

I held the dice in my open palm. She instinctively blew on them. I cast the little guys down the chute. They clattered down the way and settled near the wall. Snake eyes. I grimaced as the dealer stretched out to collect the bets on the passline.

High Roller Airways

"Let's try it again," I said. Jennifer leaned closer and blew on the dice. "Harder!" I joked. I felt her smile radiate on my shoulder. She placed her hand on my back and away the dice went. Three jumps before hitting the wall and two more ones stretched to the sky.

"You know what, let's try slots?" I suggested.

"Hmm," an old-timer sighed next to me. I shot him a displeased glance. His eyes returned to the table.

As a serious player, I never liked slot machines. The odds are so low that making a profit was a foregone conclusion. Jennifer sat me down next to her claimed machine. She slipped some cash without saying a word. The game roared up with a paper dragon flowing across the screen before resting on top of the 3x3 square. Looking at my own screen, I realized how tall these machines actually were, towering over me as I sat down. The screen took up my whole vision. The dragon's claws encapsulated all I could see.

I threw in a twenty. *No harm, no foul*. The square buzzed as the slots rolled. The possible combinations whizzed by. Lanterns, diamonds, and a golden dragon statue in the middle caught my eye. The wild and vibrating machine stopped, anticipating my next bet. I looked for the red button near my lap and popped it down.

Like a fish on the line, the slots reeled around and around. After a few more revolutions, I faced a similar result. The golden dragon dared me to hit the button again. I checked the bet I was making. $1.50. *Man, what a rip off!* Sure, I'd just lost $100 at the craps table in a few minutes, but this was just insulting. I slapped the red button, waiting in haste. I felt my tongue hang in my mouth, pleading in suspense for a change of fate.

A variety of gems appeared before me, but none made a pair. The dragon perched on top of the slots flared his nostrils. *Did that thing just taunt me?* I leaned my head side to side, letting out a good crack. *Fine, let's do it again.*

As the slots spun again, I felt a thrill of excitement run through me. I squinted and turned my head. Kelly's painted nails brushed against my cheek.

"Hey, Mr. Big Winner," she slurred into my ear.

Kelly wasn't the first woman I'd met to flirt with a guy just to make him squirm, but it sure didn't make me squirm any less when she started massaging my shoulders.

"Having a good time?" I asked, the crack in my voice betraying my confidence.

High Roller Airways

"I love coming to Vegas," she said, a lilt in her laugh as she threw back her hair. "You never know what you'll take home with you."

Woman, you need to chill out! I thanked my lucky stars when Jennifer turned a curious glance in Kelly's direction.

"Kelly, where's Crystal?"

"She was over by the bar just a minute ago."

I escorted myself out of their conversation by hitting the red button again. My eyes narrowed at the dragon up there, so smug. The wheel spun around again and presented me with a bunch of gongs and firecrackers that won me 20 cents, leaving me with 68 cents on a $1.50 minimum game.

"And there it goes… Well that was fun."

One of the girls came around to our side of the machines with tons of slips in her hands. I remember someone calling her Missy. She had round cheeks and a deep hazelnut haircut that looked like it was from the fifties, but her soft eyes and genuine smile made it easy to talk to her.

"Hey, Missy, how'd you do?" I asked.

"I just won fifty bucks! I'm on cloud nine right now!" The smile that took up her whole face suddenly dropped when she looked past me. I twisted my head up to see Kelly throwing her a look and then glancing down at me, daring me not to notice.

"Hey, Missy," Jennifer piped up. "Why don't you try this one? I'm gonna get a drink."

"I'll come with you," Missy said. She shot a serious glance at Kelly before she left.

"That just leaves you and me," Kelly said, running her hand across the back of my neck.

"Welp…" I stood, pulling up my jeans with my thumbs in the belt loops. "I'm gonna look for Crystal. I'll see you around."

The dark playfulness in her eyes dropped like I was a pet that didn't want to play anymore.

I found Crystal alone at the bar. Seeing the bride-to-be on her own the first night of her bachelorette weekend sank my mood. Seeing her swirl the olives in her martini with a lost look in her eye only added to the sad, dull feeling in my gut when I thought of losing more customers.

I hesitated to approach her, a near stranger on one of her worst nights. It wasn't what I had signed up for, but I had to give service with a smile. My palms eked out sweat and my throat clenched. There was the pressure of a peace talk on my shoulders as she looked up at me.

"Hey, Crystal," I piped up. I tried to keep it simple. I didn't want to stir the pot any further.

"Hi," she muttered, sinking away from me. I heard the gulp in my throat as I attempted this diplomatic tightrope walk.

"Mind if I join you?" I asked. She watched me sit down. "Something on your mind?"

"I'm fine, thanks," she said, just above a whisper.

"Sometimes it's better to talk to a complete stranger with two ears than worry about it on your own." *F—k, I hope that helps. This is so bad.*

"The party's going about how I expected it to."

"Not well?"

"Not well," she echoed. She lifted a full martini glass to her lips.

"Anything your pilot can do to help?"

"Fly me back and leave the rest of them here?"

"Doesn't sound like a bad idea, but... you just got here. Things can change."

"It's not the place, it's the people. There's a lot of bad blood, but I had to bring them all."

"I know how it is. Social expectations can be a drag."

"They're a b—h."

"That too," I chuckled. My eye caught the corner of her mouth twitch before giving in to a delicate smile. She started to look warmer, less desolate than before.

"I wanted to ask you: Do you have a crush on the receptionist?" she asked.

"The receptionist?"

"The redhead who checked us in."

"She's the manager," I guffawed. "She'd love to hear you say that."

"Do you like her?" Crystal repeated.

The prompt return to the question sat me up in my chair. "Everybody likes Susan," I said with a wave, dismissing her prying question.

"So you must really like her." She giggled, blushing as she sipped her olive soup.

"What about you? How'd you and the groom meet?"

Her eyes flexed before looking where to set her drink. She licked her lips, tasting the residue from her drink while purposely thinking of my question. "We met at a bar… just like in the fairytales."

"You don't have to play the cynic for me."

High Roller Airways

Her eyes softened. She swayed upright, looking at me. "It wasn't really a bar. It was one of those beer garden things, you know old Wisconsin. He just got back from golfing with some buddies, burnt to a crisp, but I loved his smile. I knew some of his friends, so I included myself in their little circle, and before I knew it, it was just us…" A stiff inhale rattled her bones. "I didn't know it could be that easy before."

"Sounds like a perfect match," I said. She simply answered with a smile. I chuckled. *Mission accomplished.* Then an idea sprang into my mind.

"Also, can you keep your friend Kelly away from me? I think she's trying to-"

A flash of blonde swept into the corner of my eye. "Kelly, hi!" I said at an unexpected octave.

"Hi, David, we miss you."

"Oh yeah?" I asked, looking at Crystal. Her head slumped down onto her fist. Kelly started pushing my buttons again, literally. The light touch of her fingertips pressed against my skin.

"Hey, you know, there's a karaoke bar not too far from here? You girls game?" I asked.

215

"Only if you promise to sing us a song," Kelly cooed, pressing my shirt button into my stomach.

"Sure, what do you say, Crystal? A little embarrassment to pass the time?"

A helpless smile ran across her face. "Sure," she said. We slowly wrangled the other girls and walked down the strip to indulge in Japan's worst export. To keep my customers happy, I serenaded them with "Hero" by Enrique Iglesias. There is no bottle deep enough for me to ever live that down.

From the blackness of sleep, I was thrust back into my hotel bed, covered in sweat. The unwelcome gray swirling in my mind almost made me sick. My heavy head looked up to the bright desert sun piercing through my window. Gut rot wrenched my stomach, ebbing with constant pain. I groaned at every movement it took to flop onto my side. My hand slapped against the hotel room phone. I squinted to find the right number for room service.

After forking an eggy breakfast into my mouth, I rinsed myself off in the shower, strung on my swimsuit and took the elevator to the rooftop pool. I sighed and moaned against the dozens of straps that made up the back of my chair. My head throbbed with red pain to match the burning behind my eyes. I just hoped I could fly tomorrow. My limp hand pointed at the waiter walking toward me.

"Bloody Mary, please," I muttered.

"A Bloody Mary?" he asked. I realized my ragged voice wasn't loud enough for him to hear.

"Yes," I nearly shouted as I sat up, closer to him. "And a Coke, please."

"Right away," he said, rushing back to the tiki bar. I kept one eye open on him while the other slept. As soon as he lowered my drinks onto my table, I sucked down the meat skewer and chugged my soda. *Gotta look alive.*

My stomach churned with this dark concoction but stirring the ice in my Bloody took my mind back to carefree Wisconsin summers. The salty taste smothered my tongue. Another sip and the throbbing dulled in my head.

"Rough night?" A baritone voice intoned. I looked over my shoulder at a Fat Cat in a big Hawaiian shirt.

"Nothing Mary can't handle," I said, raising my glass.

"The name's Charles," he said.

"David," I said, twirling in my seat to offer him a hand. He took it softly in his big mitt. "Are you a regular around here?"

"Oh, yes, I'm here quite a bit."

"Me too, so what do you do?"

"I'm retired," he said, almost reluctantly. Maybe he was a company man back in the day. "What about you?"

"I run a private airline called High Roller Airways."

"That name does ring a bell."

"I have a deal with the hotel. My passengers stay here, so we've probably crossed paths before."

"Maybe," he said in his slow, easy way. "Do you get a lot of business?"

I cleared my throat to stall for time. We were making money, but my flight plan for the next month was nearly empty. I put on a brave face and started nodding.

"We're doing well, making good relationships, getting our name out there. Do you come here often?" I asked, my face jolted with embarrassment, but he didn't seem to notice.

"It's like a second home. Maybe I will charter a flight with you someday."

"Anytime," I said. I pulled a business card from my wallet. "Here, give me a call sometime."

He took the card carefully and looked it over. I watched his lips form a slight impressed smile. My grin curled.

"Now, if you don't mind, I really do like talking to you, but I need some rest."

"Oh, sure, sure," he whispered in a reassuring tone. He put his feet up and basked in the sun. I relaxed my back against the warm straps of the chair, let the rumbling inside me fade to the soundless, ebbing darkness of my afternoon sun nap.

After waking up at the pool and noticing the sun was in a considerably different position in the sky, I hustled back to my room. The heat stayed with me on my cheeks and shoulders even as the AC blasted from all directions. I caught myself in the mirror with a sobering look.

I'd seen that harsh stare of regret in my reflection countless times before, but this time my big blue eyes sat in the middle of my beet-red face. My eyebrows flinched at every touch of aloe on my cheek.

"Last time I sleep at the pool," I muttered to myself. My phone buzzed on the counter. *No, not now.*

Jennifer's name popped up with a message reading, "We're getting dinner. Why don't you come with us?"

I sighed, weighing the options. *Be a good host. Don't say no.* I looked up from my phone and saw how my face looked, like I was holding my breath for too long.

I typed, "I'll be down in a bit." I squinted my eyes and winced, which caused more rubbing against my air-tight skin. *I'm tied up now, but I'll meet you later.*

I took a cold shower, applied more aloe to every inch of my exposed body, and lowered myself into bed. My whole body felt like it had clenched together like a "snakebite" kids give each other on the playground.

"Just one of the many hazards of working in Vegas," I said to myself. "Ow."

After agreeing on meeting the girls downstairs, I threw on a Hawaiian shirt and the thinnest pants I had in my bag. I felt like I was covered by a cloud. I tried not to move my arms too much as I walked down.

A woman glanced at me as she watched me enter the elevator. My arms hung away from my sides, so they didn't rub against me. My eye glanced down at her as she kept her cold stare at me, as if I were behaving like a child. *It really hurts, lady.*

Once the elevator doors opened, I saw Kelly's mouth form a shocked oval before her unblinking laugh. She wanted to remember every inch of the splotchy red lobster she saw standing before her. *Oh crap, what an entrance.*

"Please, be gentle," I said with raised hands, resigned to Kelly's lack of discretion.

"David got too much sun," she said. Her friends' giggles disappeared into the sound of the casino. In the corner of my eye, I saw Jennifer nervously power-walking near me. The look on her face hinted that she was also curious about my massive sunburn.

"What'd you do?" she asked.

"I flew too close to the sun." The corner of her mouth curled up. That soothed my skin for a moment.

"Let's hit up the slots!" Missy said, her lips fumbling the words as they came out.

"We will," Kelly said with an unsubtle eyeroll.

"Let's have some fun, girls!" Jennifer shouted. The rest of the group shuffled out to the casino. I felt something brush against my sleeve. Crystal stood there, giving me a serious look.

"Crystal, what's up?"

"I'm glad you're here," she said with a grave expression.

"What, is there some drama going on?" I asked. She raised an eyebrow like I already knew the answer.

"Missy and Kelly have been fighting this whole time," she muttered.

"I'm sorry to hear that. Any way to split them up?"

She sighed. "I didn't want it to go this way… That's why I need you to-"

"Distract Kelly?"

"I normally wouldn't want a guy hanging around at my bachelorette party, but…"

"You need an overcooked pilot to tame the beast."

A laugh leapt out of her chest.

"Thanks," she said, placing a hand on my shoulder.

"Ow, don't do that."

"Sorry," she giggled. That gave us the confidence to march into the dragon's lair.

♠

"F—k me!" I shouted at the slot machine. I peeled off another hundred from my pocket and threw it into the machine. I felt my finger bend as I jammed it against the glass. $1.50, $2, $2.50, $5 a pop. The screen vibrated as the wheel rolled on with a whimsical zhim. The slots halted and showed three gold medallions in a row. Fireworks went off and the money started to climb. Fifty bucks in my pocket.

"Yes!" I kept under my breath, clenching my fist. I hit it again for another $5 bet. The dragon flew around the spinning blur before returning to its nest. Its roar rumbled through the machine. The slots slapped shut. Three lines cut across the screen, connecting jades, pearls, and sapphires. $67 came running into my pockets. A burst of purple light forced me to blink. I was now fighting for the jackpot.

"Here we go. Come on, baby!"

"What is it?" Jennifer asked, leaning back in her seat to see my screen.

"I'm winning!"

"You're due for one. Win us something big!"

"One jackpot coming up," I said, licking my lips.

Three golden dragon statues appeared and then vanished from their mantles. The dragon up top clung to them. Suddenly, a horde of gold coins rose above him and crashed down like a tidal wave. Instead of the usual slots, this time there was only one square that held a golden dragon in the center. I pressed the button. The square spun with every kind of symbol running past in a haze.

I tried counting the different shapes to know my odds, but the square stopped in its tracks. A gong looked back at me. My eyes glanced up at the dragon. He showed his teeth. He was smiling. The scaly beast threw its head back. *He's laughing at me!* The second time he leaned back for another uproarious howl I slapped the button to go again. A red X burned into the stone above the square. Two more strikes and the jackpot is gone.

I took a deep breath and slapped the button. The wheel swirled and came to a quick stop. A golden dragon shined in the light. My arch nemesis flared its nostrils as one of its treasures left its talons.

Just two more to win $19,500. My eye left the screen momentarily to see a familiar face. Mario was waiting on folks, coming our way.

"Mario!" I shouted. He came over, not as enthused as I had hoped.

"What can I get for you?" he asked formally.

High Roller Airways

"Grab me a beer, whatever's closest. I'm trying to win the jackpot. I just need two more."

I looked back and Mario was gone. The center of my throat burned with thirst. I turned back and saw Jennifer leaning over to see my screen. I realized I wasn't alone with this box. My hands slapped together and rubbed for warmth and good luck.

"Come on, let's get a win." I pawed the button, and the wheel spun again. Two strikes left; I was still in this. I could make it happen. Gold, red, and blue streamed past like headlights on the highway and came to a standstill. The vibration of the gong rang through my hands. Another golden dragon slammed into the empty space.

"Yes!" I cried.

The machine pulsated with impending good fortune. New promises and new horizons.

"One more! One more!" Missy chanted.

Her fists bobbed up and down. Some of the other girls closed in. Kelly bent over my seat and tapped her fingernails across my shoulders. I could feel the taste of excitement on everyone's tongue. It was so close.

"One more! One more! One more!" I chanted. I pounded the button. My eyes stretched open, red, gold, gold, green, and then gray took over. I had to wait and hope now. *Gold dragon! Gold dragon! Gold dragon!*

Emerald. A red X slammed into the stonework. The dragon cackled with delight.

"You have one more shot," Missy cheered.

"This is it. Go," Jennifer insisted.

She clutched the back of my seat. Kelly leaned in closer and gave my shoulder a squeeze.

"Come on, David," she slithered into my ear.

"Last one! All or nothing!" I announced. The wheel scurried around and around. This time I could see the colors more clearly. The world slowed down. The chants behind me lost their rhythm, but I could still hear the vibrations against my ears. The jackpot is right there. More money than I've ever won was right there. The slot slammed into its tracks.

A ruby, a ruby for a red X. The final dagger slammed into the stone arch above and the dragon sprayed his fire across the screen, transitioning us to the original screen.

"Oh," my entourage sighed. I glanced at my credits in the machine: $95. Back where I started — or at least where my last hundred started. The encouragement from my audience seemed to spill onto the floor, evaporating into thin air. I peeled my eyes away from the machine. Everyone else returned to theirs, except Kelly. Her nails burned into my shoulders. I didn't realize Mario was standing beside her, my drink still on his tray.

"Thanks, pal," I said, reaching for the can. Mario, miles away, locked back into service mode and lowered the tray for me. I cracked it open and started again.

I could feel the time pass me by. My throat dried up, but I was too focused on the game. I couldn't give up now. I had lost most of my winnings by now, but I could change my fate with another spin of the wheel.

Kelly sipped her cocktail with a straw and watched me from behind. I let her stare. The whirling wheel took my mind away from the world.

Lines cut across the screen, tallying a measly $5.10. *Another dime for me.* The wheel spun again. Nothing. My fingers thudded against the machine. Zero. Its room-temperature touch made me feel all the more alone, totally indifferent to all the heart and dough I was putting into this thing. Red, blue, green, gold. Not a pair in sight.

"It's alright, sweetie," Kelly said in her syrupy baby voice. My face tightened. I felt like my lunch was going to come back up.

She dug her claws into my roasted shoulders. I stifled a growl as I focused my energy on the dragon. Somehow the pain melted away as I saw the wheel roll again. I needed it so bad. The dragon's nostrils let out plumes of smoke. *Once more into battle, dear foe.* The screen rattled. *Something big! Something big! Something big!*

The slots stood still. Nothing connected, not a single row, column, or anything. I couldn't keep my eyes from falling on the credit that I had left in the machine. $4.95. I had to lower my bet. I had lost $200 on this machine. A cold bath ran down my spine. I was a sap. I threw money at this machine, taunted a dragon, and it was all a f—king game!

Something in me snapped. Maybe it was Kelly's wandering hands, maybe it was anger at this game for making me look like a loser, or maybe for falling asleep in the sun, or maybe it was that the whole bachelorette party was a disaster for Crystal, and I would never get their business again. So I lost it. I lost my cool.

"That's enough, Kelly." Her hands glided over my chest. "I said that's enough!" My voice climbed to an angry register. The sly look in her eye disappeared, a wave of embarrassment crashed over her eyes. She backed away, quickly glancing for another warm body to cling to. She found Mario handing out drinks to her friends. She laced her claws over his shoulders.

"Mario, sweetie, can you help me back to my room?"

A little shocked by the question, Mario nodded affirmatively. His eyes, full of surprise, looked back at me. I don't know if he was looking at me for help, but he took her under his wing and guided her across the casino. Her friends followed, giggling between sips of Long Island Iced Tea. I hung back a bit, tailing them to see where they were going, but I knew as soon as they reached the elevators were. Something tightened in my chest, and doubt crept in.

He's not my responsibility, he's a man. He can do what he likes, I thought.

I stood my ground across the lobby and watched Kelly drape her arm around him and cheer loudly to her friends. She and Mario exchanged an intimate look as the elevator door slid shut. *Not on my watch.*

I strode to the elevators, the room number glaring in my mind. The elevator was taking its time. A flock of old folks stood in the chute waiting for me to move. I guess bingo was about to start. As I waited for the old-timers to clear out of the way, I thought of my speech. I couldn't just barge in with nothing prepared.

This is stupid, I told myself. *You're not his babysitter. You're not his guardian angel. So what if he screws up?* I felt my lungs packed with air. My chest depressed into me, letting the air flow out of my nose. The elevator showed their floor was up next.

"It's stupid to care, but I can't just stand by." The door slid out of my way. I leaned out of the door. The hall was empty. Just bright lamplights and curling carpet were in sight. I felt my spine straighten as I walked. I tried to will confidence into myself. My arms hung at my sides, and they weren't getting up anytime soon. I worried they could see me through the peephole, just waiting to get my courage up. I took in a breath, when two large men walked my way.

They didn't seem like security, but maybe they had a few plainclothes guys on hand. Either way, they were looking right at me. One stepped ahead of the other and leaned closer to me, keeping some distance.

"Are the girls in there?" The human refrigerator asked.

"Uh, yeah, yeah," I said, stepping out of the way.

He and his friend looked like professional wrestlers. They both wore baggy suits and sparkling rings. While one knocked, the other looked at me. "So, where are you from?"

"Oshkosh," I said.

He squinted like that wasn't the answer he was expecting. "No, like-"

"Hello, ladies," his friend announced into the room.

"We can share the room, it's all good," he said, tapping my chest with the back of his hand. I stared, blinking as one of the girls jumped up in excitement, seeing the two Red Grants march through the door chest first. Thinking on my feet, I slipped in behind them.

They swept the girls into their arms and sat them down on chairs in the center room. My eyes turned right onto Mario, legs hanging over the arm of the couch while his Blue Stallion Hotel polo was riding high. Kelly's French tips spread and flexed across his chest. So many opposing emotions swam across his face that in that moment I thought he might *really* need my help. Some song by Pitbull blared from a speaker.

"Mario!" I shouted over the noise. His mouth sprang open like he got caught by his mother. Kelly threw me a layered look. Her eyebrows jumped at first, before her tongue rolled into her cheek. Her eyes stared with a bold possessiveness, held afloat by a look of fiery wantonness. *That's my luggage boy!*

"Come on, this isn't for you," I said.

"He's a big boy. He can stay," Kelly said, pressing her claws into him.

I felt a shirt hit the top of my foot and saw the wide backs of the two male strippers gyrating, taking up all the space in the room. Infuriated, I stared at Mario one last time. "Do you want to lose this job?"

Mario sighed and tried to sit up. Kelly finally let him go. She didn't look my way as I took Mario outside. The harsh party music subsided to a throbbing memory as I closed the door. It was just me and Mario in the hallway, not sure what to do.

"You need to get out of this place," I said.

"What do you mean?" he asked.

"I'm talking about this job, Vegas, the whole thing. When are you starting school again?"

His tongue held still in his mouth; mine did too. My eyes looked at him, egging him to say something.

"I'm not sure I'm going to college."

I stopped in my tracks. "Whoa, whoa, whoa," I said, reaching out for his arm. He stopped for me, turning back with an indignant look. I could see he was waiting for me to give the "not angry, just disappointed" routine.

"What do you mean you're not going?"

"I mean I'm not going. I make good money here. It's fun. Chicks want me, man."

"What about Carson State or Reno Tech?"

"I don't want to go back to school. I'm good." He turned his back on me. He didn't want to have this conversation, or any conversation with me.

Once I felt his footsteps disappear, I muttered to myself. "You lost the customers, you lost your padawan, and ah, your top layer of skin." I shuffled down the hall to the elevators. I could feel a wet patch on the back of my tongue. I was craving a bottle of something cold.

The games of chance didn't entice me anymore. I was chewed up and spat out for the night. As soon as the bar was in reach, I slid into a chair and raised my finger for the bartender to come over. It was a little slow at that time of night, so he came right down.

"Beer, whatever you got." Most bartenders hesitate, but he could tell I really didn't care what he brought back to me. His hand gingerly placed my mystery beer on a coaster in front of me. I let the foam spread across my lips, letting the familiar taste run across my tongue. *Beautiful.*

I glanced around the bar and saw Crystal with her hair down, head down too. The glass of beer she was holding looked bigger than her. We were sharing the same half-shut, drifting eyes. We thought we liked it here, but plans changed. I took a big drink and moseyed on over to her. As I got closer, her eyes lifted up to meet me. I gave a reluctant smirk.

"Trouble in paradise?" I asked.

She let out a gravelly laugh. "This might be the worst bachelorette party I've ever been to," she confessed. Her eyes lost their focus somewhere in the distance. A kind of cold, sublime clarity fell across her face.

"On the bright side you only get one of these," I chuckled. A black, bitter laugh wheezed out of her, and I couldn't help but join her.

"At this point, I don't know what I expected," she said, shocked at herself. She let out a breathy "ha" and let her body sink closer to the bar. A peaceful dejection seemed to fill the space around us. "This is it. This is my party, and I can cry if I want to."

Her hair flew to the side. She lifted her glass towards me. This was the first time I'd seen her face since coming to the bar. Her pale cheeks gave way to red plums.

High Roller Airways

"Whatever floats your boat," I said, clinking her glass. She let the rest of her beer slide down her throat.

"Bartender, another round!" Her voice cracked the stratosphere and heads turned around. I moved in closer and lowered my voice.

"Shh, you gotta be quiet," I couldn't help but chuckle.

"Oh, sorry!" she said louder. The bartender placed another pair of drinks in front of us. Her mischievous grin hovered over the foam.

"You're a little troublemaker, huh?" I asked.

"I like to laugh things off, keeps things going."

"That's a good way to look at it."

"Kelly was picking me apart back there," I mentioned. "Did you see that?"

Crystal seethed, shaking her weightless head. She took another big slug.

"She's like that with every guy. Sorry if you thought you were special."

I coughed hoarsely. Some beer hit the wrong pipe. My lungs knocked out a few more smoker coughs before settling back. "No, I've met a few girls like her. Still hurts every time," I said, massaging my hurting shoulders.

"She just doesn't know when to stop."

"Mmm," I grunted.

A twirl of arriving blonde hair showed Kelly's burning eyes staring me down as she found an empty space at the end of the bar.

"She might've heard you." I told Crystal.

"Who cares?" She sighed. "We're leaving tomorrow."

I had nothing to add, just another nail in the coffin for this trip. I looked down the bar, not at Kelly directly, although her piercing eyes never left me, even when the bartender came with her drink. Missy stood next to her. Kelly followed my eyes and recoiled. *Oh boy*.

"What's your problem?" Missy said. I looked around the bar, most people had moved on, and only a few stragglers hung around. I could hear their conversation, crystal clear.

"You've been such a b—h," Missy shouted. "And I've kept my mouth shut, but you know what? F—k you."

"F—k you too," Kelly raised her thin middle finger. Once I saw that, I clenched my teeth.

"When Crystal said she had to invite you, I didn't want to come, but I came here for her, and you've been nothing but mean to me this whole time, making this whole trip about you, not what she wants.

"You could have had anyone else, and you stole him from me, and you feel nothing."

The sides of my mouth pulled down. *Yikes*.

"Oh, honey, if he was really yours, it wouldn't have been so easy."

"I'm gonna kill you!" Missy leaned back and threw a heavy punch.

Kelly belted out a scream that sent shockwaves through the whole bar. I've seen a few girls fight in my day, none of them were very good at fighting, but if I were a woman who's never expected to be hit before, I'd be scared too. In fact, seeing those two girls wailing on each other freaked me out. It's not something you see every day.

"Cat fight!" Some drunk tourist shouted, exposing the potbelly under his shirt.

"Dave, do something!" Crystal cried. I twisted my hat backwards and waded through the stunned witnesses in my way. After propelling myself through the crowd, the two girls swirled around. I opened my arms to catch them. *Thud*.

Missy's big elbow cratered into my sternum. Suddenly, I wasn't thinking about the sunburn anymore. I locked my eyes on Missy. Her fiery eyes only looked one way. I was just a speedbump to them.

"Hey, that's enough!" I shouted. Like a drowning elephant, Kelly pulled me with her to the ground. My head skipped across the fender that wrapped around the bar. It hurt so bad I didn't make a sound.

Now that Kelly was off her feet, I only had to push a wild Missy away. She already had some heft to her, but I took her wrists and threw her off of me. Finally, she saw me. The big, heaving lobster wasn't just a part of the scenery now. I saw the shame in her eyes and let my guard down. Kelly's whimper on the floor turned my head. She wasn't having fun anymore. Her eyes looked scared and brimming with tears. She reached out, straining to pull herself up.

I lowered my hand, and she gripped it, shaking the whole way up. Crystal, and the rest of the bar, were staring at us. The shock of shame kept our mouths shut. I looked reluctantly at Missy. She seemed willing to follow me and Kelly out of the bar and try our best to return to normal. I guided Kelly and Missy through the crowd, who weren't sure what to do, watch us leave or pretend they hadn't just seen us make a great World Star video?

High Roller Airways

Crystal walked past the standing bodies that made a barrier between us. Once I stepped out into the open gaming floor, she came to my side, looking at me for answers. I tried to speak but could only shrug with an open mouth.

"Let's just sleep on this and let me know when you want to leave tomorrow, okay?" Crystal nodded, astounded. She reached out to Kelly and Missy, walking silently with their heads hanging low.

I slept in late, not looking forward to the day. My phone sat there waiting for me. I imagined missed calls from Susan, wanting to hear her voice when she said she was banning my guests, a drunken voicemail from Kelly, or a short text message from Mario saying, "Don't talk to me."

I groaned as I threw my hand from under the covers, letting it slap onto the phone. I plucked it from its charger and, not wanting to see any bad news completely, looked at the home screen with one eye open. There was nothing.

They must have been waiting to talk to me in person. Susan's stern look, Mario's cold shoulder, or the girls' awkward, disheveled appearance as they waited for me to take them home in total silence.

Room service brought me breakfast and a ginger ale on ice. I pressed the highball glass to my mouth and felt the cold drink dissipate the shower steam behind me.

There was a lot to do, a lot of time to do it, and no desire to leave. My lips pressed against the glass again, sending the rest of its contents past my teeth.

I stepped out of the elevator and looked at the front desk. Mario was waiting. My blinders came on. I marched right at him, my thundering footsteps echoing across the hall. His eyebrows stretched up his forehead.

He was scared of me. *He should be*. Susan flipped her attention to me, barging ahead. I took Mario by the arm, pushing him back a bit with the momentum.

"I need help with my bags," I said through gritted teeth. He didn't protest, and I pulled him back with me to the elevators.

"Mr. Jennings," Susan said in her particular tone to avoid social embarrassment while still remaining composed.

"It'll just be a second," I said over my shoulder. I saw a family of tourists had just arrived at the counter with lots of heavy suitcases. I felt her sting of embarrassment with her being a hotelier without a luggage boy, but I pressed on with Mario in tow. I hit the rooftop button in the elevator.

"What is wrong with you?" I asked.

"What?" he asked with a shocked open mouth.

"Are you really-?"

A woman approached the elevator just as the doors started to close.

"We're full," I said with my hand out. Her face dropped at my rudeness and stopped before the closing doors. I locked eyes with Mario.

"Are you really going to waste your life working at this dump?"

"What're you talking about?"

"Last night you said you weren't going to college!"

"Yeah, well, I don't know." He crossed his arms.

"You can do better than this place. Do you really want to be here for the rest of your life?" He shifted in his shoes, not meeting my eye.

"This place is a trap, man. You have to get out of here now, or you'll never get out."

"You don't know that."

"I've seen so many guys like you do this because it's easy, or they quit and work another dead-end job for the next six months and just move around like that until they're a forty-year-old fry cook somewhere, wake up, man!"

"What do you care? You're just some guy."

That gut punch sent me back. I tried to read his eyes. Did he really feel this way?

"I thought we were pals. I like you, and I don't want to see you f—k it up."

Air steamed out his nose. His crossed arms tightened. Neither of us knew what to say next.

"I care because you're a good worker, because you're a good kid. I want you to be happy. I want you to have choices in life. I can see you doing anything you set your mind to. You don't need to settle for this."

The elevator doors opened. A couple in swimsuits stood on the other sides of the doors. I jammed the close doors button with my thumb.

"Occupied," I muttered with a raised hand, the words barely slipped past my teeth. I hit the button back to the first floor. Mario didn't stop me, not sure what to do. We both just looked at our shoes and waited for the other to speak.

"You don't have to settle for anything in life," I said, shaking my head. "You don't have to be a genius to get what you want in this world. You have to work hard and use your head, but you don't have to settle, and getting back in school is going to give you what you need to have a chance, a real chance to do something worthwhile with your life."

The elevator lowered us to the ground floor. He waited for my parting words.

"Go ahead," I said. "I've done enough talking."

His blank, thinking face turned to the open doors and headed out. I didn't know if he was going to listen. I realized something else as we descended to the lobby. I had no one else to look after, and I desperately wanted to.

Susan didn't forgive me for my antics. After talking to Mario, I caught myself aimlessly strolling through the lobby when she lifted a finger for me to see. Not that one. I stopped in my tracks. She gave instructions to her underling behind the desk before stepping away. Her hospitable charms shifted to hawkish precision.

"I need to speak with you," she said in a terse tone. A cold feeling filled my stomach. I was too tired to talk back. She led the way, expecting me to follow. She wanted to give me a talking to, and I thought to hear her out, but the more I thought about it the more ridiculous it was to follow her into a side office and have her read me the riot act.

As soon as I made it past the door, I shut it tight. She threw her head around and stepped to me with crossed arms.

"Your behavior and lack of control over your clients are unacceptable," she said. I held my rolling eyes in check before responding.

"Technically, they're your clients too, so we should both share the blame," I said with a shrug. Behind her frown I could see her tongue turn over her teeth.

"You overstepped today. I expect better from you."

"I had to talk to the kid. He is making a big mistake."

"*I'm* responsible for my employees."

"It wasn't about the job. He needs to get out of here. I know he works for you, but you have people coming in and out of this place all the time. I was just trying to make sure he doesn't get stuck here for the rest of his life."

"I run a very nice hotel. He's lucky to work here."

A dark scowl ran down my face. "I didn't think you were some heartless bean counter."

"I run a good hotel. Not by accident, not by chance… I'm not going to tolerate anyone screwing things up for me because he feels like he owns the place."

"What is this?" I asked, my arms hitting my sides. "What is this even about? Did the customers complain? Or was it just you?" She hesitated, holding her tongue.

Now I was on offense. "If they didn't complain then you have nothing to worry about."

"People talk," she said in a blurted whisper.

"To them I'm just one jerk in one hotel. It happens. It's not going to ruin your perfect record." Her jaw stayed shut, no sign of breaking free. She wouldn't admit defeat. She wanted to lecture me. *What? Not good enough for ya? Gotta make me look like a jerk?*

"Is that what this job is? Another way to show to the world that you're perfect? Were you always this Type A?"

She gave her snotty scoff; my knuckles tightened, and her tongue whipped back.

"Don't psychoanalyze me. Get your s—t together."

"Hey, I'm not some toothless hick, alright? I bring money into this place. I'm not some nobody."

"Oh please, this deal is lopsided in your favor, and you know it. With the fight and you pulling my employees away like they work for *you*… I'll remind you we can always renegotiate that deal."

A stone formed in my throat. I shifted in my shoes, peering into her eyes. "You wouldn't do that."

"I have that power."

"Is that what you do? Is that your plan? Every time we argue about something, you're gonna pull out that card?"

She didn't respond immediately. The same cool, confident look in her eyes told me everything. She had no fear, and I was something to scrape off the bottom of her shoe. "Just act like a professional," she said.

"You'll know when I don't." I pulled my jacket forward and showed myself out. I knew I had to find the girls soon to get them back on the plane. The sagging feeling in my shoulders didn't pair well with the fact that I had to stay awake all that time, no rest in the cockpit.

I texted Jennifer when to show up. I waited patiently after I knocked on their door. It opened to the girls filing out, silent and hungover. After all the girls stepped into the hall, I led the walk of shame down to the lobby.

Missy and Kelly looked the most miserable, Crystal wore a mask of long-reconciled defeat, and Jennifer looked down, seeming, only that morning, to feel the group's disappointment and the failure of her matronly duties, wash over her. I didn't speak a word. With traffic as hectic as it was on every drive back, I didn't let my anger show.

We felt like strangers sharing a car. You don't show your real self to strangers. I didn't even bother to broadcast the rules again on the way back. That minibar wasn't going to be touched, too many bad memories, decisions that they'd like not to relive again.

Flying over the Rockies wasn't picturesque, floating above the mesmerizing country beneath us wasn't joyful. We were washed up. Maybe I shouldn't have become too familiar with my clients. Maybe it wasn't worth the risk. Maybe it'd be better if I hunkered down at a table and lost what I've earned on my own. They were never my friends to begin with, and maybe that's what got me in trouble: putting my nose in other people's business.

Chapter 12: Blue Christmas

After a late flight back home, I fell asleep in my jeans. Feeling the cold, gray morning air through the window, I launched my body through the doorway and clambered to the couch for another two hours of jarring, swirling sleep. Wrestling the damp clothes off my back in the early hours of the morning came with a startling call.

I sighed, deciding to leave it for my voicemail, and sighed again as my back felt the corduroy comfort of my old musty couch. I closed my eyes tightly before they settled into a relaxed, tenseless position.

My phone rattled again in my pocket, this time more aggressively than the last. I wriggled myself up and extended my leg to easily pull it out of my pants. I answered, leaning over the side of the couch like I might be sick.

"Dave, why didn't you answer?" Jack Flambeau asked, half concerned, half angry.

"Sorry, Jack, I got back late. What is it?"

"I'm calling because I'm surprising Bonnie and the kids with a trip to Florida for Christmas."

"Oh yeah? That's nice," I said, groaning softly into the arm of my couch.

"Eh, no, you – I need you to fly us down. The kids haven't seen the jet yet, so we're taking it down to Miami… That means I'll need you."

"Just for Christmas, or…?" I squinted hard, trying to remember my flight schedule.

"No, not just for Christmas, til New Year's."

"We have clients flying out for New Year's," I said.

"When are they flying out?"

"The 30th."

"What time on the 30th?"

"Sometime in the afternoon, four or something."

"That's fine."

"So you want the plane from Christmas Eve to the 29th. Should I mark you down?"

"What? No, the 30th. We'll fly in the morning, noon at the latest, and you can make that afternoon flight for Vegas."

"You want to double book me?" I sprang up from the couch, sitting on the edge of the worn-out cushion with my nails in my mouth.

"You've done it before, come on."

"With a night in-between. By the time I land and refuel it'll be three, three-thirty."

"That's fine. They have to be there at four; you can leave when you want." My head shook like a bobblehead. My sighing cut through my teeth like hot steam.

"That's not going to be a problem, is it?" Jack's voice dripped like black tar through the phone. I held back my answer for one indignant second.

"You know you have to pay for gas, right? That's a lot to get to Florida."

"Yeah, I know. I can pay for it with my real job. Keep it open. I'm still not sure when we'll leave. Sound good?"

"Yeah, sounds good." I don't know how I could hide how tired or unmotivated I was.

"I'll text you when I know more."

"Alright," I grumbled. He ended the call, and I threw myself back onto the couch.

After my morning coffee, I made the arrangements. I'd be working for two weeks straight, over the holidays. I gripped the handle on the mug so tight I thought it would break apart in my hands. I thought of that hotel room in Buffalo, hating to work over the holidays, but at least there was a payoff.

Now I was working for nothing, and then I was working for half of what Jack would earn. He'd just sit there on Miami beach, toes in the sand, while I caddy his family around. Then I remembered my dad.

"Shoot!" I reached for my phone and gave him a call. This wasn't going to be pretty. A moment went by, then another, then another. *Maybe I could leave a voicemail. No, it has to be over the phone. Can't avoid it now.*

"Hey, Dad."

"Hey, Dave, what's going on?"

"I just wanted to call and say that I got roped into something with work, so I can't make it to Christmas." I couldn't hear anything. The quiet carried on for a moment longer, making me swallow and start to say something.

"Well… that's disappointing. I thought you said you had more flexibility."

"It was just a spur of the moment thing."

"Just tell them you have off. I thought being the boss means you can get off on holidays."

"Listen, Dad, it's just one time."

"I respected it more when it came from the airline."

I gulped again. I felt my head slip past the phone, his voice still talking to me. I raised my head to listen to me getting chewed out.

"It was a last-minute thing, it happens… Maybe, you know, you can meet me out there or something…" The silence plunged to the floor. "I'll see you the week of the 5th."

"Yup…" the word hardly got out of his mouth.

"Alright, see you later." I waited for his goodbye, then rushed to hit "End Call". I didn't want to know that he had given up on me. I rubbed my eyes, thinking about what I had to do to prepare. The anxious weight of it all sank me back down into the couch where I lay there, feeling more tired than I had started.

It wasn't a white Christmas this year. The grass was wilted and turned over by previous rain and snowfall that

High Roller Airways

winter, which made it look like a foreign wasteland in the morning mist, not the cheery winter wonderland I knew Wisconsin to be. The morning fog had disappeared as Jack and I helped put his family's bags away. I felt relieved to leave it all behind, hoping to find some joy over the next few days in the Florida sun.

Taxiing into Miami for Christmas was not the reward I had hoped for. Starting and stopping in a parade of bigger planes prompted me to check the security feed in the main cabin. I looked back and watched Jack's miserably resentful face bounce forward as I braked.

Inside the airport, Jack and his family waited for their luggage. I stood with my arms crossed, my gear already at my feet. Jack rubbed his temples and looked over his shoulder at me. It wasn't a good sign for my upcoming performance review. Under the rumble of the moving flowage of travelers, the luggage cart came into view from some unseen location. Once I looked up from the cart, I saw Jack put out his hand. A smile I hadn't seen in months rose across his big cheeks.

"Thanks for the ride," he said. Before I could get a word in, he turned to his family. His meaty hands guided his wife and kids towards the flow of people exiting the gate. I was shocked to realize two things: I can't follow them, and I wouldn't be staying with them. *Oh crap, I'm homeless.*

My feet stuttered out of the place where I was standing, not wanting to get in the way of anyone else's vacation plans. I joined the flowing mob and looked up hotels near the airport. *Guh, hotel airports.*

I veered out of the way of travelers and leaned against a beam. I flicked through a few hotel options, something by the beach. That's when I was introduced to Miami prices and had to draw up a new plan. But then again, seeing the pictures of slot machines and poker tournaments under the hotel's website, I thought, *when in Rome*.

After a short, scenic drive through the city, my taxi pulled under the massive façade of the Hialeah Beach Hotel. Images of performers under the bright lights flashed down at me. The glamor absorbed me, taking my mind away from anyone else I was sharing the street with. My cabbie knocked me out of the spell by promptly putting the handle of a suitcase in my hand.

"Sorry, thanks," I muttered and stepped out of his way. A heavy-set doorman nodded and smiled. His smile reassured me that this would be my kind of place. That was until I sat on the bed. The blank, white walls of the hotel gave

High Roller Airways

me a nice view of the city and a hint that the beach wasn't too far away with the number of seagulls pecking around on rooftops. The sterile atmosphere drained the energy right out of me. I was already trapped, being stuck for half a week alone in a gaudy city like Miami, so I turned the lights out and closed the shades to freeze under well-tucked blankets.

A steamy shower and a shave didn't help me. I got an energy drink from the hallway vending machine, feeling a blood bubble stiffen against my neck. The cold air kept pestering me, reminding me of the hard work the HVAC guys did on this place. My best bet for some rest had to be the bar in the hotel's Italian bistro. The wall opposite the bar let in the afternoon sunshine, glistening every glass and piece of silverware. I chugged the energy drink and ditched it in a trash can before knocking bellies with the bar and making eye contact with the server behind it.

"Can I get a Coors?" I said through a burp.

"Sure," he answered, trying to hold back a grin.

I sat on the stool and stretched my back. Even though I was sitting behind the wheel of a plane for hours, it felt so much nicer to stop moving and knowing I wasn't going to move for a long time.

255

As I settled in, a figure caught my eye. A woman sat two stools from me at the corner of the bar. She had a short dark brown hairdo and a crisp white pilot uniform. Her luggage sat at her feet with the handle meeting her shoulder.

"Gin and tonic, thanks," she said.

As the bartender moved out of my view, I popped over to the next stool. "So, you're a pilot," I said.

"Yes, I am," she said with all the formality she could put in such a simple sentence.

"So am I," I replied.

She looked at me directly with a puzzle going on in her head. "What company?"

"It's a small one. You've probably never heard of it. What about you?"

"Cambridge Airlines. I'm from Boston originally."

"Oh yeah, like Boston Boston or like western Mass?"

A little puff of air came out her nose. "Boston Boston. I have the Bruins tickets to prove it."

"Oh, I believe you," I said, leaning in with my glass of Coors trailing behind. "So, what's a pilot like you doing in a small town like Miami?"

She pursed her lips a little, thinking of the right thing to say. She flung her hand over the bar and angled her face towards me. "Did you not notice my wedding ring?" she asked, flashing it around. It looked like a 2-carat headlight in the Miami sun.

"I did. Did you buy it yourself?"

She couldn't help but laugh. "No, my husband did."

"That's very traditional of you."

Her smirk rose again. "So, Mr. Charmer, what are you looking for?"

My hands sprang up in surrender. "I'll tell you the truth," I offered, leaning back into my seat. "My boss had me fly him and his family down for Christmas, and now I'm just biding my time."

"Oh really? That's a shame. Are you a private pilot?"

"Sort of," I pondered. "I'm more of a… well, I run a service for gamblers. Here." I reached for my wallet and pulled out one of the slick black cards.

"High Roller Airways," she said to herself.

"I fly folks who are looking for that a first-class Las Vegas experience. So, if you know anyone near Chicago, you should let them know."

"Interesting," she said.

"Don't worry. I don't just talk to people to sell them on this. I just-"

"No, no, I know what you meant. You must lead an interesting life."

"I do. It's a lot of laughs and headaches, but I guess that's with every job."

"So does your boss own the plane, and you just fly it?"

"No, I own 50% of it. I shouldn't have said he's my boss, but… being his chauffeur in the sky doesn't make me feel like I'm my own boss either."

"So your partner has you working over Christmas?"

I heard her words that matched what I'd told myself before I started this company, but with a fresh sense of self-hatred all I could utter was, "Yeah."

"You should tell him to f—k off," she said with a scrunched brow.

"But then he'd take a wing in the divorce," I replied. I laughed a little louder than her, but it warmed my heart to know I wasn't laughing alone. "After the pandemic," I started. "I just… didn't have it in me anymore. Flying commercial, I mean. How's flying these days?"

"It's good. I've been flying for fourteen years. Those extra flights really helped us out with my husband being laid off. We have two daughters, so we were afraid that we would have to make sacrifices, but it all worked out."

"I blew my overtime on a jet, how about you?"

"We bought a new house, which in Boston is impossible, but we made it work." She flashed her phone screen at me. I saw her family sitting on the stoop of a large stone house.

"Cute kids," I said. "Are you flying back tomorrow?"

"No, Henry and the girls are flying down tonight. Christmas by the beach didn't sound too bad."

I felt my smile fall a bit and my eyes haze over. "I'm happy for you," I said, placing my glass to my lips.

"What about you?" she asked. "Have any family?"

"No, I never wanted to stay in one place. I've been renting an apartment in my hometown for the last twenty years because I still think I might leave it…"

The warmth in her face shrunk down to a look of concern. "As funny as that sounds," I added.

"Is there any place you'd like to travel?" she asked.

"Hawaii might be nice. I've always done domestic. The only place out of the country I've been to is Toronto."

She let me hear a relaxed laugh. "But being from the Midwest it's really not much different." Her smile shined before sipping her G&T.

"It's just as snowy. Boston can get pretty cold, huh?"

"Oh yeah," she said. "As much as I like a white Christmas in the city, I prefer going somewhere warm."

"It's not a bad choice, no," I almost murmured.

She gave me a concerned look and thought to say something but a vibration in her pocket caught her attention. She plucked it up and answered it, facing away.

"You are… already? I thought it was late… Okay, okay, good. Alright, love you." She stepped out of her stool and drained her glass. "I have to go," she said, gathering her suitcase.

"It was nice talking with you," I said.

She stopped her hurry for a second and took a slow pace to get herself sorted. "It was nice. I don't meet too many undercover pilots. Thanks for keeping me company."

"Anytime," I said. She rolled her suitcase behind her and waved back. My hand lilted upward, watching her happy, expectant face before she disappeared around the corner. A relieved and satisfied sigh escaped my lungs. In a few moments, the warmth in my cheeks paled in the reflection of

High Roller Airways

the mirror behind the bar. I felt the oppressive air on my skin again. Even the bartender seemed like a lukewarm body taking up space, not a friend nor a companion, just there.

"You guys have a casino, right?"

I shuffled down the hall, searching for the next sign to point me toward the casino floor. For a place that doesn't move, it was hard to find in this maze of hallways and tucked-away rooms. Two double doors, each with large porthole, waited for me. I pushed through them and took in the climbing ceiling over the stacks of slots and table games.

Purple lights cascaded over the black machines that rested on copper carpet, lulling my eyes into the comfort of an endless sea of lights and screens. I felt fresh enough to do something daring, not just plug away at a slot machine. I needed to crunch numbers in my head. A man picking up his jacket and leaving the craps table caught my eye.

I took his seat and threw $20 on the passline, waiting anxiously for the shooter to throw. An older couple at the end of the table muttered to each other about their luck before the husband threw the dice. Rattling against my side of the table, I looked down at the red cubes, holding my breath.

"Snake eyes!" The dealer shouted.

His crook swept our chips towards his partner. The second dealer stacked the chips. Click. Click. Click. Click. He swung his hands out, signaling the dealer with the crook to pass the set of dice to the missus.

"Come on, honey," a fella at the table cheered. She had a clamped frown on her face, one that looked more calculating than upset. She passed her steely glance at each die individually and took one from the side nearest her and then the one from the other. As soon as the second die left the field, the dealer corralled the rest and spoke in his announcing voice.

"New shooter! New shooter!"

"Let's see what you can do, come on!" A man shouted. She clawed her dice with her short-nailed twig-like fingers and chucked them down the table. The dice clattered against the felt and rolled up a 3 and a 2.

"Fiver!" The dealer shouted. I threw a $10 chip on the 6 and 8. I paused, waiting for a sign. I took a chance and put another chip on the Field.

"Let's see something good," the vocal man next to me piped up. She put a cage around the dice and lifted them up. The dice came crashing down with a dull thud and knocked into the port and starboard side of the table.

"Yeleven! Chips back to the Field," the dealer said. A cuffed hand dropped an identical chip next to mine. I stroked it into my groove on the table. The dice slid back to the shooter. She played with them in her fingers. They jumped apart with a cracking ricochet.

"Six!" the dealer said. I picked up two $10 chips from my spot on the 6, keeping them around for a crazy bet. *What's on the menu? A hard eight? Boxcars? Double fives?* I put another one on the Field just to play it safe.

"Place your bets," the dealer warned us, watching the woman claw the dice again, her beady eyes on my end of the table. In a slow pendulum movement, the red pair dashed across the felt.

"Seven," the dealer said beneath the groans around the table. The chips I had on the table disappeared. That one took a bite out of me. I put another $20 on the passline.

"Same shooter, dice coming back," the dealer announced. I tried not to look at her; I didn't want a nervous hurler. She jiggled her dice and let them fly.

"Easy eight!" A steady hand dropped the white button above the big yellow 8. I put a chip behind the passline. I threw my two $10 chips down the table.

"Hard eight!" I said, looking the dealer in the eye. He nodded and put them into place. The talker next to me let out a weaselly laugh.

"I'll join ya," he said. He threw a $10 on the table. "Hard eight." He looked at me and offered me his closed fist. I tapped it, not letting the fear of bad juju get to my head.

"Colombian breakfast," the dealer shouted. My eyes shot back to the dice, a pair of threes. Even the veteran gambler next to me squinted at that one. My bet on the hard eight still had a chance. The dice scattered again.

"Double fives!" The dealer declared. *Oh!*

"I was thinking about that one," I muttered.

"You always see one before the other," he said. Maybe that was folksy wisdom or just gambler gibberish, but before I knew it, the roller plucked the dice from the table. I slipped another chip on the Field. I shot my hand back before she threw. The dice clanked against each other and settled under my hands.

"Niner!" The dealer shouted.

"Good call," my chatty neighbor said.

"Thanks," I said, a little bashful. I left the chip out there, feeling good.

High Roller Airways

"Fiver!" The chip went away. I put back the one I won and braced for impact. She laced the dice against the backboard, spinning them out into the center of the table.

"Seven, unlucky," the dealer muttered. His partner palmed my chips from around the table and slapped them into place in the bank. I stared at all the red chips I lost. I stroked a few chips into my palm and put them on the passline.

"Second chance, coming back," the dealer said. The same woman had picked two new dice from the bunch and rattled them between her twiggy digits.

"Come on, girl," my compadre said just above the noise of the gambling floor. The red dice popped onto the felt. Rolling closer a five and a four appeared.

"Niner!" The dealer shouted. "Place your bets." The second dealer shifted chips around for the players, shouting out commands for longshot combos. I focused on the dice, shifting on the green mat between little fingers. Her thumb pinched them together and let them fly. They slid under the table, out of sight. Every players' necks craned over the side to see. I kept my eyes on the chips I lost.

"Seven!" The dealer shouted. He refrained from a witty comment as the groans swelled around the table.

More of my chips slipped into the grooves on the other side. My remaining chips took up much less space than before. I dug into my pocket and threw out three hundreds on the table. The second dealer took them gladly, shoving the green bills down the chute with a low clap. The table waited as he gathered a medley of chips in his hand before dropping them in matching stacks. I threw $50 on the passline.

"Let's see it, baby!" I shouted.

The old-timer next to me clapped his hands together. "We got a ball game now, ha ha!"

I licked my teeth waiting for the next player to select his dice. A wiry Asian fella with sunglasses sunken into his head and a red Hawaiian shirt threw his dice as soon as the dealer gave him the go-ahead.

"Black as midnight," the dealer said, sharing our disappointment. A pair of 6's dared me to look back at them. I blinked and looked down the table.

Some of the players took their chips with them, but my neighbor stayed and the little woman down at the end kept her stony eye on those deadly dice.

The dealer reined them into his little bamboo stick and presented them to the unlucky shooter. He rattled his head, shaking out the bad luck. Our eyes settled on him. We couldn't see behind his shades, but the muscles around his neck stiffened. We all stood taller in our shoes, waiting for him to take off. He tossed them down. They rattled long enough for players to cheer them on until they went belly up.

"Yeleven! Everybody wins!" The dealer shouted. My fading eyes shot up. The pile of red chips on the passline in front of me doubled in size. I snatched the new pile, adding it to my mix in the grooves. The rush of a big win got me going, but I knew I was down deep. I had to pull a few wins together; I just needed the dice to fall my way.

"Dice back to shooter," the dealer shouted. The fella in red knocked the dice against the mat; one, two, then sent them flying. I backed up in case they hit my chest on the way down. The backspin shot them back to the center of the table.

"Three's company," the dealer announced. His partner swiped all our chips into his clutches. I pursed my lips at having to throw my recent winnings back onto the passline.

I thumbed the chip at the end of my line, let the soothing familiarity of its round edge help pass the time for the unlucky shooter to try again.

"Could be anything," my friend muttered, fanning our worried spirits to catch flame. Two knocks and the dice soared under my knuckles. One rolled flat, a 6. *Come on, give us a 1*. The die hung on the dice tray off the main mat. The edge of the die wobbled. The dealers hadn't called it off. Their stern eyes widened, wet and white at what could happen. The thick red die toppled over and showed a haze of white dots. 6.

"Twelve," the dealer said, hardly a mutter. He knew mad customers were bad customers. The fella in the red shirt passed on the dice with a wave of the hand, saying, "No more, no more."

The dealer sent the crowd of dice over to my neighbor. He gladly took the first two dice he saw and rubbed his fingertips across the red pair. The sharp edges dug and fled from his skin as he rolled them in a short circle. When the dealer gave the all-clear, my friend shook them in his overhand grip and shot them at the lower wall. They landed so far away my eyes turned to the dealer to confirm.

"Eight, lucky number eight," the dealer said, a little relieved. I let out a sighing laugh, having spent the last few rolls thinking the bad luck would never end.

"Finally!" I said. "Let's see something good," I smacked my friend on the back. He chuckled and threw some chips behind his previous bet. I bet on the 6 and 8, easy numbers that would bring me something back over time.

"Ah, why not?" I said. I threw a hundred on the field. The woman at the end let her mouth drop at the black chip.

"Let's see something big," I said. My encouragement didn't seem to put him at ease. He knocked the dice against the wall and flung them away from us. I licked my lips and strained my eyes to see.

"Nine!" The dealer announced.

"Yeah!" I shouted with my arms raised. My claps thundered across the room. The second dealer placed another black chip down. I took it and stacked it on top.

"Come on, let's see it again!" An unexpected laugh came from the woman down the way. Seeing a big winner really excited the bunch. They threw in chips on crazy rolls and waited for my friend to make his move. His mouth formed an oval before clearing his throat. He threw the dice down and watched them go.

"Seven!" The dealer shouted. A pale splash slammed against my insides. I stared at the 3 and 4 down the table, bold and out in the open. My friend took his chips and put them in his shirt pocket. He leaned close to my ear.

"Good luck, partner." He slipped past my shoulder into the dim lights behind me. The dealer glanced at me and down again. He used his crook to deliver the new set of dice.

"Take your pick," he said with waning enthusiasm.

I took two on the left side of the bunch and jiggled them in my hand while he slid the rest back to his side of the table. *You think I don't know what I'm doing? You think I'm some chump?*

My fist lowered a stack of chips on the passline, watching the dealer look at me with a shocked, watchful expression. So did the rest of the table. Once I knew they were waiting for me I chucked them down the felt.

"Snake eyes," the dealer said, holding his breath as he brought the dice back to me. His comrade smoothed my lost chips across the table, pooling them back into his tray. *Just a bad run. It's gotta get better.*

When the rest of the table looked at me expectantly, I tossed those suckers down the whole way.

"Twelve. Sorry, folks," the dealer said. I looked down, seeing the mess of chips I wagered quickly swallowed whole by the dealer's white sleeves. I knew I had enough. You can only get knocked around the ring so many times before you have to hang up your gloves. The dealer pushed the same two dice to me again with an unsure look.

I palmed my chips and waved him off. He understood and turned back to the few stragglers who stayed behind. I stepped away from the table. My remaining chips hung weightless in my pocket.

The stiffness in my neck helped me know that I had been hunched over the craps table for too long. The doors leading out to the marina were full of orange sunset. I could taste the waning heat and sea breeze. My lead foot held still in my shoe. The chiming bells and clinking coins echoed in my ears. I took my eyes off the outside world and saw the golden frames of slot machines and overhead lamps at the tables. I settled into the next seat I could find.

My head throbbed against the window of my hotel room. The shabbier, industrial side of Miami was laid out before me in the late afternoon sun. I had no place to be, waiting for Jack's phone call. Who knew when that would come? A city has so many possibilities, but around the holidays, alone, I had none.

I looked at my phone and found my dad's number. Once I saw it, I paused. I assured him that I'd never have to fly over a holiday again. I told myself that a few times.

Being away from family over the holidays made me want to reach out. Then he'd be right, get the last laugh, scoff at my grand adventure. My finger hovered over the call button. I chose to forget the idea.

High Roller Airways

Chapter 13: Three Old Ladies and a Pilot

I guided my clients to the hangar, explaining over my shoulder how the trip would go. They were three old Chinese ladies who kept a deliberate pace behind me. When I received their reservation, I was shocked there were only three of them, and no husbands, or at least on this trip.

They held stern frowns, analyzing every word of my presentation. Except for Mei, she was a sweet, old lady and was clearly the youngest of the bunch. She took great pride in how she looked; she had the same hairdo she must've had in the 80s, but it still kept its youthful shape.

Bao trotted beside her. She was a crotchety-looking woman with layers of hair that had the color of an old chalkboard. Fang stood head and shoulders above the other two. She frowned the deepest as I explained the rules of the aircraft. Her arms folded as I turned to face them, not giving anything away. Maybe she was a poker shark.

"Do you ladies have any questions?" The wind passed through the hangar, the only response I got. My hands clasped together; I had to do something to get the nervous tension out. Hearing none, I cleared my throat and clapped my hands.

"Well, we can head inside; I'll take your bags." I reached out to take their suitcases. They rolled them over to me and I set them aside as they formed a line for the stairs into the cabin. I held onto the rail on the stairs for them, bowing as they passed. Bao passed without any hint that I was doing a good job; Mei grinned at me, as if to say thank you for being so helpful; and Fang gave me a cold glance that chilled my insides. *This will be fun.*

I felt my steps sag behind a bit to let the old ladies catch up. The Blue Stallion's lobby seemed especially elegant for my guests. I looked back and saw the slightest nods of approval, just to show they like this part of the hotel. They weren't completely sold just yet.

I managed to reach the desk before the receptionist noticed me. Feeling mischievous I took one long step before drumming the desk with my hands. Her blue eyes popped up, shocked that she hadn't noticed me.

"Didn't mean to scare ya," I said.

Her embarrassed look disappeared into her shining smile. "Welcome to the Blue Stallion Hotel," she said, still getting used to the phrase. She looked young, like she came from money, and her head tilted to the side, keeping her eyes on me.

"Thanks," I chuckled.

Susan slipped through the gap behind the front desk. Her eyes shot down to her feet as she saw me.

"Hey, Susan," I called. "Long time no see."

She tossed her hair over her shoulder and lifted her chin, letting us hear her clanking, stiletto footfalls.

I looked back at the receptionist, maintaining my self-assured smile. "It's a funny little routine we have. I say hello and she ignores me."

Her smile warmed her face. "How can I help you?"

"We have some rooms for my clients. The room should be reserved under Bao Ling."

Her flowing head of blonde hair swished to the side, looking over my shoulder, to see Bao, Mei, and Fang waiting for more information. She flashed them a big smile, one that wasn't reciprocated. Her long curls flopped back onto her lapel as she typed away on her keyboard with her nimble French tips.

"Alright, I have the room keys and players cards right here." She planted the black cards in two neat rows.

I stepped aside for the ladies to take them, but they kept their expectant stare on me. I cleared my throat and palmed two cards at a time, checking the names on the player cards before reaching out to meet their hands.

"He'll take your bags," I explained to the group. They each looked over in their own time at the teenage boy standing by the luggage cart. I had half expected Mario to be working, but almost felt relieved that he wasn't.

"And will you be staying with us?" she asked.

"Yes, Dave Jennings." I waited for her to type my name into the computer. I looked at the nameplate she wore. Against a gold bar the black script read "Brittany".

"So, Brittany, how long have you been working here?"

"Just a few months," she said, still staring at the screen. Her eyes suddenly traded confidence for fear. "I'm sorry," she said. "But I don't see a reservation in your name."

High Roller Airways

A suit came into vision. Susan had some business to return to at the front desk. Her glare didn't go unnoticed.

My cheeks stretched up as my wily smile rose underneath. "A few months, you said? I'm a regular here — a business partner. I always have a room waiting for me. I'm sure Susan forgot to put it in." I flicked through my wallet and tossed my card on the desk.

Brittany glanced down at it, recognizing it immediately. "Oh, that's who you are," she said, a breathy sigh of relief seeped through her teeth. She took the card in her fingers. "Very official. I've heard of you." Her mouse bounced around finding where I'd sleep that night. "So you fly for the company?"

"I own the company."

"Impressive, I never knew there were companies like that out there."

"We're the only one." I chuckled. *What is this? LinkedIn?*

She handed me the key to my room. "So," she nearly whispered, leaning in. "You must fly a lot, right?"

"I fly all over."

"Have you ever been to Monaco?"

"I can fly *you* to Monaco."

Her tongue turned in her mouth, holding back that exquisite smile. "That sounds nice," she said, looking at nothing in particular. Once she got tired of holding that coy, wondering look, her sharp blue eyes snapped back at me.

"Are you free tomorrow night?" My eyebrows jumped up. Her smile curled.

"It just so happens I am," she replied.

"Do you have a number?"

Her eyes looked shocked. She padded around for a card and pen. She looked past me. The coast was clear. Her manicured hands stretched against the top of the desk, revealing the blank side of a hotel card. She finely wobbled the edge of her ballpoint pen across it.

"Call whenever you like." She passed it to me. I pawed it, but not before her slight fingers inched over mine. My eyes jumped up to meet hers. I tried, with all my focus, not to look away.

"Oh, I will," I said. I winked at her. It was funny to see her regain her composure, standing at the ready for the next boring tourist. She'd be thinking about me all day. As I felt my feet move away from the desk, I looked up to see Bao, Mei, and Fang all looking at me with dull eyes. Even the bellboy was waiting patiently.

"What floor?" He asked.

Once the bellboy emptied their belongings into their suite, I thought it would be my time to say sayonara.

"Well, ladies, I'm gonna relax in my room. I hope you enjoy your stay."

"Where's casino?" Mei asked, leaning forward on the couch to hear my answer.

"I'll show you," I answered eagerly. Newly found energy flashed across their faces. I could barely get out the door without them tripping up my shoes.

Moving down the hall, I tried to keep a respectful distance. I looked over my shoulder once, seeing them keep a closer than comfortable distance. I just kept walking and never looked back.

Feeling the pressure to keep it short, I opened the door and threw my gear inside. I closed it shut and came across three waiting faces. I hesitated to move, but they had no interest in finding their own way without my help.

I escorted them into the elevator. Once they were inside, I tiptoed my way in, avoiding touching Bao as I reached for the lobby button on the wall.

As soon as I hit the button, I slid back against the opposing wall. Bao gave me a cantankerous look. She waited for the doors to close before speaking.

"You like Blackjack?" Bao asked.

"Blackjack, you say? Sure, I'll play."

"Are you good?" she challenged.

My eyes squinted a little. *I respect your chops, old lady.* "Oh yeah, you'll see."

Unsure, she gave a curt nod. The elevator doors opened. She led; I followed.

Once we crossed the hall into the gaming floor, I looked back a few times to make sure I hadn't lost them in the shuffle. Mei was looking around me, trying to get a sneak peek at all the action that was happening on the floor. Bao kept walking the same speed, keeping her eyes on my back, while Fang gave me a cold look that turned my head around to find the nearest table.

At the first Blackjack table I found, I pointed at the open seats. Bao looked up with depthless eyes. Fang leaned forward; her Mandarin cut through the air. Bao looked up at me and pulled my sleeve.

"This is baby table, where's the bigger bet?"

High Roller Airways

I looked at the minimum bet sign that read "$10". I gulped, thinking of where I was in the casino. Mei, darting her head around, pointed at a table a few lengths away.

"There, Bao, over there," she said.

I cleared my throat and waved them to come with me. We found the next table that permitted bets for $25, not anything less.

At this ritzier Blackjack table, Bao pointed with her open hand to first base. I took my seat. Bao, Mei, and Fang sat in the next seats.

"Welcome, welcome," a heavy fella with a bun of hair greeted us. Mei popped open the clasp of her sleek onyx purse and cut her deck of hundred-dollar bills, handing over the smaller half to the dealer. My eyebrows shot up, leading me to take a few more twenties out of my wallet. Once all our chips were neatly placed in front of us, our man-bunned dealer gestured to me to place my bet. I threw down the minimum bet. Bao and Fang wagered $100, while Mei looked at her friends' bets before deciding to slim hers down to $50.

"Let's have some fun," the dealer insisted. He slipped some cards from the shoe. I had a sturdy-looking 9 to start. Once he got back to me, the *thwip* of the second card showed I was doomed. A 7, 16 total. I glanced at his red Queen. I sighed and waved him off. The rest of the ladies stuck with their upper teen hands. The dealer flipped his hidden card to show a black 7.

"That's about right," I muttered. The dealer chuckled as he plucked my chips from the table.

"That's a tough break, but your luck'll change." He passed my chips to Bao and pressed his fist into the table in front of Mei and Fang.

The next round started off worse, with a pair of 2s. *There's no point in splitting these is there?* I tapped the felt. He flipped the next card over. I sucked in some air. A 10. He had one just like it. I shrugged a little.

"What else can I do?" I said, hitting the green. He turned another one over. 24. My stomach flipped.

I was losing badly. I looked at Bao's cards. She was in the clear with 19. I looked up at her. She was already looking at me. *You were supposed to be good, you said.* I let out a deep sigh to let her know I wasn't a clueless schmuck. It was just one of those days. Fang was up with a pair of 6s. She looked at the shoe, her eyelids hovering halfway over her eyes, tabulating. Her little finger drilled into the table. The dealer's eyebrows flexed but did as he was told. He flipped her a new card. A bright, red 8, 20 total.

"Ah," Mei reacted, clapping at the professional's work. Fang bowed her head. We caught each other's look. She nodded slightly, acknowledging my round of applause.

As soon as I threw my chip down, the dealer started again. My second card fell, and I could see that I had a 10 and a 3 versus his 10.

"Another one, huh?" I grumbled to the dealer. His hands and shoulders reached up. I shook off the bad feeling I had and looked down the table to see what had been dealt out. Then I noticed something touching my wrist. It was Bao's hand. Under her wrinkled, painted fingers was a $25 chip.

"No hit," she said with a glare. I didn't have to think about it twice.

"Stand," I said, waving my hand. Bao hit. The dealer flopped a bright red Queen at her feet.

"I told you," she said, raising her eyebrows as she thwapped the mat with her finger. The dealer went down the line. He revealed a hidden 2, making 12. Then a 4 and then an 8, bust. I chuckled to myself and looked over at Bao. Her eyes flashed down at the chip. I guess I wasn't quick enough to return the favor. I slid the chip back to her area. She wordlessly placed it in her rung and faced the dealer.

After a few rounds with their ups and downs, I started to feel my throat dry. I didn't really mind it at first, but I thought if I didn't take a second to wave the waitress over, I would get lost in the game again. The waitress took her time to come over and asked me what I wanted to order.

"Coors for me. Bao, would you like a drink?"

She looked at me with a confused expression. "Ah?" She chirped, then she saw the waitress. "Oh," she said after seeing her. My eye caught Mei waving at the waitress with a wide grin.

"Amaretto sour!" She piped up. Fang looked up from her chips, tiredly leaning over the table.

"Two," she said, holding up her fingers. Bao swung her head over to hear. Her face dropped; all of her focus was centered on thinking of an answer. A moment later she popped back into our world.

"Gin," she said. She nodded to herself that that was the right answer.

"And a gin, neat," I conferred to the waitress. She punched our orders into the bright blue light of her tablet screen. Sometimes I wish they would just write this stuff down. *Why does everything have to be through a touchscreen?* She stood there, trying to find the button for an Amaretto in their catalogue. As I waited, I heard a voice rise to a quick screech.

"You were talking to that girl," Mei said, cutting through the noise. It sounded more like an accusation. I felt the waitress next to me looking down my neck. I turned my head, and she made herself scarce. I tried to put on an undisturbed face.

"Yes, I did," I said, raising my voice like I was making a phone call in a tunnel.

"She's pretty, like Grace Kelly," Mei piped up. *Not even close. How did she hear that over all this noise?*

Sensing the silence was left for me to answer, I spoke up. "Thank you."

"You take her on a date?" Bao asked, seemingly very focused on pulling the answer out of me.

"Yes, tomorrow night at the restaurant." Her face held its inquisitive scowl. "Here, the restaurant here," I clarified.

"What's pretty girl name?" Mei asked. With all the noise and confusion, I started to flounder. As I started to sputter, I saw Susan's jacket slip past.

"Susan," I spat out. She stopped as if I had called for her like a rolling taxi.

"No," I sputtered. "Brittany, Brittany is her name. This is Susan. How are you, Susan?"

Susan's sloped nose glared down at me. My hand gripped some of my chips, like I was bracing for a slap.

"I've heard of the *kindness* you showed Brittany today, showing her the best places in town, just outside your doorstep. If I may be so bold, Mr. Jennings, the shrimp ceviche is the best thing on the menu. Do you require anything else?" I gulped as my eyes could only absorb her inescapable, paralyzing stare.

"That sounds lovely, Susan. Thank you," I muttered. She kept her scowl turned towards me as her feet carried her away. Suddenly, I realized the blood had rushed into my eardrums, and the crowd continued chatting again.

"Brittany and David, like real Hollywood couple," Mei said, clasping her hands. Fang scoffed and shook her head. Bao kept her eye on me, not sure whether she approved or disapproved of my answer.

Deep in the womb of sleep I threw my arms around, struggling against the covers.

"No, no, why?" I mumbled in desperation. My muscles rattled under my skin, leaving me too alert to sink back into the black sleep. I then realized it wasn't just the late-night jitters. Someone was knocking on my door, a little knock, like the pruny claw of an old Chinese woman.

"Guh... Please, let me rest." The sound was so faint, and my head felt so soft and heavy against the pillow that I convinced myself it was nothing, and then I imagined all three of them were on the other side of the door with their sagging faces, disappointed that I made them wait.

"One moment!" I grumbled towards the door. I fell out of bed and crawled to where my pants had laid crumpled on the floor. Jumping into each leg, I reached for the doorknob and opened it. Bao stood nearest the door and before she could see me completely, her nose jumped up to her eyebrows. I turned my face into my armpit. *Do I smell?*

"Why are you naked?" she asked.

I looked down at my white undershirt and jeans. "What? Is it my feet?" I picked up my foot to see if I stepped in something.

She kept her disappointed glare on my face. "Get dressed and meet us in room. You're taking us shopping."

After a speed shower and a shave, I called a taxi to take Bao, Mei, and Fang to the closest Chinese grocery store.

"We need tea," Bao said.

I thought it was silly to go shopping for tea when we had room service, but I obliged. As soon as we got there, they started throwing rice and tea leaves into my arms. I cradled the pile of groceries like a football to keep the tea leaf packets from sliding off. Bao led us through the next aisle. The shelves were packed close together, so I'd have to walk in sideways sometimes. The tendons in my arms started to stretch under the strain of the big bag of rice.

Once Fang placed a ginger root on my precarious pile, she looked at Bao with a reluctant glance, like I was a mule that was packed to the brim, and my limited endurance was a burden to them. Bao mercifully agreed enough was enough by taking the last item herself.

She led the way to the cashier. I dropped my heap onto the conveyor belt, causing it to shake. Bao let us pass. We waited for her to pay for the groceries. Mei flashed a big smile at me as she saddled me with the grocery bags. Fang stood by Bao, watching the prices pile up.

Once the cashier finished swiping the food, he nodded to Bao to use her card. She leaned into the card reader with her whole weight. The card stuck. She relaxed, folding her arms and waited. I blinked, and her face dropped again. I'd seen that look before.

The climbing chime of the card machine rang once, twice, and our eyes shifted to her before the third time. Fang bumped Bao's elbow and muttered something in Mandarin. Bao turned her face down to the card and snapped it away.

"Hard of hearing," Fang explained to the cashier. He looked to the next customer in line. I made room for us to leave. I kept my eye on Bao. The spacey look in her eye made me feel less resentful for being their errand boy for the weekend. I stayed close behind her until I saw her sit neatly in her seat.

Mei sat on the couch in a huff, like *she* carried sacks of rice up the stairs. *Elevator maintenance, is Susan that angry with me?* I kept my shoulders from popping out by setting the bags by the fridge. As soon as it closed, Bao looked back at me. She waved me over wordlessly. I let out a tormented sigh. Maybe she wanted me to lift up the refrigerator to retrieve an ice cube.

She pointed into the sink where I found a little black kettle. She brushed against my back and segregated me to my corner of the room with what sounded like a complaint in Mandarin to Fang.

"Sink, Dave," I muttered to myself. "Haven't you seen a sink before?"

"Huh?" Bao shouted to me.

"Nothing!" I shouted back and slapped the faucet on. After filling the kettle, I walked back to a room of noisy jibber jabber. When there was a pause in the bickering, they turned their heads to me; the heavy kettle dipping down in my hand.

"Wha?" Bao asked.

"What do you want me to do with this?"

"Stove," Fang explained.

"Stove!" Bao screeched.

"Alright, alright," I said. As I turned to the stove, I thought to ask what level to turn it to but decided somewhere in the middle would work. I watched the water bubble with folded arms until Mei placed her hand on my shoulder. She gestured to three chairs.

I lowered myself down with a heavy sigh, closing my eyes to see if I could pretend that I wasn't there. I felt the faint, wafting heat of the kettle and looked down at the table in front of me. Bao had set a wooden tray there. Various porcelain cups stood around it, including three short bowls in front of us.

Mei and Fang sat beside me. Bao held up a finger to catch my attention. She lifted a wooden sheath to her face. She slid the top of it open, exposing the packed tea leaves inside. She breathed in their bitter fragrance and brought them closer to me. Her arms could only reach so far, so I obliged and leaned in. I placed my nose just above the tea leaves and gave them a sniff, looking up at Bao for approval.

She moved the leaves away and gave them to Mei for approval. She nodded with satisfaction. Fang followed suit with a demure subtlety. Bao returned the sheath back to her side of the table and lowered the leaves into a glass.

After letting the limp leaves fall in, she reached for the kettle. The steaming water flooded the glass and churned up the tea leaves, releasing black specs in the muddied waters. She then spread the leaves to the side of the glass with its matching transparent lid. Steam billowed out of the top, but Bao grasped the top of the glass effortlessly and strained the tea into a porcelain cup with a spout.

The tea-infused water leapt into the cup until the last few drops left the soggy leaves. Waiting for the last of it to drop down, Bao then returned the strained glass back to her side of the table and waited a moment. Then her right hand took the porcelain cup and turned it over Fang's bowl, filling it with the familiar brown liquid. She lifted the cup above Mei's and did the same.

She transferred it to my bowl with a slow, calculated motion. The tea warmed my cup, heating my folded hands nearby. Bits of tea leaves swirled around inside. There was something peaceful about the slow, patient practice of serving tea this way.

The little imperfections in the bowl brought my mind away from the crisp, clean perfection of the modern world. That moment seemed timeless and without place, like we were no longer in the same city as we were that morning.

I waited to reach for the cup as I watched her pour her own. After Bao gave herself some tea, I sat up straight, relieved to finally enjoy this special tea that Bao had invited me to partake in. A few moments went by before Bao poured the rest of the strained water into a larger porcelain bowl. *Not enough for a second cup, I guess.*

Bao made her hands into fists and set them down on the table shoulder width apart. I waited for her to start, but she reached for my bowl first and poured it into the larger bowl where the excess tea had been poured. My eyebrows shot up, embarrassed, knowing that I easily could have disrupted this peaceful ceremony.

Once Bao had emptied all the bowls, she started again, pouring the still steaming water from the black kettle over the tea leaves. She strained the glass again into the cup with the spout. Out of the corner of my eye I saw Fang stroke her finger against the table. Bao tipped the cup and let the tea flow into Fang's bowl. Mei stroked the table the same way. Bao obliged her with more tea. I looked at Bao sheepishly, looking for the hint that I should do the same.

Her eyes concentrated on Mei's bowl. My finger pet the table like Fang and Mei had done. Then Bao brought her slow movements to a stop. Mei looked at me and closed her first two fingers, making a big knuckle. She pet the table like before. So I dug my closed fingers against the table like a bull digging up dirt with its hoof.

Bao turned her attention to pouring me some tea. Once everyone had a whirling bowl of tea in front of them, Fang and Mei raised theirs with both hands. I did the same, sensing the heat of the tea against the pads of my fingers.

It was delicious. It spread through my core and radiated inside my chest. The bits of tea leaves hung to my upper lip. I licked them off, and they stuck to the back of my teeth. Bao glanced at me and looked down, nearly stopping me from seeing her smile.

After tea, Bao instructed Fang to cook some rice. Bao and Mei spoke to each other in Mandarin as I waited for Fang to finish some meal that they never bothered to name. Being left out of the conversation, I started to remember where I was, and who I was, and why I was there.

The cold, gray sunlight entering the room made me sink into myself. I felt totally trapped, not just by my clients cooking for me, but by the sad fact that I had nowhere else to go until that evening. Brittany was the only thing I had to look forward to, and everything about it felt bittersweet.

My gratitude for the meal was deflated as my hostesses treated me less like a peer and more like a trough for extra rice and chicken. I looked at Bao. I realized how unusually I sat. My eyes drooped; my back was hunched.

Do you feel as lonely as I do? Once her eyes flicked up at me, I turned my head. I kept my hands folded and waited for Fang's hard work to warm me as I felt the persistent chill of the AC. *These gray walls*.

When our food arrived, Fang dropped chopsticks in front of Mei and Bao. She sat my plate down with the corner of a cloth napkin holding a knife and fork tucked underneath. I noticed and snorted. Nobody else seemed to notice, but it brought something out of me, a fleeting moment of acknowledgement.

I started to unravel the cloth napkin that held my knife and fork until I felt a tug. The silverware budged from the pinch of Bao's little hand. My eyebrows bent downward.

"What're you doing?" I asked.

She pulled away my knife and fork and placed a pair of wrapped chopsticks in my hand.

"Oh," I mumbled. I let a moment pass before casting my eye at Fang. She blew onto the rising steam from her plate. Mei held a wad of sauce-stained rice in front of her mouth as she conversed with Bao. The longer Bao and Mei talked, and the more Fang hung over her plate, the more uninterested they felt. I was stuck in the corner, at my own little kid's table.

There's gotta be something I can do. Fang let the other two talk, but their animated speech got so loud I couldn't hear myself think. When a lull started to form, I piped up.

"Is this your first time in Vegas?" I asked. Bao and Fang looked at me like I was dense. "Any favorite casinos?"

"They're same but different," Bao said. Fang nodded. Mei politely placed more food in her mouth, pretending to listen.

"What about your date?" Bao asked. "What are you doing after dinner?"

"I'm not sure. It's a first date, nothing crazy."

She gave me the same dull look. "She's a pretty girl. She'll want to go out."

"I'll play it by ear. I don't want to be too pushy."

"You should take her to the club. Do you like to dance?" Bao asked.

"Oh, I don't dance much," I said, shaking my head. All three of their jaws sank deeper beneath their closed mouths. My desperate eyes looked to Mei for understanding, but she looked away. Fang seemed to sit taller over me. I cleared my throat and ate some rice. After a moment, I thought I'd try again, anything to escape the gray malaise.

"So besides gambling, what do you like to do for fun?" Another pause, I swallowed my tongue.

Then Bao picked her head up and spoke to Mei, whispering in Mandarin.

What? Do you think you're better than me? What is this? Why am I even here?

"Hey! I'm talking to you! You can't just ignore me. I'm not your nephew. I'm not your grandson. I don't have to put up with this!"

Bao raised her eyebrows, stunned. As soon as I raised my voice, she dropped her chopsticks on the plate. Her face swirled with mixed emotions, all of which I caused. Fang and Mei's faces sank into their bowls. I'd shut myself out. There was no coming back from this.

"I'm sorry," I muttered into my chest. "Excuse me." I bolted for the door.

"Nice job, idiot," I told myself in the hallway. "You couldn't keep your cool for one more minute, could you? They're never coming back after this. How many more failures can you afford? Moron!"

I laid back on the bed. The back of my eyes ached. I looked at the time. I had all the time in the world before my date. I hated it. My eyelids flapped down. *Sleep*.

Maybe I could nap for an hour or two, and then what? I kicked my shoes off and sank my head into the pillow, hoping to rest until I had forgotten about all of this.

I flung myself out of bed at the sound of a knock at my door. I didn't care what I looked like. I threw the door open and saw Fang. She stood there unfazed, having expected me.

"Fang," I said, caught off guard. "What is it?"

"I'm sorry about Bao…" she said.

I waited to hear more. "I don't know what to say."

"We don't know you, but Bao seems to like you," she explained carefully.

"What do you mean?"

"She's hard on you, but she didn't want to be alone."

"Wouldn't she have you?"

"She feels how lonely you are. She sees potential in you, but as a middle-aged man you should have shaped up by now." A laugh rattled out of my stomach until I couldn't stop. I put my hand in front of my mouth to stifle it.

"That… I wouldn't expect anything less," I laughed.

"She has a son she doesn't talk to anymore," she said.

The gray light in the room caught my eye again. My smile dipped into a thin line.

"It's been a year, she says. She thinks she can try again with you, that you'll listen. You did well for a while."

"I really tried," I admitted.

"I'll tell her you are sorry and that you're not mad." She waited for my response, but her eyes hung still like she would say that no matter what I said. Another test.

"Please do," I said.

Fang nodded slightly and took her leave. I closed the door and blinked.

My eyes snapped open, and I whirled out of bed. My nose and mouth slammed against the thin carpet. The air thrust through my nose like I got hit with a basketball. Then I remembered the wisp of images of Fang at my door in my dream and sighted. I jerked my head enough so I could see the door, but my temple dug into the carpet again. The door was closed. I bent my body up like a seal and checked my phone for any missed calls or texts. There was nothing, no reconciliation, no communication, just the slog of post-nap consciousness.

"Ahhh!"

The lines of cold water raced down my back in the shower. I hopped around to relieve my neck and chest from the constant stream of frigid water pelting my skin. I leaned out of the shower, still feeling the heavy, sinking feeling behind my eyes. I found myself in the mirror and saw the five o'clock shadow had set in. *Did I shave this morning?*

I let the water stream through my hand, my throbbing palm inching away from the heat. I shaved as lightly as I could, only covering inch-by-inch squares at a time. I grumbled after I saw a red line under my jaw. After washing my face, I threw on a shirt and some cologne I had found ages ago. I turned over the bottle and looked at the label and scoffed. They just went out of business the previous week.

Taking in the smell again, I didn't think Brittany would mind. My lip curled thinking about a back-and-forth. It was funny, I couldn't remember the last time I was on a date, and here I was wearing an old shirt and old cologne.

After carrying this dream on my shoulders, all the convincing talks it took, and after all this work I was finally reaping some of the rewards.

Brittany suggested we meet in front of the restaurant. I agreed, only to avoid the whole building seeing us together. Maybe that was a dumb idea since I hardly remember seeing anyone more than once in that place, but as soon as I saw Susan behind the front desk, I knew Brittany had a good idea.

I felt clean and fresh, no clients on my mind, no future to worry about. It was just a date. It might actually be fun for once.

High Roller Airways

Susan spotted me a mile away. There were a few tourists in the lobby, but it felt a lot bigger seeing Susan stare me down as I walked across the front desk. Her hawk eyes clamped onto me. She knew exactly what I was doing and was expecting the worst. I tried to put on a smile like she didn't scare the tar out of me. I took another one of her devastating looks and the icy cold feeling in my gut made me look down at my feet.

I checked the time to make sure I wouldn't keep her waiting but there was nobody there. The open doors led to a dark hall, hiding the restaurant from sight. I looked around the corners to see, but there was no one standing in front of the blazing white walls.

"You're an idiot," I told myself. "Still getting stood up. You're friggin' embarrassing." I searched around the lobby, not going too far out to run across Susan again, but she wasn't hurrying across the floor either. I sighed and posted up against the wall. *Should I text her?*

After scrolling on my phone for fifteen minutes, I saw someone round the corner. I lifted my head to see her. A fluffy white jacket hung from her shoulders and peach pumps elongated her narrow frame. I wasn't sure why she chose to wear that jacket when it was 88 degrees outside, but her chest glistened in the light. Her smoky eyes caught my attention.

"Hello, David," she said with a lilt in her voice.

"Hello," I said with a smile. "I love that jacket."

"Thank you. I hope you haven't been waiting long."

"Oh no, don't sweat it. This place is the best."

I led her inside, letting the host show us around the joint. The dimly lit restaurant had red paper lanterns hanging overhead and Chinese dragons etched into obsidian glass partitions throughout the restaurant.

The host placed us down along the wall to give us some privacy. Her hair glowed in the supple lighting and looking at her smiling at me let me sink into my seat.

"You look gorgeous tonight," I heard myself say.

She ducked her head and smiled. "Thank you. My mom always said I look like Nicole Kidman." She did not. "You clean up pretty good yourself." *Not really*.

"Thanks," I grinned. "They have some world-class chefs here. The whole menu's to die for."

"I can't wait," she said. She still had that furry white coat over her shoulders.

I cleared my throat and whispered. "Aren't you going to take your jacket off?"

"Oh," she said, stripping it from her shoulders as soon as she could. "I forgot I had it on." I smiled and returned to the menu. Underneath the rumble of casual conversations throughout the room, I turned my head up at the sound of loud footfalls. Susan's black suit cut down the aisle where we were seated. She pivoted to us and clasped her hands, grinning ear to ear. Brittany welcomed her with a blissful grin, while my stomach turned.

"Hello to you both, thank you for choosing Macau Harbor this evening. Our kitchen has a delicious Minchi they have been preparing and a classic Serradura for dessert which I'm sure you'll like." She leaned closer to me. "I'll make sure they add extra sawdust to yours, David," she whispered. "I hope you enjoy your meal," she said to Brittany.

"Thank you, Susan, that's nice of you," Brittany said.

"Oh, dear, you have something on your cheek. David, you really should have told her."

"I didn't-"

"It's okay," Brittany said. "I'll be back in a second." She scooted out of the booth and headed for the doors.

Only a moment passed before Susan turned to me. She leaned close to my ear, bringing her eyes level with mine and she stared until I turned to her.

"If you break my employee, there will be consequences." She brushed past me.

All I saw was her red hair fly past between blinks. Then I registered Bao and Fang watching me with concerned looks on their faces. I saw Mei tip back in her chair behind Bao, seeing how I looked. I squared myself with the table again and waited for Brittany to come back. My foot started tapping the floor at 80 beats per minute. I took out a business card and flipped it over. I wrote down a note. *What're you doing here? You just got groceries.*

I flung it over to their table. Their necks craned over it as soon as it landed. I straightened up in case Brittany was coming back. My eyes glanced over to see Fang pulling out her cellphone.

"What are you doing?" I whispered. My voice cut through the chatter in the room, and I flinched as I saw a few heads turn. Fang paid no mind and kept typing.

"I'm sitting right here," I said. "You can talk to me." She put her phone away and watched me. I glanced where Brittany had turned the corner. I folded my hands on the table and waited as if nothing had happened.

High Roller Airways

A few seconds later, a buzz sprung from my pocket. I looked at the screen and read her message. *We slept too late to make dinner. Text is for discretion.*

I threw her an angry glare. I caught her putting her phone down again. Mei looked winsomely over Bao's shoulder to see that I got the next text. *Be discreet.*

I looked up and saw Brittany coming back. I slipped the phone back in my pocket and showed her a staged grin.

"How was the bathroom?" I chuckled, immediately regretting the question.

"Clean," she said with a shine in her smile. She picked up her menu and panned the options. "Did you decide what you wanted to order?"

"I know I like what I'm looking at."

A twinge in her smile let me know she heard. "What made you want to ask me out, of all the girls in this hotel?"

My suave expression loosened as I actually thought of my answer. Her eyes rose from her menu.

"I liked the way you looked at me when I came up to the desk. I don't know. Just the way you waved your hair and smiled at me, you put me at ease." She seemed pleased to hear it. I couldn't be happy with that as I traced back my memories to assure myself that wasn't a lie.

"What made you want to become a pilot?" The question threw me out of my spell.

"I just love being on top of the world," I shrugged. She let out a laugh. "It's true. Really, a lot of people love to travel, but sitting in the back?"

"Right!"

"It's the worst. It's much better behind the wheel. You know that's why I started my company, because I-"

"You like to fly," she said with a point.

My tongue ducked behind my teeth. "Well, sure, it cuts down on overhead, you know, but-"

"So when can you fly me out?"

I hesitated. "Whenever you like…" A waitress in black, pleated slacks and an open black silk shirt approached our table with a tablet floating in her hand.

"Have you decided on what you'll be having this evening?" she asked.

"The special," I said thoughtlessly.

"Could I get the dumplings and the lo mai gai, but can you leave the egg, please?" Brittany asked. I could feel my tongue running against my front two teeth. I peeked at the table across the aisle and Mei had her eyes glued to me as she sipped her Coke through a straw. Her lips parted from it with a satisfied sigh, but she kept her eyes on me, analyzing my every move. I turned back to the table.

"I'll have a Wild Turkey on the rocks," I added.

"I'll be back soon," she said, slipping out of view.

"So where are you from?" Brittany asked.

"North of Chicago, you've never heard of it."

"Where in Chicago? I've been a few times."

"Wisconsin," I chuckled.

"Oh, isn't it just farms up there?"

"No," I said, almost offended. Then I laughed as I said, "That's not all that's up there. I don't live in the sticks, you know."

"What do you do there then?"

"I don't know. I work." Our waitress brought us our drinks, and I pressed the glass to my lips, feeling the comfort of an icy bourbon to cool my nerves.

"Where's home for you?" I asked.

"Thousand Oaks."

"Where's that?"

"California."

"Why'd you leave California?"

"I always wanted to go to Vegas."

"I mean, doesn't California have… everything?"

"It doesn't have Vegas."

"That's it? What about Monaco? Don't you want to go anywhere else?"

"Yeah, but I like working here. Everyone wants to come here at least once. I like to make sure they enjoy it."

"That makes sense. That's why I do what I do."

"So why don't you leave?"

"I can't go back. I'm locked into my business, and my business is here."

"So… besides your business, what other goals do you have?"

I blinked a few times and a ringing echoed in my ear. "What do you mean?"

"Do you want to travel, have a family? Anything?"

"Uh…" I closed my mouth, thinking before speaking. I tried to put something out there, but I could only open my mouth when a crowd leapt to the side of our table.

"Bon appetit," Susan declared with open arms.

Two waiters brought us our meals and set them in front of us. Another brought us a plate of crab puffs that lofted an oily butter into our noses.

I raised my eyebrows and said, "That was quick."

"This smells amazing," Brittany said, wholly distracted by the service Susan had provided. I looked up at her. She watched me acknowledge what she'd done.

"I made your dishes the first priority. I couldn't make you two wait."

"That's so sweet of you," Brittany said.

Susan's grin flicked up. The disdain she had for this girl. She had no idea. "Of course, we want to treat all our guests like… they're the only couple in the world."

Brittany ducked her head and blushed. She looked to see how I was taking this all in. I let out a laugh and looked away. I tried to tell her with my eyes that she should go. The look she wore told me she knew no mercy.

"I always like to help David when he comes here. This seems to be a favorite place for his, uhm, clients?"

I nodded like an idiot. *Just act normal.* The nodding didn't stop as I tried to assure Brittany that everything was normal and there was nothing funny going on. "It's just uh, the food here is fantastic." She smiled at me, but a shard of her eye, I could see, lacked confidence in what I was saying. "Here," I said, "Try some." I pointed with my fork, insisting that this third wheel fly off the side.

"Oh I wouldn't do that," Susan said with an open, parental hand. "It's still steaming. Enjoy a little company from me before you dig in."

I was cracking up. *Please, get out of here, Susan.* Brittany could see the panic in my eyes. I smiled and gave a throaty, "Ha," to smooth the tension.

Susan, in control of the conversation, let us sit in her manufactured pause. The spit in the back of my throat pounded as I gulped.

"So, have you had a nice evening?" I directed at Susan. Maybe some senseless chit-chat would give her the cue to leave us alone.

"Oh yes, lots to keep an eye on. Oh not yet, Brittany," Susan said in a sweet, chirping voice. I squinted at her. *Who's she pretending to be, Snow White?* Brittany got all red with embarrassment, hiding her fork under the plate.

"What would we do without you, Susan?" I asked. Brittany seemed to snap back to the conversation Susan was forcing on us.

"Always happy to help. Oh dear, maybe I should have let them sit on the shelf before we brought them out here, I just wanted to surprise you."

"Oh, you have," I said, raising the napkin to my collar. I stuffed it in my shirt and took up the knife and fork like I was going to eat the whole thing at once, and I would if Susan kept pestering us.

"Thank you again," I said, politely wrapping the cane around her waist to yank her offstage.

"Anything for you, David. I only want the best for you," she said slyly. Her lips jumped back to reveal her gigantic smile. I pretended to feel anything other than worry about how Brittany was handling all this. My cheeks sagged after my insincere smile receded. Brittany's eyes slid away from Susan and locked onto me. A curious look spread across her face. But it slowly diminished, dripping into her plate.

We made conversation as we ate the meal but didn't have strong feelings about either of them. The spark of the evening had gone, and now there was only the check. I raised my hand at the waitress. She didn't see me and was too far down the aisle. Brittany looked back and glumly returned to the table knowing that we'd stay there for a moment longer. I waved my hand again and caught her eye. After telling her my room number, she wished us a happy evening. The vacuum of silence after she went left Brittany and I blinking at each other, wondering what to do next.

"Should we get going?" I suggested.

"Sure." The dull tone in her voice sent me sinking.

I stood up and helped her with her coat. I followed her, catching Mei's sad eyes like it was all going to be okay, just not right now.

Around the corner, Susan was drilling the maître d on the kitchen's performance.

"Have a good night, you two," she said with her patented, insincere inflection.

Brittany tried to grin as we passed. I ignored her and walked with Brittany until we were out of earshot.

"Should I walk you to your car?" I asked.

"No, I walked, and it's far away, so…"

"I had a nice time."

"Me too," she lied. "Good night." Her eye flicked up, over my shoulder before she headed to the front doors. I looked back and saw Susan standing there. She looked at me with firm defiance in her eyes. I felt my fists close. She didn't look away. She was daring me to come over there. *Let it go*.

My feet pressed against the floor as I marched towards her. There was a private wing of the restaurant across the hall. She stepped inside. It was dark and cramped. She turned to face me only when I flicked the light switch.

"Are you happy now?" I shouted.

"Keep your voice down."

"You got what you wanted. You ruined my date."

"You didn't need my help to screw it all up."

"Why couldn't you just leave it alone? Do you dislike me? Did I do something to you?"

"I did nothing but give you a nice dinner."

"Nobody wants their boss around the dinner table when they're on a date. You did this deliberately."

"Oh please, don't flatter yourself."

"You can lie all you want; I won't believe it. You're just jealous. She was nice, and we were having a good time until you came around."

"Oh please, you're a pig."

"What did you say?"

"You heard me. She's twenty-two years old! What did you talk about, her favorite crayon?"

"Hey! She's a good employee. She's trustworthy."

"Oh, well I'm glad you approve. I hope you give us a good review on Yelp!"

"You know what? I will. It'll start off with, 'She made me feel *very* welcome. I got a nice dinner out of it, but the hotel manager blew it.' You ruined my night!"

"You don't own the place! I thought you would understand there are personal and professional boundaries. You think you can just date any one of my employees and throw them away? You pilots are all the same."

"You know me… I'm not here to mess things up. It's just that… those ladies have been driving me crazy, and I wanted to talk to somebody who didn't look at me the way you're looking at me right now."

"What did you think was going to happen?"

"I don't know. I just feel shut out all the time, and when you pulled me aside last time I was here, you made me feel that way too. So I had to find somebody else…"

"For what…?" Her eyes locked onto me again. As scared as I was, I couldn't take my eyes off her face in the glow of the lantern light.

"Somebody to… somebody I wanted to be with." Suddenly, I realized how quiet it was, how anyone could hear us, but I couldn't take my eyes off her.

"You know what this means, don't you?" Her grin curled, filling with riveting expectation.

I looked at her lips, then her green, emerald eyes. The shine they had made her irresistible. I cut the distance between us, sliding my hands around her waist. Her eyes flared; her cheeks blushed. I pressed in past her nose. Her wet lips receiving mine. The softness of her hands caressed the back of my head. I pressed my lips deeper, feeling the tender warmth of our breath hang in midair.

"I've wanted to do that for a long time," I whispered.

"You have?"

"You know I have." I pulled her waist closer. Her soft lips slipped off of mine. "Are you sure you want to be caught kissing one of your guests?"

Her little hand scrunched up my lapel. She sighed, leaning away. "As tempting as this is, I should get back."

"Maybe we can go on a real date next time."

"Next time," she said.

Her words rang with cool assurance as she rounded the corner. I didn't stay far behind. She looked back at me and saw me all puppy-eyed at her, just my head and shoulder past the partition. I could feel the vibrations of her laugh from down the hall. My eyes kept on her, totally magnetic.

I watched her go with a grin so tight my cheek got stuck. But I didn't mind. She made me happy. I was happy. For just a brief moment, I didn't care what came next. I just knew I had her. I looked down at my shoes to get my bearings and saw Bao, Mei, and Fang standing behind me. They watched me, perhaps watched the whole exchange.

"Did uh…?"

"We take your luck with us to the Blackjack table," Bao said, whipping her pointer finger to the gaming floor.

Mei showed her gleaming white teeth and clapped her hands from an inch apart. My cheek got stuck again. Fang wore a less happy expression, but a little wry warmth crept into the corner of her eye as she tilted her head to follow her. What an odd, happy bunch.

High Roller Airways

Chapter 14: Mayday

I was back in Vegas on my own time. A knot in my gut twisted again knowing I had no flights coming in the next few weeks. We'd barely cover expenses this month. If we didn't score another group soon, we'd be bleeding money.

On one of those treadmills they have in the airport, I stood to the right and let the commuters and late-from-the-martini-bar businessmen rush past me. There were some jazzy paintings and neon lights along the walls before I saw some dazzlingly bright screens, rolling up new content like a slot machine. One of the promotions was for the boxing arena, the other for one of the crazy circus acts they had year-round, and the next had the same blue horse I'd seen a thousand times. *Blackjack Tournament.*

I stepped off the treadmill. I froggered through the passing travelers and stood next to the machine. It rolled through the other promotions before it got back to the Blue Stallion Hotel's Blackjack Tournament, starting tonight. The Buy-In? $25,000. I didn't stop to think. I pulled up the nearest branch of my bank on my phone.

The straps of my backpack dug into my shoulders as I crossed the Blue Stallion's lobby. Stacks of cash sagged down in the bottom of the bag. I kept my eyes on the room in the far corner of the casino. A buzzing vibrated against my thigh. The name Tre Austin popped up on my phone.

I never wanted to see that name again. It made me feel like I was his dealer. I ignored it. *I'm not ruining his life even if he wants to.* Another buzz sprung from my phone. He left a voicemail. I placed it to my ear.

"Dave, it's Tre. Hey, you want to hook a friend up with a flight to Vegas? I know what you're thinking, man, but I'm better now. You can hear it in my voice, right? Let's talk and set something up. My girlfriend and a few of her friends want to hit the Strip. Get back to me, man. Thanks."

I sighed but heard a hard "no" in my mind. The money burning a hole in my backpack pushed me forward. A man in a black suit and an earpiece made eye contact. He sized me up and gave a nod, opening the door for me. I slipped in and caught eyes with the cashier.

Once my hands hit the counter, I realized how dark the room was when the cashier's white shirt glowed in a faded blue outline between her black sleeves. I held the backpack by its strings and unzipped them down the sides. The wads of cash jumped like a fish and submerged back into the bag.

I jostled it over the counter and said, "That should be twenty-five there."

A smirk disappeared from her face as she started counting the cash. Once she and another colleague finished their calculations, they handed me a box of chips. There was a signature chip on top to show what I would be dishing out over the afternoon.

I pinched its edges and turned it over. It was black with a glittery orange melded together like marble. They were specialty chips made for the big boys. I carefully placed the chip on top of the others and found a chair where other players were sitting, waiting for the game to begin.

There were older, executive types sulking in the shadows, others in long track suits and Hoka sneakers slumming it with the rest of us. One or two of my fellow players sat jittery while they listened to music and mumbled numbers under their breath. I started to feel heat rise off my shoulders against my jacket. This was the real deal.

I looked at my watch and saw we were running a few minutes late. A thin man in a suit muttered something to a veteran dealer. The dealer nodded and stepped aside to convene with his colleagues. The suit stepped into the spotlight around the tables.

"Gentlemen, welcome to the Blue Stallion Marathon Blackjack tournament. The rules are simple. Every player begins with twenty-five thousand dollars. You may play as long as you like unless you exhaust your chips. Seats will be assigned at random, and after the first hour of play, seats and tables will be assigned based on chip count.

Once all players under the initial buy-in have been eliminated, the last remaining table will play one final shoe. The top two players will receive a cash prize of one-hundred thousand dollars and fifty thousand dollars, along with their remaining chips, respectively. Chips must be visible on the table at all times. There are no special bets, and no contestant may play more than one hand at a time. Splits and double downs are welcome."

High Roller Airways

He paused while he scanned the room for any confused faces. He gave a curt nod before motioning to the dealers to take their places. There were eight tables ready for us under the white-hot spotlights.

"Table assignments are based on the box number you have, players one through five here," the gentleman pointed with his open hand. A few players took their seats. I checked the side of my box for a number. A crisp white 38 shined back at me. I was one of the last players called up. They stuck us in the far corner by the door. Old tourists passed by the open door, letting in their chatter. I had to stay focused.

"Welcome, gentlemen," the dealer greeted us. She had slick black hair and penciled eyebrows. She looked like she just came out of the tanning booth and had a softened New Jersey accent. Her posture and draw on our attention let me know this wasn't her first rodeo.

"My name is Gina," she said. "Waitresses will be here shortly. We'll pull cards for seats."

She reached under the table and returned with a deck of cards. She parted them, raised their backs, and let them slap together one after another with a crisp sound that cut through the chatter on the other side of the room. She placed the deck in front of her to cut. One of the guys reached for it and separated a sliver of the cards off the top.

She smirked and dealt the remaining cards. I was standing at the end of the table, where she dealt first, a red ace. I forgot whether aces were high or low in this count, so I watched the others grimace at their cards.

"Ace high takes first base," Gina announced. She gestured for me to sit. *You're locked in now*.

As soon as we sat down, the dealer started flipping cards out of the shoe.

A jack and 10 of spades fell in front of me. I felt the air rush out of me, completely relieved. Everyone stayed except for the fifth player at the table, who hit on a twelve. Gina had an eight under her face-down card. She flicked it up and a king of diamonds floundered on the felt. A thousand dollars came my way in one shiny chip.

A thought came to me saying, "You could walk out now, with a G in your pocket." I could, but I was going to need much more than that. I had to play it smart to get to the final table.

She swept the cards into a stack and doled out the next set. Two eights rushed to a stop in front of my hands. I watched the rest of the table receive face cards and single-digit hands.

Gina tucked her queen under the hidden card. I blinked, lost for a second. She gestured to me to begin. I split my fingers apart and placed a chip beneath the other eight. She flipped another eight on top. She cocked her head slightly, curious to learn what I would do.

I split again. I was down three grand on three eights, hoping for a high or low number. On the newest eight she laid a ten. *Great.* I swiped my head through the air. She patted the felt next to the next eight. She gave me a four. I heard someone hissing in the air at my bad luck. I waved her off to move to the next one. She plucked another card from the shoe. A six, making 14. I threw my hands up and tapped the table. She gave me another six. 20. I waved her off.

The others stuck with what they had except for the last seat. He doubled down on a nine and got a 2 in return. He cursed under his breath. His nails dug into his scalp as he hid his face from the table.

She flipped her face-down card and showed a ten. 20. Sharp groans shot out from the table. I sank into my chair. Down a grand. The sweat started to set in around my neck.

The dealer flicked me an 8 and a 9. She showed a 9. A grand wasn't worth risking on a such a low number. I stayed. She showed an ace and took my chip.

Down again. I put another chip forward. My hands brushed against my mouth. I heard my heel pound against the footrest of my chair.

Two glowing white cards shot out in front of me. A 4 and a 3 stared back. I lifted my eyes to the dealer's cards. She had an ace. *Oh boy*.

I knocked the table with my knuckle. She slid me a 9, making an unenviable 16. I shrugged and tapped again.

"Twenty-six," Gina said, straight-faced. She slid my chip in one hand and opened her palm with the other. The strain in my neck tightened like a vice. I knew this game had its good and bad streaks, but I hoped I could count on the bad streak ending soon.

Gina swept the spent cards away and tossed us a new pair. She showed an 8. I had an eighteen and decided to stay. She revealed her hidden card with a thwap.

"Nineteen," she said, knowing the news wouldn't be appreciated by the table. Most of us lost on that round. I caught glances from the other players. We all wished we couldn't split the weight of that hit.

High Roller Airways

"Place your bets," Gina said, shocking us out of our glum dejectedness. She dealt me a pair of aces. My eyes shot out of my head like I'd seen water in the desert. I split the aces and thumbed another chip onto the felt.

"Good luck," she said, flipping over two cards. Both were red 3s. 4 or 14, either way, I was not going to be popular at the table for siphoning more face cards from the other players. I knocked on the table. She delivered me a 10. I waved my hand to move onto the next hand. I tapped for the next card. She swept up 4, making 18. I called uncle and let her deal to the next player. With a 14 and an 18 I watched her measly black 3 sit there. One of the players hit on his pair of 4s. He got the 10. I hid my anger. *Just let the dealer bust.*

Once it was Gina's turn, she flicked up her second card. 3 and 7 showed on the table. She brought the dagger down with a black queen. Another two chips slipped out of reach. I felt a hand on my shoulder. It was one of the casino employees. I saw more of them at the other tables, managing the game.

"Come this way, sir," he said.

I took my chips and followed him to the next table. He sat me down with the other unlucky losers. I was at the end of the line. Fourth, basically the runt of the litter at a blackjack table. Whatever crumbs were left would fall to me.

I felt like a boxer sitting on his stool between rounds. The cold sweat seeped into my shoulders. The first round was over, and I needed to endure the next few rounds if I was going to stand a chance of outlasting the others.

The dealer handed out the cards. I got a 7 followed by a crisp red 8. He tucked in his little King under his facedown card, looking smug. There wasn't much choice in the matter, so I pounded the table when he looked to me.

A glowing white card flopped onto the green. 7. A big breath ran through my nostrils, my eyes half open as he took another chip. I begrudgingly pulled another from my stack and pressed it into the table.

I looked down the table as the dealer flopped their cards out in front of them. 19, 20, 17, and I had the low pair of 3s. I could split or hope for a few smaller numbers to hit 17. I shook my head and gestured to the dealer to split them.

Pulling another chip from my stack took the strength of Excalibur but I saw no other way. All eyes were on me and my two 3s. I tapped the table.

High Roller Airways

The first card was a ten, as expected. I sighed again. *Might as well.* I hit. 6, that's 19. I blew the air out of my lungs and gestured to the next card. Another 6, up to 9.

"Come on, come on," I whispered. I hit again. 8. 17 and 19 isn't bad. "I'll take it," I said with a hand wave.

The dealer had a 4 and exposed his second card. A 7. Every head flew back and winced with a deep hiss.

"Please don't do this to me," I pleaded. He swept another card out of the shoe. He set it beside the others in a nice line. A Queen. A red Queen that took out the whole table. I pinched my nose and sighed into myself. I looked at my tablemates. None of them had any hope left. The fun of the game was left. They were just survivors.

The next few hands zipped by like a felon in a Corvette. 10 and a seven, dealer wins. Automatic dealer blackjack. No insurance, no refunds, goodbye. I looked down at my few remaining chips and tossed them onto the table.

I'm getting back into this thing. No fear. Balls of steel. The dealer gave me an 18. I watched his 7 lay on the table. *Just be a ten so I can get back in this. Please. Please.*

He pinched the head and tail of the facedown card and flipped it over. It showed a 2. I slumped in my chair. He snatched another card from the shoe and slammed down a crimson red jack.

I felt the color sap from my face. My heartbeat throbbed in my ears. I heard mumbling behind me as I watched the chips drift from me like the returning tide.

"Thank you for playing, sir," I heard a voice say, like we were gambling with pennies. Just another whisper, no gong, no drums, no sirens to point out my whole plan had fallen apart. It was all for nothing.

I stumbled out of my chair. I staggered down the steps into the casino floor. The normal grannies at the slots and bachelor party guests had no idea what had just happened. It just happened, like it meant nothing at all.

I made it to my room and stripped off my clothes. I threw them at the bathroom wall and snatched my swimsuit from my open suitcase. I caught myself in the mirror. My eyes glanced down, throwing my vision to the tile floor.

You idiot. You ruined your life. Look at yourself. You're nothing. You're trash. You're going to be a deadbeat. Even if you go back to the airline, you're going to live paycheck to paycheck for the rest of your life.

I had to cool off. I took deep breaths all the way to the pool and sat on the side, letting the water cool my legs. I lifted my head up, feeling the sun on my cheeks. One last breath. *You'll find a way. You'll find a way.*

"Would you like a drink, sir?" a waiter asked me, crowing over my shoulder.

"Rum and coke, make it a double." He went away, leaving me to lower myself under the surface. Feeling the cold water around my temples refreshed me.

I came back up and held my face up to the sun. The water bounced off my ears. A few moments passed where I felt the pull of the water run across my arms under the surface, the slow draw that kept me afloat. *It didn't happen. I have enough stowed away. It's fine.*

"Sir?" I heard in a concerned voice. I opened my eyes. I might have fallen asleep if he hadn't called me. He had a dark, sweaty drink in his hand.

"Thank you," I replied and swam to the ladder. The water rushing off my sides wasn't nearly as refreshing as the anticipation I felt before closing my hand on that drink.

"Thank you," I said again. I took my seat and drained half of my drink through the pair of thin black straws. I could feel the rum pulsing through my veins. I closed my eyes as I laid back but caught round Charles sitting next to me.

"Hey, David, remember me?"

"Charles, I remember. We were talking about business a while ago."

"That's right. Glad you remembered. Sorry the tournament didn't turn out your way."

"You were there?"

"I watched you. You're a sharp player, but the cards are the cards."

"Something like that," I muttered.

Charles covered one hand with the other and rubbed it, waiting for something to say. "You remember me, but you don't know who I am, do you?"

"You're… sorry, I don't remember your last name."

"Charles Chandler," he said, stretching out his hand.

My face dropped in disbelief. I absent-mindedly shook his hand. "Do you own the hotel?"

"Yes, I do."

"So you're the heir to the Blue Stallion fortune."

"Yes," he answered, clearly wanting to move on from the subject. "I'm interested in your company, David. How long have you been in business?" He shot me a sly but serious look.

"Three years or so," I said.

"And you're turning a profit?"

High Roller Airways

"We have. We've made six figures the past three years," I said with a grin on my face. It was true, actually, but I was only making eighty grand with my half of the profits.

"How's your debt situation?"

"How's my debt?" I asked. "Why would you want to know about that?" As soon as I said it, I felt his tightened incredulous face loosen as his intention became clearer.

"You have something very interesting going on at High Roller Airways. You own the majority share, correct?"

"No one has majority, it's fifty-fifty. My partner and I split the costs."

"How much were they?"

"What aren't you telling me, Charles?"

He sighed. He looked away at the buildings beyond the pool, letting the cogs roll in his mind.

"I think your business could grow, if it had the right investor. I also think that you're enough of a businessman to know that the travel industry is a fickle beast…" His head hung low; his eyes deep and penetrating in thought. He turned to me again and wouldn't let go of my eyes.

"You lost big today. A gamble you haven't made before in all your time at this casino. We track your member card, watch your average bets, what games you play and when, we know your MO. Business must be going sour for you, otherwise, why take such a big risk?"

"Maybe I wanted to win big for the thrill of it," I lied through my teeth.

He clicked his tongue and looked down at his thumbs before trying to reason with me. "I can give you the out you want. Being based in the Midwest is not where the clients are." I sat up with a defiant stare.

His two hands shot up to appease me. "And you've done well in taking this company off the ground, but you've dried up that well. Maybe you'll get some more ball players on your logs but that's it. I have the connections and the capital to make it what you've always wanted it to be… Let me be frank. I want to buy your company."

My heartbeat pounded in my ears again. The water droplets across my body had evaporated in the red-hot sun. I felt my hand bring the little black straws to my lips as I stalled. I swallowed the rest of my drink.

"Would you like another one, sir?" The waiter asked, oddly just in time.

"Yes, please," I said. The waiter looked to Charles who looked back at the young man with a grin that hung over his large meaty hands.

"Thank you, Kevin," Charles said. His arresting gaze turned back to me. Out of options I crossed my arms and gave him an answer.

"I'm willing to hear you out."

He stretched his back and refocused himself to make his pitch. "I'm willing to offer a price that is above market value, but I have to know how much this company means to you so I can make an offer that benefits us both. How much do you want for it?" he asked.

I squinted at him. I wouldn't know how to put a price on any of this besides what I was getting out of it. I also didn't want to get short-handed by some Fat Cat on the deck of a pool when I could have taken the time to have the airline assessed. Maybe they'd shortchange me too.

"Shouldn't you be making me an offer?"

A low chuckle rose from his chest. "Without knowing much about your company's financials, I can't offer you a fair price that's fair for me. How much do you still owe on the plane?"

"Thirty grand a month for the next two years."

"So I'd still have to pay off the jet, even after buying you out?" he asked.

"It's not just the jet; it's the business."

He padded his hands while keeping his eyes on me. "Five hundred thousand," he said.

"Five twenty-five…" His cheek twitched upward, betraying his cold expression. I held my stare until he answered.

"We can do that," he replied.

"Good," I said, breathing in as much air as my lungs could take. "Do you want fifty percent or the whole thing?"

"Do you think your partner would be interested?"

"I think he could be persuaded."

"When can you set a meet?"

"Give me your number, and I'll get back to you." He flicked a business card out of his back pocket. He pointed it down at me, letting me grasp it. My get out of jail free card, if I played my cards right. Charles groaned as he stood. I had to look up his white, fur-covered chest to see his round chin squeeze down at me.

"I look forward to it," he said. His sandals slapped against the cement. I watched him go before Kevin returned with my second drink.

"Thank you, Kevin," I muttered. I traded him my empty glass and pressed the rum-soaked ice against my teeth. I reached for my phone and called Jack. The tone came in and out. A bobbing head cut across the surface of the water. The sun beat on my shoulders. A robotic voice chirped up.

"The person you are trying to reach… Jack Flambeau… is not available. Leave your message at the tone." I moved the phone away from my face as I sighed.

"Hey, Jack, it's Dave. I have an interesting proposition that I think you'd like. I just talked to the owner of the Blue Stallion, and he's interested in our company. Get back to me."

I relaxed into my chair and closed my eyes. At first a chuckle bubbled in my chest. Then it turned into a roaring eruption of laughs. I couldn't help it. I felt nothing but air underneath me.

I could finally cut out. I didn't have to sweat it out at the tables anymore. I didn't have to worry about debt. There was a path, a choice. I didn't have to hold on any longer.

Later that night, Jack called back asking for details. The conversation didn't start off as smoothly as I had hoped.

"S—t, Dave, how much did you lose?" Jack asked.

"Nothin'!" I shouted. "Well, not nothing, but he wants to buy us out, and I think we should take it."

"How much do you owe him?"

"Nothing, honest."

"How much does he want?"

"For my half, over half a mill. But make sure we're not getting ripped off for that price. Fact check that."

"I'll have someone look into it. You didn't sign anything did you?"

"No, I convinced him to talk to you for your half. That way we can get a better price together. Not a bad idea, huh?"

"No, not too bad, are you still in Vegas?" he asked.

"Yeah, we can do an online call and get everything sorted out."

"Alright, I'll hear him out, but let me check how much we're worth first. It might take a day or two."

I set up a time to meet. Since I was still in Vegas, I took the meeting in Charles' office. The whole place was decked out like a southern cabin. Paintings of the Appalachia mountains covered the walls, a stone fireplace with a black bear's head hanging over a digital flame, and classic snapshots of Kentucky thoroughbreds breaking out of the gate at Churchill Downs.

It seemed kind of odd in a place like Las Vegas, but when I heard Charles' voice ringing down the hall, I felt like I knew more about the man.

High Roller Airways

"Welcome, David, how are you feeling?"

"Good," I said. "I like your office."

"Everything's from Kentucky, even old Smokey over there," he said, pointing to the bear. The ferocity of the animal held still in its frame.

"Reminds me of home, kind of."

"You ever been to Kentucky?"

"A few times, it's a pretty place."

"Well I tell you what, once we finish this deal, I'll let you in on some hidden gems."

I chuckled. "I'd like that," I said. "Are we in here?"

"Yes, right this way," he said.

I followed him to his desk where he sat gleefully in his large leather chair. I saw his computer was facing him, so I cleared my throat.

"Where should I sit?" I asked.

"Pull up a chair over here," he said, pointing to his side of the desk. There was hardly enough room for him to turn it. I sheepishly looked at the nearest chair and lifted it up as I brushed past his desk and a tall, green-leafed plant.

Jack appeared on the screen in his office back home. He looked at me with his hawkish face.

"Hey, Jack, how've you been?" I asked.

"Good," he said with his lips. "And you must be Charles, how are you?"

"I'm fine, thank you. What has David told you so far?"

"He said that you wanted to buy our company, and I'm willing to sell for the right price."

"And if we can't come to an arrangement, David and I could still settle on a number for his half of the business?"

"We'll see how this goes first," Jack said.

"David and I have met on several occasions; we have spoken about your business, and I was curious about bringing it to Las Vegas for my West Coast clients. So that's why we're here today. David and I have had some very good discussions, and he's told me you're a savvy businessman who might be interested in my proposal."

"I had our company assessed," Jack started. "He estimates that we're worth 2.5 million." My throat closed up. You idiot, I thought to myself. Charles seemed unfazed.

"How much more do you have to pay off on that plane?" he asked. Jack licked his lips and cleared his throat.

"We have some payments left to make."

"David knows how much you still owe. Do you really expect me to pay that much for over seven hundred thousand dollars of debt?"

"You don't have to pay, because I don't have to sell."

Charles stirred up in his seat. "This is your chance to get out of a business that could cost you more money than you're willing to lose. This is the highest point you'll be able to sell. Over the next few months, maybe you'll scrape by, but the profit model isn't there. We need to move it to Las Vegas, and I'm willing to pay you fairly for it."

Jack's stone face started to crumble. His crossed arms loosened, and he sat forward in his chair.

"What do you have in mind?"

"I'm willing to buy your company for 1.1 million."

"1.25," Jack said.

Charles turned to face me. I nodded.

"Then we're agreed, one and a quarter million." Charles said. He leaned back to shake my hand. My hand shot out to grasp his. *It's done. It's finally over.*

Chapter 15: Descent

I thumbed the side of the rosewood counter at the bar. Looking out the window past the shelves of scotch, I saw the rain spray off the tarmac and spread out into waves of mist behind a speeding plane. I heard a voice ask me what I'd like to drink. I kept my eye on the puffs of rain fall back to earth.

"Brandy old-fashioned," I said. He moved to collect the necessary ingredients. I settled into my seat. Passengers' chatter and rolling suitcases hummed along behind me. I looked up at the TV in the corner. A college football game came to life as both teams lined up, ready for another make-it or break-it play.

It was heartwarming to see two teams on the gridiron from some sophomore SEC conference. Some kids from

High Roller Airways

Nowhere, Arkansas could be seen on TV by their parents and even curious pilots in airport bars. Maybe I'd heard of these two schools before, but they didn't have a good reputation as a place of higher learning or as a school with a good football team. Analesco State looked to gain more ground on South Mississippi Tech's half of the field.

A lean 19-year-old squatted behind the center. He jogged back and knew exactly where he was throwing it. Down the right sideline a receiver cut back and up the line, losing the defender. The quarterback flicked the ball right to his man. As it hung in mid-air, a corner ripped up some turf and barreled to the kid reaching up with both hands.

I gritted my teeth as I saw the harrowing shoulder drop down. The ball closed in and stopped in the receiver's hands. The defender flew past. He missed. *He missed!*

The receiver softened the spiraling football in his gloved hands and stuck a stiff landing on one foot while the other was a mile behind him. The momentum keeled him over onto the sideline for a first down.

I shifted my seat forward and turned to the corner with the TV. *Go little Analesco State. You can do it!* The center snapped the ball back into the quarterback's hands and a second pair of arms zipped past with the ball in tow. The fullback bounced off the guard and had to reorient himself to gain some yardage. The thick crack of helmets and pads came through the toned-down speakers of the TV.

I squinted at how fast and heavy that hit must have felt. The officials dug the ball out of the pile and let the game continue. The men were curled over themselves, ready to pounce. Even I was leaning over in my chair when South Mississippi Tech jumped over the line and caused yellow flags to fly in from the corners of the screen. I let out a sigh of relief. I couldn't help it. I was hooked.

The officials settled Analesco State into striking distance of the endzone. They ran the ball to the 5-yard line as I was polishing off my drink, only three more plays to make it in the endzone or settle for a field goal.

It reminded me of the time Judd and I were in the casino. He would have loved to see me now. Well, at the beginning he would have. The melancholic chill ran through my insides. There were still happy memories somewhere I knew. I focused on that night, that young happy night where all the roads were wide and open for me.

I felt a quarter loose in my pocket. Remembering that bet I made with Judd, I made a bet with myself. If the offense scores a touchdown, I win; simple as that. I pulled the quarter from my pocket and sat it up on the bar. I rubbed my thumb over its little grooves, watching with my full attention. My thumb started firing up with the quarter rubbing my skin raw.

The ball was snapped. The quarterback stepped back. The offensive line caved in, but he saw an opening. Feeling the pressure, he let the ball loose out of his hand, heading straight for the corner of the endzone. Six arms sprang up, falling, waiting for the ball to drop. The receiver spread out to give himself some room before the ball fell into his hands, but the safety reached over his head, getting a hand on the ball. The Analesco State player fell on his back, leaving the defiant defender standing over his supine opponent.

My fist smacked the bar, clutching the quarter in my palm. Then a wave of relief washed over me. I hadn't lost. I made the wrong call, but I didn't lose anything. I didn't have to fork over another bill. I didn't have to rub my remaining chips together for good luck. It was fine. It was just another play during a football game. A hint of perfume thrust itself over my shoulder. Long red hair caught the corner of my eye as she nuzzled into my back.

"I missed you," Susan said.

"I'm right here," I said, letting her duck under my arm. I held her close and looked back at the chaos on the field.

"Big game?" Susan asked.

"Huh? Oh no, it's – it's just football."

"They're going to start boarding soon. We should get in line. Are you ready to go?"

"Um… give me a sec."

"Sure," her eyes followed me as I walked to a lonely corner near the gate. I scrolled through my phone to find my dad's number. My breathing stopped. I had to do it.

I hit the call button before I could talk myself out of it, taking a deep breath, waiting for the dial tone to stop. Each time I heard it I thought he'd pick up, sending my heart racing. Then it stopped. The tone stopped and a robotic voice replaced it.

"Please leave a message after the tone."

Beep.

I thought to run, to let him call me back instead. I cleared my throat.

"Hey, Dad, I uh… hope you're doing good. I got good news for you. I… I sold the jet. So, I'll be set for a while…" I looked around, trying to find the courage.

"I got us tickets to the air show, back home. I'll be back next week. I'd really like to catch up. Bye, Dad, thanks."

I felt a hand on my back.

"Ready, honey?"

"Yeah, I'm ready."

I felt a serene sense of peace wash over me. No more loose ends. With two tickets to Hawaii in hand, I led Susan to our gate. I let the quarter fall back in my pocket. I figured there'd be casinos there, but I kept my eye on the wide-open horizon, the blue waters, and the white sand beaches. I'd even try standing on a two-by-four with a paddle. I bet Susan would get a kick out of that. The thought of her smile brought one out of me.

Things come and go. I've had a million dreams in my life, and this one came true, for a while. But there are no shortcuts, just the path you take. I tried to leap into early retirement with a dream and a hand-me-down jet, but it turned out to be another chapter of my life.

I couldn't be mad about it. I could've crashed and burned. I could've been Jack's chauffeur for the rest of my career, but now, with a little extra cash, I could eke out a living doing something I wanted to do. Holding Susan's hand in an airport in Seattle, I knew whatever I was going to do, I'd be coming back to her after every flight.

www.ingramcontent.com/pod-product-compliance
Lightning Source LLC
LaVergne TN
LVHW010307070526
838199LV00065B/5476